NICK MONTE

AND THE ESCAPE FROM THE REALM OF SHADOWS

G.K. MONTILLA

NICK MONTE

AND THE ESCAPE FROM THE REALM OF SHADOWS

G.K. MONTILLA

ISBN: 978-1-965943-00-7

"I am come, a light into the world, that whosoever

believeth on me

should not abide in darkness."

John 12:46

Index

Introduction

We live in two worlds simultaneously. There is a spiritual world, and of course the natural one. The two are linked together—intertwined if you will. This story reveals some details of the dark side of the world we live in. There are people out there that are ordained, anointed, and taught to entangle the world with magic, and the powers of darkness. But there are a few people out there that have the true power of God, and these are the only ones with the ability to destroy evil. Everyday people are deceived and seduced into darkness and choose to follow its path. There are others, however, that are born into this evil. They are, from the womb, introduced and raised in a world of darkness, a world of magic, a world of shadows and demons.

Nick was born into one of these families, shaped and raised from the time he was born, to be an agent of hell. His family brought him up to carry their mantle of darkness, and he worked right alongside demons, which were handed down from one generation to another, to do supernatural things.

But somewhere along the line, Nick stumbled upon a little church, where the true power of God resided—more powerful than anything he had ever seen—and a people that truly do care about him. He found himself between the powers of darkness that didn't want to let him go and the power of God that strove to bring him out of darkness.

The battle for his soul was in full force.

In the Beginning

It was almost dawn. I could feel it. Though I was deep underground and in the depths of the Earth, I knew my time was running out, so I hurried to get the snare set. There was a high priest we were going to kill the following night, and I was preparing the bait that would lure him to his death...

As I rushed the ritual, I cast the spells that would seal the man's fate. The spirit of lust ran through my being as the magic took hold, the powers of darkness overshadowed me, and it changed my body into a giant lizard-like creature. It was more delicious than having sex, and though I had felt it many times before, it always felt special when murder was involved.

I worked the spell, my eyes began to glow red, and my tongue divided into two…when, without notice, a realization of where I really was suddenly took hold of me. My mind became unplugged from what I was doing for a moment, and I looked to my left, and gazed beyond the cliff where I was kneeling. I stood up and saw the enormous cave I was in, my neck extending higher to see that it was larger in length than the island of Manhattan, and taller than its highest buildings. Different shades of brown and black covered the hills within it, and the walls moved as if they were breathing. Fires burned in the distance…

I was in Hell.

I looked down toward the bottom of the cavern and saw bat-like creatures flying from one fire pit to another.

This is where the disobedient spend eternity, I thought. The reality of it became evident just for a moment. It was not the first or last time I would be there, but it was the first time I felt its dread.

As quickly as it came, the reality and chilling truth of where I was quickly left, and insanity took hold of me again. My focus returned to the spell. I ran back to what I was doing, and hurriedly spoke the last chant, and it came out of my mouth with violence in the shape of a bloody snake, and then tied itself to the skull I was holding. Then, it disappeared... It was done. I knew the high priest would be done as well. I changed back to my shadow form, placed the skull in the side of a mount by the cliff and flew up through a hole in the ceiling of the cave. I hurried back to the surface…back to my physical body.

As I was flying—and gloating in the evil I had done—I thought about a test I had in high school that day. I just had to get a good grade.

As I traveled through the Earth, up through spouts, through caves and onto the surface, my thoughts went to the blindness of most people. Like a lot of my classmates, some people had no clue that there was an invisible world—a spiritual world. We were all part of it, but it couldn't be seen with our natural eyes. We've all experienced it in some way or another.

When you feel like you're being watched, you probably are. When you think you saw something in the shadows, turn on the lights and see nothing, you know what? There just may be something there your natural eyes are not able to see, but your spirit can sense it. Many people claim to know all about the spirit world, but the truth is, the ones that know the most—the ones that have seen the most—usually talk the least. They, like me, have been supernaturally opened to it, know how dangerous it really is, and know that there are consequences for talking.

I'm late. I'm late, I thought. I had to get back to my body because dawn approached, and my day was about to start. I flew through the air and as I traveled, I saw other witches and wizards making their way back from their night travels as well. I knew some of them; I waved, they waved back, but I didn't stop to chat. I made it back to my house and turned my head to look at the park across the street, and I saw the sun's rays begin to light up the sky. I flew through the open window into my second-floor bedroom, and I stopped to look at my body for a moment as it rested on my bed—quite peaceful, actually.

I had made it in time after all.

I looked around my room, and everything was quiet. I could hear my mom moving about downstairs, and my body breathing on the bed. I said hi to Dorzener, the demon that watched my body while I traveled, but he said nothing in return, only giving me a stone-rigid stare. I scrutinized him for a minute and began admiring the monstrous being—the hairy back, the bat-like ears, the deep black eyes, and those razor-thin, sharp teeth. To me he did not look like a monster. To me, he was beautiful. He stood by my feet with a hatchet in his hand, and as we looked at each other, I waited to see if he would say anything, but he didn't. He just looked away and looked straight on in disgust. I looked at the alarm clock, and it was about to go off, so I jumped into my body, and quickly turned it off before it buzzed.

I felt a sense of relief come over me and felt a little bit safer. I made it back into my own skin again and I was happy about that. That was because I knew a lot of people who had died out there in the spirit world, and never made it back to their bodies. In some cases, where people just don't wake up, or fell into comas, that's because the body of the person lived for a while, but their spirit was not there. Sometimes, no one knew where their spirit was. They were lost, and they stayed like that for years.

I had been in some of those spiritual search parties…looking everywhere for the missing soul of the person, while the body lays in a coma-like state. I'd also heard some say that God put people in comas sometimes to deal with them directly…

I didn't know. I was just happy to be back...

"Wait a minute," the pastor said, interrupting my story. "Before you continue, I need to know. What is the real reason you've asked me to come down to the church, to meet with you?" she asked.

I looked at the pastor with an overwhelming feeling of sorrow. I knew she could see it in my eyes, but she was not moved. She looked at me, picked up the hot cup of tea on her desk, took a small sip, and asked again.

"Why?"

"I'm at the point where I cannot hold things together anymore." I put my hands together on my lap. "You've been very good to me. I know you are a real minister of God, and I feel something is urging me to tell you who I am and where I come from," I replied.

"I knew from the moment you came into our church that you were an enemy." The pastor leaned forward on her desk. "But God is merciful, and you needed a fair opportunity to repent. So, we allowed you to be amongst us and hear the Word of God. You've been in our services; you've seen that we are just striving to serve God," she said and then leaned closer.

"Who sent you? Who are you…really?"

I looked at her and realized the moment was upon us. If I was really going to tell her, that was going to be it. I would not hold back, and I knew she would probably be completely shocked.

"I'm part of a secret government organization that specializes in the spiritual realm of espionage, intelligence, and assassination," I replied. I looked into her eyes, and she was not moved.

She leaned back on her office chair. "I know…" she said and looked at me like I was an idiot. "You think that God is not going to reveal someone as deadly as you to the one that is responsible for keeping his sheep safe? I'm responsible for the spiritual welfare of the people that come into this church. God will always warn His people," she said.

"If you knew, why did you ask me?" I wondered, a little baffled by her response.

"I was giving you the opportunity to confess. The Bible says that if we confess our sins, God will forgive and cleanse us from our wickedness," she said. "Revealing the evils that you've done will only help you if you believe that God can cleanse you, and save you… Do you believe that?" she asked.

I put both hands on her desk. "I believe that in revealing to you what I've done, I will be in a better place, where God can help me," I replied.

The pastor nodded. "Well, at least that's a good place to start. So, tell me, where did it all begin for you?"

I nodded my head and started to tell her how my story really began around 1977, in Argentina—the province of San Juan to be exact.

In the city of San Juan, in a two-bedroom apartment on the living room floor, I sat, dressed in brown overalls and a yellow shirt. I was four years old, playing with my toys, like every little boy does. We lived in a small apartment in the city. It was nothing fancy. A lot of it was set in brown décor: a brown loveseat, with matching chairs, a brown bookshelf, and a brown living room set. It was the seventies, and everything seemed to be comprised of earthy

colors and patterns.

My mom went back and forth, busy with everyday

chores, talking to me as she entered and left the room I was

in. I was transfixed and could not stop watching what was

going on. It was not my mother I was interested in, but the

shadow that followed my mom. It was like a puff of gray or

black smoke, and it looked like a liquid at times. I could

sometimes make out a face looking back at me, and

sometimes almost a whole torso. Wherever my mom went

it followed, sometimes beating her to her destination as it

hovered beside her. I don't think my mom knew I could see

it, because she never addressed it at the time.

She would also react to the spirit. Sometimes I

could see mom turn her head as if she was listening to it,

and sometimes her face would take on a countenance like

the one the figure had at the time. I discovered later that it was a familiar spirit—a spirit that she communed with and relied on for day-to-day tasks and such.

My mom came out of the kitchen and went to the living room, talking out loud, and I saw the spirit. It began to whisper something in her ear, and she leaned in to listen.

She turned around to look at me, and her visage was again changed. Her eyes and expression looked exactly like the spirit that was with her.

My mom went over to the phone on the wall and made a phone call, looking back at me as she did. The shadow spirit wrapped itself around my mother's body. I did not understand it then, but looking back, I realized she was being controlled by that thing.

She hurried off the phone with fidgety hands and looked down at me. She gave me a half-crooked smile as the shadow continued to wrap itself around her. A head formed out of the black mist, and it looked back at me and grinned wickedly, knowing exactly what he was doing. She hurried out of the living room and into the bathroom in the hallway, slamming the door behind her.

As I watched my mom and her "friend" disappear into the bathroom, something caught my eye. I looked down the hallway, and by the doorway of one of the bedrooms, there was something looking back at me! It was a small figure, just a little creature, like a gnome, a little bit taller than me, with tiny red eyes. I remember being afraid, and wondered what it was really after.

It was not the first time I had seen a creature like that. I had seen them before, watching me from afar as I played. I did not know what they were, but they seemed to keep their distance, at least for the time being.

The small creature then ran into the hallway and slipped under the bathroom door. I heard my mom giggle. I looked down and stared at my toys for a bit, and then I continued to play.

The hours went by slowly. Time itself seemed to move at a snail's pace back then, but I kept myself entertained in the small apartment. It was common for me to see eyes watching me from across the room, hovering in midair, and then suddenly vanish.

Later that evening, I found out what the phone call was about. I was in the hallway of the apartment, playing. I heard a soft knock on the door, and my mom hurried to answer it. She opened the door and greeted someone. It was a man. I heard him come in, and he carried on a conversation with my mom for a little while, so I assumed that it was one of her friends.

A little bit of time went by, and I did not hear them anymore—I was concerned more with playing. Suddenly I heard my mom call me into the living room. I walked in, and saw a man I did not recognize sitting on our couch, my mom sitting beside him. The man introduced himself as Simon. He had a brown suit with a black turtleneck, black combed hair, and a trimmed beard. He smiled and asked me to come closer. I did.

We talked for a while, and then he looked at my mom, received a nod of approval from her, and continued. "So, your mom tells me that you like superheroes. Is that right?"

I nodded in approval.

"Me too," he said. "What if I told you, there was a way for you to actually fly, to levitate and move as if you weighed absolutely nothing?" he asked.

I remember just looking at him, and feeling a bit puzzled, not really understanding what he was talking about…

"I can give you the ability to fly like Superman. Would you like that?" he asked.

"Yes," I replied, thinking it was just an obvious answer to a stupid question.

He put his hands on my shoulders and gave me a kiss on the cheek.

"Well, I can give you something better, actually…something special," he said with a smile as he opened his arms and waved them about, pointing all around the room.

"I have friends that are here with me. You cannot see them yet, but with them, I can make you fly. Will you allow us to help you?" he asked.

"I don't know," I said, in my mind thinking of the things I had seen around me already.

"You can trust me, and my invisible friends as well. They won't hurt you," he said.

I looked over at my mom. She smiled at me and nodded her head in approval. I slowly turned my head to look back at Simon.

"Ok," I replied hesitantly.

I didn't know what to expect, but my mom seemed to be ok with it. She kept smiling and nodding her head for me to do it.

Simon asked my mom to put her hands on my shoulders and hold me. Simon opened a little leather pouch, took out a syringe, and proceeded to inject me in the arm with something. After the injection, my arm felt warm, and the feeling traveled all the way up to my chest and began to spread throughout my body. I felt dizzy, and lightheaded, like someone had removed the top portion of my skull. I looked at my mom, and she looked on with anticipation.

Simon said something repeatedly, like a chant or something, and my mom joined him. Everything became blurry. Immediately after that, I felt like I exploded

upwards and away from them, as if I was blown out of a

cannon. I thought I was going to hit the ceiling of the room

but stopped suddenly about an inch away. I turned my

head, and I looked around, and realized I was not standing

on the floor anymore.

I…was floating.

I had been propelled out of my body and was

floating in spirit form. My head felt like it was ablaze. I

looked down and saw my mom looking up at me, smiling.

Simon looked up as well, and grinned. I did not understand

anything that was happening. All at once, I felt extremely

cold, but I did not understand how.

I felt a scratch on my hand, and when I looked to

see, I realized that there were others—spirits—in the room.

There were demons floating all around me, just looking at

me. Brown ones, black ones, gray ones; they looked like

they wanted to eat me up. I looked down again, and I saw

that there was something embracing my mom from behind

that did not look human. It was the same color as the smoke

I had previously seen so many times beside her, but I could

clearly see it then. I tried to talk but could not communicate

with my mom.

Then I heard her voice in my head saying, "It's ok,

it'll be ok," as she opened her hands up to me.

I saw my little body down there on the floor, and I

realized then that I would never be the same again;

something had changed in me forever. I did not know what

to do and I felt scared.

"Good job" said Simon. "Let's bring you back

down now."

Some of the demons came up to me and began to

poke me. They looked like they wanted to do evil things to

me. One of them grabbed me and dragged me around the

ceiling like a rag doll. Then I felt a force begin to pull me back down, and slowly I descended. I looked at Simon, and he chanted something repeatedly with a somber expression on his face. My mom had joined him. I entered back into my body…and it was over.

That was how I was opened wide to the spiritual world, and it was also my first walk in the spirit realm. To this day, I still don't know exactly what was in that needle. I later learned that it was Simon's specialty, and he had been called upon by my mom to prepare me.

My mom did not bring anything up about that event in the days that followed. She didn't talk about it, but there was a knowing between us. When her eyes would catch mine sometimes, I could see her thinking about it, and I am certain she knew it was on my mind. But the memory became almost like a dream after a while. I would continue to see things around the apartment—figures walking around, eyes looking at me from the shadows, objects moving by themselves—and I learned to live with the things happening around me.

It was my new normal.

As I told my story to the pastor, in the church office, she looked deep into my eyes. I never could tell what it was that she was thinking, but I felt like she knew more about me than she let on.

"Well son," she started, "thank you for sharing that with me. I have been to many parts of the world and have seen a lot of people who have been deep in the devil's kingdom. And I've heard things like what you're telling me now. This is nothing new to me.

"The devil does a lot of evil to his own people in order to break them," she continued. "He does that so he can rebuild them for his evil purpose, to manipulate and control them, like he did you. He needs your feelings to be raw, he needs you hurt, and for you to feel betrayed by everyone in the world around you. He can use those feelings against you and against others by making you believe that he's the only one that cares—the only one that would be willing to help you. Sound familiar?" the pastor asked.

"It does," I answer.

"God allows you to suffer, and to go through things so that He can cultivate the fruits of His Spirit in you. Love, mercy, patience, understanding… But He doesn't leave you there in that pain. He's a healer, you see. He heals our pain, dries our tears. He comforts us. Our suffering is not in vain."

She paused for a moment, as she considered her words. "I'm sorry," she said. "Please continue."

I nodded, ready to continue my story.

It's not easy for me to talk about, but I was sexually abused from a very young age, by many different people, over a long period of time. I don't even know where to start, because there were so many instances…

"It's okay, take your time." Said the pastor.

Well, my memory is a bit choppy, But I'll do my best to tell it. I remembered that one day, my grandmother on my dad's side came over to the apartment. It seemed like a casual visit at first, but it did not turn out that way. I was playing on the floor when my mom opened the door and let my grandmother in. There was another woman with her. She was someone I did not recognize, but my mom said she was grandma's friend. The woman brought a little boy with her, and she introduced him as her son. His name has escaped me after all these years.

My grandmother took me by the hand and guided me to the master bedroom. To my shock, she very quickly began to undress me, and as she did, my mom entered the room with the other boy. Mom quickly began to undress the little boy, who looked terrified as he looked at me while my grandmother continued to undress me. My mom and grandmother began to say things that did not make any sense to me at the time.

I understood later that they were casting spells.

I looked on, surprised and frozen by fear. My grandmother took dead animal body parts and containers with blood from the bag she had brought, and they began to rub our bodies with the animal parts, and the blood, casting spells as they did so. As they moved from animal part to animal part, and from the other boy back to me, they began to undress themselves, feeling moved by the dark taboo of what they were doing. They took blood out of a bottle and began to paint things all over our bodies.

I was traumatized. I wanted to escape but I did not know how. I wanted to make them stop, but I could not. I could not even speak. I felt like I was trapped within myself and could not break out.

"Wow. That's horrible," the pastor said, sounding more like a therapist in those moments. "I'm sorry that happened to you." She paused then, humming to herself as she considered what she knew of me. "You told me you had a sister, right?" the pastor asked.

"Yeah, I do," I replied.

"So did they do the same type of things to her?" she asked.

"Yes…they did," I replied.

I looked at the pastor and then over to her son Jay sitting on a chair in the corner of the room. He took a sip of his coffee and nodded.

A friend of mine, Jay, closer than a brother, was the one who convinced me to talk to his mother, so that I could get some help. I took a deep breath and continued explaining my story. I told her about a memory that was burned into my mind.

One night when I was a little kid and was in bed, I was awakened by a noise. I couldn't make out what it was. I just knew the sound was coming from the hallway. I was afraid to investigate, but I mustered the courage and climbed out of bed. I moved to the hallway and realized the noise was coming from my parents' room, and the door was slightly ajar, with light coming from within. I walked up and slowly opened the door.

There, on the master bed was my mom, naked, with my father and my little sister. My dad was on top of my sister, raping her, and when I gasped, they all looked back at me. My sister's face was etched in terror and shock. I know she wanted to cry for help, but she couldn't say a word. My dad just turned around and kept going, and my mom looked at me and gave me a devilish grin. I ran back to my bedroom and jumped into my bed. Moments later my mom came into my room, picked me up and walked me back to their room, where my dad did the same to me. My sister and I went through that type of abuse constantly.

"I'm sorry that happened to you and your sister. It really is horrible for anyone to go through something like that," the pastor said, her face covered in pain. "But God can cleanse you and heal you. You just need to allow Him, okay? One of the biggest mistakes that people make when they come to God, especially from the kind of hell that you've been involved in, is that they don't reveal the works of darkness, so they are eventually dragged back. The devil is able to blackmail them," she said. "That's why it's important to talk about these things, get them out in the open. What you're doing takes a lot of courage."

The Government Came Knocking

"I'm just tired—tired of living like this," I said to the Pastor. "I feel like I'm carrying an enormous weight that is choking me, not letting me live, not letting me be who I really am. I know that they will come after me for telling you this. I'm never supposed to reveal anything about the world that I live in, but I don't care anymore. I want out…"

"Who is going to come after you?" she asked.

"The people I work for… The ones who sent me to your church," I answered.

The pastor swept her hand under her chin and rested her elbows on her desk. "God can protect you from anyone and everyone. Trust Him, and don't you be afraid." She narrowed her eyes as she looked at me a little more intently. "Tell me, what did you get yourself involved in?

Who are these people, and why did they send you to our church?" she asked.

I told the pastor that the people that sent me her way…I was involved with them when I was in High School. Originally, it was because of my desire to break away from the hold that my family had on me—that I actually joined the group. I was already working for spiritual organizations that my family had been involved in, but one of the biggest things that nagged at me was the control that my parents held over me. They were able to keep authority over me and make me do things that I didn't want to do within those groups.

I hated that. It felt like they owned me, and I know they enjoyed bending me to their will.

I think I was a junior in high school when this happened. I had sent out demons a few times to see if there was any way that I could break away from my parents, and nothing positive had ever come back.

Not until that one night.

I was coming back from one of my endeavors in the night, flying through the air when I heard someone call me from below. I looked down and there was a man standing on a rooftop, motioning for me to come down to where he stood. I flew down and stood before him and got a good look. He was a tall, slender, White man. His hair was presented in a buzz cut, and he dressed in a long gray cloak, which emanated hazy white smoke as he moved. He slowly approached me, parting his lips to speak.

"Very impressive work you do," he said.

As he spoke, one of the little spirits in my employ realized that I was no longer flying home. It came back toward me, sensing my presence, and once it found me, it slowly circled around the stranger, until it landed, perched upon my shoulder.

"What do you want?" I asked the man.

"I believe I have the answer to what you're looking for," he replied.

"Oh yeah?" I asked. "What are you talking about?"

"You want to be more…independent, right?"

He had my interest then, but I still did not know who he was, or where he came from.

"Go ahead," I said.

"Officially, I'm a government agent," the man admitted. "I work behind a desk, and I do boring analytical work all day. Unofficially, I'm in charge of a group that specializes in the supernatural. We work with law enforcement to—"

As he spoke, I cut him off. "I'm not interested," I replied and began to fly away.

"Your parents and those people you're with won't hold you back anymore…" he yelled.

I stopped short and turned around midflight to look at him.

"You don't know anything about me," I said.

"Actually, your little friend…told me everything," he replied. "Just, let me show you what I have to offer. No strings attached. If you don't want any part of it, then, at least you'll know what it is you rejected."

And that's really all it took. I turned around and followed the man into what I thought was an abandoned warehouse…but I was in for a big surprise.

We walked down a staircase, four floors down into what seemed to be a large holding area. The warehouse had high ceilings, and seemed like something left over from the late 1800's. There were small windows everywhere, but the place overall was expansive. There were large open areas with a lot of open space in the middle, and what seemed like side rooms that used to hold passing freight to the sides.

We entered the main area. There were spirits flying to and fro, in and out of different rooms. People and demons flew around, some carrying on in serious conversation while looking into open portals that led to other locations. There were spirits forming circles in the air and chanting as their spells manifested in front of them. Others laughed and joked around on the warehouse floor as they looked into orbs. The people there were all young. A lot of them were just teenagers and kids, and it left me wondering what was happening.

"Name's Edward," my host said. "I recruit young talent, but not just anyone out there that dabbles in magic. I look for…the special ones. Those that are unique, with very special abilities, and talents, like you," Edward explained.

As we stepped onto the warehouse's main floor, I began to understand what transpired there. I looked around, and my eyes went directly to a small office in the back of the warehouse. There, a demon worked right beside an agent, both of them producing some kind of electrical magic. I was at the other side of the warehouse with Edward, but I could still feel the energy in that room.

There were dark, shadowy forms swirling around the demon and the man, who was dressed in black smoke. As they sat there, other people that had been paired up with demons would fly into the warehouse, come into the office briefly, stand in front of those two, and then they would fly out of the warehouse once more. It seemed to me as if they were reporting back from a mission and then given a new one immediately. Sometimes some of the swirling black shadows that were around the main demon and the man would follow those that left that room.

"We've been tracking you for a while now, but it was just recently that we decided to approach you. We need someone like you," Edward said.

"So, what is it that you really do around here?" I asked.

"We do the dirty work," he said, flashing a smile my way. "There are people in power that need someone to facilitate certain business dealings for them, and sometimes, regular methods are not enough."

I looked around and saw people working right alongside demons in a way I had never seen before. There was no sense of hierarchy, no one was jockeying for someone else's position, and there was unity there. All around me they opened portals, channeled spells, and harnessed all different types of magic together. It seemed like they were all unified. It was not like the coven I was raised in. Everyone was young, there was no-one trying to outshine the other. There was a sense of community there.

"We are a family here," Edward said. "We're a group of very special individuals. We don't have elders we have to bow down to. Of course, we still all work under the same lord. But if you join us, the hold your parents have on you will be broken, and you will be one of us going forward…" Edward put his hand on my shoulder. "Tell you what," he added. "Why don't you follow one of my teams and see the kind of work they do? If you don't like this sort of work, you will never hear from us again."

I looked around and all I could think about was the fact that I wanted to be free from my parents' power. This would be a way out for me—a way for me to do something different.

I looked at Edward and nodded in approval.

He smiled in return and raised his hand. Immediately two girls appeared beside him.

"This is Olga," he said as his hand gestured toward a tall and skinny White girl with short red hair. She was dressed in a red and black cloak that looked like it was stuck to her skin, and it dripped with some kind of liquid.

"This is Rishi," he said as he gestured toward the other girl. The small Asian girl was not human. I knew she was the demon companion. The girl was dressed in black jeans and a yellow bomber jacket, which seemed normal, but her eyes glowed red. She gave me a smile and revealed long, razor-sharp yellow-brown teeth.

No, not human at all.

Edward then looked at me, and when he did, the girls flew up like lightning out through a window in the warehouse. Edward looked over at me. "Well…?" he asked.

I realized I was just standing there, so I flew up out of the warehouse to follow them. As I reached the night sky, I could see them in the distance toward the east. They traveled fast—faster than I was used to. I followed from a distance and tried not to get close. They held hands as they traveled in the sky, teasing and taunting one another. It seemed as if they had been together for a while. Every now and then they would look back at me and giggle.

We slowed down as we neared a prominent mansion in the woods. As they descended to one of the windows, I followed.

Through the window, we saw a man raping a little girl in her bedroom. He held her mouth shut as he had his way with her, and her little sister watched in horror as she held the covers up to her mouth in the bed right beside them. When he was done, he got up, grabbed the other girl, and dragged her out of the room as she cried.

As the man dragged the girl away, Olga opened the window to the bedroom and entered, with Rishi fast behind her. I stayed outside but continued to watch them through the windows of the house, a distance away. I saw the man bring the little girl to his own bedroom, and it looked like his wife was there sleeping. She woke up when he opened the door, and when she saw the man holding the girl, she ran toward them. She tried to separate the girl from the man, but he was too strong for her.

He threw the little girl on the bed and shut the door behind him. Then, he proceeded to beat the woman relentlessly.

I watched as Olga made her way to that bedroom door, slowly opening it. I glanced back at Rishi and saw that she was talking to the older girl—the man's first victim. I could not hear what she was saying, but I knew that Rishi offered the girl some much-needed comfort.

When I looked back at the master bedroom, I could see the man was on top of the little girl, as the mother cried in a pool of blood on the floor.

Olga slipped into the room, quiet as a ghost. As she drew near to the mother, her dress wrapped around her. As it did, it brought them closer together until Olga entered the woman's body.

The mother climbed to her feet, raced to the closet, and came out with a shotgun. She screamed out, shocking the man, who reflexively jumped off the little girl. As he landed on unsteady feet upon the floor, he noticed the gun in the woman's hands. He tried to calm the woman, but he couldn't produce a single word before the trigger depressed. The muzzle flashed, and the next moment, blood and brain matter stained the bedroom wall.

Though I wasn't close to the unfolding chaos, it still seemed to grow far quieter than I expected. The woman stood there, entranced within Olga's grip, and the girl seemed too shocked to budge from her spot on the bed. Another quick glance through the window of the other room showed me that Rishi held the older sister close, soothing her and distracting her from the echoing shotgun blast.

I was distracted then as well, as a portal opened within the master bedroom, just beside the corpse of the fallen rapist. Ghostly chains flew out and grabbed the man's soul, tugging it from his body. As shocked as he was to see the shotgun, his soul seemed surprised, and he offered no resistance as the chains pulled him to hell.

The portal did not close, however, and an eerie feeling washed over me.

The little girl screamed at the view of the body by the door, finally able to rip herself from her stupor. Her mother walked slowly toward her and then sat on the bed.

At once, the traumatized girl raced from the room. I watched her as she ran into the adjacent bedroom with her sister and Rishi.

I looked back at the master bedroom, stunned to see the mother put the shotgun in front of her, resting her forehead against the barrel. Another blast rang out and temporarily blinded me, and when my vision returned, I could see the woman crumpled on the bed, dark crimson stains marring the mattress.

Olga stepped out of the woman at that point, and the woman stepped out of her body as well. She seemed surprised as she saw Olga there. She didn't have long to consider the strange occurrence, for from the portal, additional chains emerged, grabbing the woman and pulling her through. Her spirit screamed for just a moment, and then the portal closed, and she was gone.

At that point I entered through the master bedroom window and flew toward the kids' bedroom, Olga was already there, watching as Rishi held the older girl, the pair sitting on the bed. Rishi had the girl in a trance and as she whispered things in a language I could not understand, purple and black smoke emerged from her mouth and entered the little girl.

Olga stood by the smaller child, who watched her older sister intently. Rishi then stood from the bed, taking a glowing bead out of her chest. She walked toward the smaller child, knelt beside her and placed the bead inside of the child's head. I watched the little girl's head begin to grow out of proportion, until it was twice the size of her body. I realized then that it was her spirit I was watching— the demon was giving the little girls spiritual demonic gifts. As we flew out of the bedroom, I saw the older girl pick up a phone to call someone.

"So…what was that all about?" I asked.

"It was the end, and also the beginning," Rishi said.

"What?" I asked.

"The end of a long stream of abuse, the beginning of a new life for the girls," Olga replied.

"So, you guys just let them get raped, how come we didn't help them? Why didn't we save them?" I asked as we flew back to the warehouse.

"Who said anything about helping, or saving anyone? Those parents needed to die. It was the only way those girls would join us," Olga said.

"I get it. Trust me I get it," I said, "So, is it mostly this kind of stuff that you guys do?"

"Among other things," Rishi whispered as we flew into the warehouse building.

"You see that bitch's brain hit the ceiling though?" Olga said with a laugh, prodding me with an elbow.

"I'm sorry I didn't get to see that," Rishi said, grinning wide with her needle-like teeth. "The punishment is my favorite part."

As we entered the main holding area of the warehouse, my companions immediately flew toward the room in the back, where that big demon and the man were sitting. It looked like they had some type of spiritual interaction as I saw all sorts of colored smoke envelop them. They flew back out again just as fast.

I walked around a bit and I sensed someone behind me. I turned around and was face to face with Edward.

"This is your one opportunity," he said then, not giving me a beat to consider things. "It's the only time that we will ever extend this invitation to you."

"Even though I did not know who these people were, I knew that I was tired of being ruled by my parents.

I needed someone to help me get out from under their

power, so I joined them. I found out later they were

affiliated with the government—they *were* the government.

As one of their secret arms, they were affiliated through

spiritual ties. They were the ones that sent me to investigate

you, Pastor, and the ones that told me to find out what your

church was really about."

"Why?" the pastor asked.

"Well…there were many reports that I read about

your church. They spoke mostly about power, and the fact

that there was power here—real power they could not

control. And because they have no control over it, well…

That was concerning to a lot of people," I said.

"Well, that's nothing new. They sent spies after

Jesus himself after all. Those religious leaders back then

didn't want anyone affecting the hold they had on the

people. You've heard me teach about it," the pastor explained.

"I have," I replied.

"It's the true power of Jesus that they fear!" she exclaimed, sounding as though she was preaching as much to herself as to me. "So, what did you tell them? What did you tell them you found here?" she asked.

"I told them that there was nothing we could do against this power. I had no way to fight it or withstand it. All I could do was try to resist it when it came after me."

"That's the power of God you were resisting, He's been trying to move on you for a long time now," she said. "I'm glad you're taking this seriously now. Your very life is at stake."

We looked at each other for a minute, then we continued our session.

The Initiation

For days I found myself sitting in the pastor's office, and as I spoke about a topic, before I could finish, something else would come to mind. It felt like someone was pulling a string out of my mouth, and the more I talked, the more they would pull on that string. It seemed as if it would never end.

Then again, I had done so many things. Some things I had completely forgotten, until they came back to mind, sitting there in front of the pastor. Sometimes it seemed like it had been someone else that had done those things. Deep down I knew the truth. I felt it all in my heart, and I knew I was guilty.

We had been sitting there for some time, talking about the weather, or mundane things like that, when the pastor looked at me for a moment, and smiled.

"We're not the monsters they made us out to be, huh?" she asked. "Were you surprised by what you saw when you first got here?"

I paused for a moment. "Actually, I was shocked by what I saw," I replied. "Your son had invited me to church, and I remember walking in and being taken aback because everything seemed extra bright in here. I felt a presence of love that I just could not explain. I felt completely subdued, like I could not channel any magic at all, but I felt good. I was brought to one of the chairs in the sanctuary by one of the ushers, and as I sat down, I saw large figures of light that resembled tall men. They walked around the church, and I would only catch glimpses of them as they moved about," I explained.

"Angels," the pastor said.

"Yeah, I know," I replied.

Then I went on to tell her how the fact that I could not fully see them was puzzling to me. Every time I would almost get a good look, a wave of love would hit my spirit, and I would close my eyes and just suck it all in.

One time at church, I told her, I was sitting down and when I turned around, I saw some older women dressed in nice clothes come in, and I could immediately tell they were witches. They just came in, but they did not see the angels like I could, and I could not understand why. Dressed in their Sunday best, they hurriedly found a place toward the back of the church. I looked back at them, and I could see that they were trying to muster up some kind of magic, but it was not coming through. There was an unseen force hindering them.

They looked at me, and I could see they had been doing this for a while. They looked like regulars to the church scene. Frustrated by their lack of success there, one of them looked around. When she saw no one was watching, she looked right into my eyes, licked her middle finger and put it down her skirt and started playing with herself.

All at once, a large, charred black arm came out from between her legs, and then another one. They held on to her knees, and a large demon began to pull itself out of her groin. Once it had freed itself, I could see it was a bat-like creature that swept up from under her skirt and began to fly toward the center of the church.

As suddenly as it appeared though, a very large sword pierced it through the heart. I could see a massive arm coming out of a tremendous ball of light holding that sword. It was a gigantic angel in the center of the sanctuary. I could barely make out a head and a shoulder, as he shined so bright. He hurled the demon back into the woman, and she fell onto the floor, the force causing her to urinate on herself. Embarrassed, she climbed to her feet and ran out the door. Her friend wasted no time racing after her.

"God was letting you see, in part—letting you know—He is in control," the pastor said.

I told the pastor how when the music began and the people started singing praise songs, and things grew stronger for me. I began to feel as the presence of love intensified, and as the musician played, I could see a white mist descend on all of us. It was like we were being brought to a higher plane… Or heaven was coming down to us.

"Praising God in truth brings His presence close to you," the pastor added.

I continued to tell her how the atmosphere became so thick with the presence of God that I closed my eyes. I remember we began to sing a song called "Come Into My Heart Lord Jesus." And as I sang, I began to feel things inside of my heart begin to change. I started to feel the love

I had felt outside in the room, and it began to move inside of my being.

"It was like nothing I had ever felt," I said.

The pastor nodded, seeming pleased by my experience. "That was the Spirit of God. He moved within you…" she said.

"Yes, I could feel Him changing and re-arranging my heart and mind, and I felt so good. It was…euphoric," I explained.

I told her everything I could remember from that day. When the singing ended, the mist disappeared, but I could still feel the presence of God. I remembered feeling happy for the first time in a very long time. And then she came out and began to preach. That was what truly did it for me. I felt power that I had never felt before—the power of the Word of God as she spoke. It was more powerful than anything that I had ever felt in all my years in the devil's kingdom.

As she spoke, I explained, it felt like waves of power were coming out of her, and I felt like a stone that just sat there, crust and rust tearing off me. It was surreal.

It was then, at that very moment, that I knew that the Power of God truly was superior to anything that I had ever experienced in my life.

The pastor then crossed her arms. "So then why the struggle?" she asked. "I've seen you make your way to the Lord like this many times, and then turn back and resist Him?"

"I've seen so much of the devil's kingdom, I needed to make sure that God would protect me in the same way that I saw Him protect you. I mean, from everything that I had experienced, I needed to really be sure," I replied.

The pastor nodded her head. She understood what I was saying. "Can you talk a little about that? What made you believe that God would protect you?" she asked.

I explained to the pastor that it was not just one incident. It was over the course of time of me seeing God move for me that really convinced me to trust Him. And when I started to see that the devil was trying to kill me, I really had no choice at that point but to truly turn to God.

"He tried to kill you? But you were serving him…" the pastor said.

I told the pastor that the devil wants total loyalty, and he punishes you if you disobey in even the smallest of ways. After seeing that I was allowing God to take up a place within me, the devil tried to kill me numerous times, because he would rather me be dead, than lose me to God.

"Can you tell me a little bit about that?" the pastor asked.

I told her I was convinced that I needed to come and talk to her when they started making attempts on my life.

One time, I was driving home on a cold winter's night. As I stopped at an intersection, I looked at my rearview mirror, and I saw a big black shadow that moved from tree to tree. I had been at a prayer service, and I had been told to hinder the service. Instead, I allowed God to move within me and bless me that night. That was one of those times that I felt conflicted, because I knew the devil wanted me to fight the church, but I did not have it in me to do it anymore.

The light turned green, and I continued driving. I looked back and I saw the shadow following me. It raced from tree to tree, up on the buildings and even through the sidewalk. When I stopped at another light, I looked more closely at the shadow, and I confirmed it was a hulking demon following me home. It looked at me strangely, and I realized that it had been sent against me. As if it knew I made that revelation, it lunged out of the trees at me, brandishing a tremendous axe. As it lunged in midair, weapon over his head, my car stopped, and I could not accelerate. I jumped out of the car, and began to run down the street, and then into a park, the demon gaining on me with every step.

I remembered running in the snow, and looking up at the cloudy sky and thinking that this was it—this was how I would die. I fell, and as the demon jumped up in the air to strike, I just whispered "Jesus." Then suddenly, a bright flash of light came out of nowhere and knocked the demon back, halting its attack. Within the light I saw a tall, broad angel, wielding a humongous sword.

God had sent him to my rescue. The demon would not give up though. He tried to fight his way to me, attacking over and over, but every time, the angel would prevent him, striking him fiercely.

Then, at once, a spiritual gateway opened behind the demon. Smoke and ash emerged from within, but I don't think that the demon was aware. The angel struck the demon so hard that he flew into the gate and fell straight down. As the gate closed, the angel turned to look at me, offering only the quickest of glances before it disappeared, fading back to wherever it came.

The pastor studied me at that point, not really saying anything.

The birds chirping outside broke the silence in the room. She exchanged glances between her Bible, on her desk, and back to me.

"I'm glad you're taking this seriously," she said. "I know your life depends on it and…I'm glad you know this too. I want you to know that I love you, and I'm here to help you. Can you tell me a little more about your youth? What else happened when you were a child?" she asked.

"My initiation…" I said.

I began to tell the pastor of my introduction to my parent's cult when I was a child. We were still down in Argentina, and I must have been around seven years old. It was night, and my parents had kept me awake beyond my bedtime. All they told me was that we were going somewhere and that I was going to be part of their "extended family" as they liked to call it. They said it was like a club for special friends.

I waited with them. It was strange because we just sat on the living room couch and waited for what seemed like forever.

Finally, the doorbell rang. My mom got up and answered the door, and it was one of their closest friends. I knew him from the times he had visited before at the house. He had a purple garment with him on his left arm. He was very excited, and asked if I was coming. When my mother confirmed that I would be attending, he smiled and winked at me.

My parents talked with him all the way to the car downstairs. I remember being a little afraid because I felt the presence of something evil all around me. I felt like I was in danger—grave danger.

I held my mother's hand and went downstairs with them. We got into a small brown, beat-up, rusty car. It took some effort for my dad's friend to start it, but he did, and we were on our way. My mom and I sat on the back seat and my dad in the front. As we traveled, I saw a change begin to happen to my mother's features. First, she became pale, then her skin took on a yellow-green hue, and her eyes began to shine red and black. Her curly blond hair began to move on its own, and slowly darkened until it turned black. She looked at me and I realized I was looking at a very different person.

"I'm your real mother," she said as she reached for me.

I looked down to see where her hand was going. She grabbed my leg, then she said some words I could not understand. Suddenly black and brown spirits that looked like they were made of smoke appeared on the outside of the car. They flew all around us and followed us from then on.

"They will protect us as we travel," she said as she pulled her hand away from me.

There was an eerie silence in the car. As my mother's skin glowed brighter and brighter, a green, lingering mist appeared inside the car, and I remember feeling sick to my stomach.

We drove for a long time into the wilderness. San Juan is quite arid, and the city is surrounded by barren desert. We finally reached what looked like a ranch in the middle of nowhere. There were a lot of cars parked on the front lawn and all around the house. There were a few structures around the main building, though it seemed like everyone was inside of what looked to be a barn. We parked at the main house. When we all got out of the car, my dad and his friend went straight to the barn, whispering and looking back at me as they walked. My mom grabbed my hand and jerked me out of the car toward her. She hurriedly walked me to the house.

The house seemed ancient. There were cracked windows, peeling paint everywhere… It had certainly been there for many, many years.

When we walked in, there was a thick presence of evil in the air. It felt dangerous, suffocating, lustful, and enticing, all at the same time. It took you over the minute you walked in, and made you think differently—it made you act differently.

My mother led me by the hand into the house. It looked like nothing had been touched in the living room for years. The old furniture was covered in dust, and so was the carpet. We walked into the kitchen, and it was just as old and dusty. I was surprised to see that my grandmother was there. She stood in a corner with other old women and men, and it looked like they had been waiting for me. They all wore what I thought at the time to be dresses, but they were cloaks. Each one wore a different-looking cloak: my grandmother's was purple, some wore black, others black with purple stripes, and some were adorned with what looked to be gold or silver.

My mom handed me off to my grandmother. She pulled me toward her and began, with the other people, to undress me. I was scared and frozen with fear and disbelief of what was happening to me. I saw my mom across the room, with one of the women I recognized as her friend. She was helping my mom undress, and she was putting on a black cloak as well. I saw my grandmother take a small

container from one of the man's hands—to me it looked

like white grease. She began to put it all over my body with

the other people that were there. Whatever that was, it

smelled vile. I almost threw up from the smell a few times,

but it didn't seem to bother anyone else. They made sure to

cover my entire body with it.

When they finished with me, they exited the house

and left me standing there by myself in the middle of the

room. A single light bulb in the middle of the ceiling shone

on me, but every other room had gone dark. The house

grew quiet and still as everyone else made their way to the

barn. I could hear noise coming from there, but that was it.

I was frozen. For some reason, I could not move,

and was afraid to try. Goosebumps rose up from my arms

and legs as a cold breeze came in from the open door. After

enough time passed me by, I felt brave enough to move,

and to look around. Despite all the people who had been

inside the building just before, it seemed like it had not been touched in a while. Dusty dishes were stacked haphazardly in the sink. Dated, dusty appliances were on the counters, and empty pantry shelves lined the walls.

As I looked around the kitchen, I heard something enter the room. I turned to look at the doorway to the living room and there it was: it had the stature of a large man, and it wore a long black cloak, the hood covering his face. He took two steps toward me, and I felt a chill as he drew closer. He grabbed my hand then, covering the distance faster than I expected.

"Follow me," he said. He led me out of the kitchen and into the yard, bringing me toward the barn. His hand felt like it was dead, like there was no life in it. I looked at it and it was gray, like old, scaly skin.

As we neared the barn, the doors began to open by themselves. We walked in to find a multitude of people wearing black cloaks with hoods. There was hay all over the ground and it stunk so badly I had to clench my jaw shut and tighten my stomach to fight against the growing nausea.

There were people to the left and right, similar to a church, creating a walkway in the middle that led toward the back of the barn, where there was a large wooden platform, almost like a stage.

We walked up a small staircase to the platform. There were people with fancier black cloaks there, their inlays lined in gold. They faced me, staring me down, leaving me more uncomfortable than ever. A few of them wore purple cloaks, but among them there was one wearing a red cloak. I assumed these were the leaders or elders of some sort. I could not see their faces, as their hoods cast a shadow over them.

The platform was covered in blood, urine and feces, and there were pieces of flesh everywhere. An unsteady heat in the area left me breathless, and I was in such shock that I could not even think to scream—it was like I was in a trance.

I was brought in front of the elders by the man-creature that brought me in. All the other cloaked figures nodded in approval, and I was then led to the middle of the platform. The tall creature left me and walked toward the opposite side of the elders on the platform and faced me.

The presence of evil was even stronger there than outside. There was a thick, green mist moving through the people. I ventured a glance up to the ceiling and saw demons and black shadows flying around. Though I was uncomfortable, I scanned the room and recognized my mom. She had come up on stage, her head uncovered, though she still wore the black cloak. To my surprise, she stood beside the creature.

The one in red motioned for her to come to him. She walked toward him, past the middle of the platform and removed her cloak. She then kneeled at his feet naked and kissed his feet. The one in red poured something on her head. They said things I did not understand, and then my mom's skin began to move like it was alive, as if there was an invisible force moving it. One of the dark shadows came down from the ceiling and entered her. She began to convulse and vomit red and green liquid all over the place.

Then, as if it was completely normal, and nothing had happened, my mother stood up and a new robe was given to her. It had a different design and a little bit of gold trim. The elder in red gently lifted the hood, covering my mother's head.

The tall man-creature that walked me into the barn made its way to me again. It put its hand on my shoulder and walked me toward the front of the platform, where the highest concentration of blood was spilled. The platform felt both sticky and slippery as I walked to the center. I looked at the crowd and they quieted down as they gazed back at me. The creature walked back to his spot.

Suddenly, I heard a commotion on one of the sides of the platform. A small boy, smaller than me, dressed in a white garment, was brought up onstage, held by his hands and feet by strong, muscular men. As they brought the boy to where we were standing, the men raised him over their heads. Then, two cloaked members of the cult came from behind me and knelt at my sides and held me by my arms. Even though they were wearing black hoods, I knew they were women by the touch of their hands. The men brought the boy and held him over my head. I didn't know what was happening, I looked around and saw the person in the red cloak give a golden knife to my mother. The boy above me was screaming for his mom. Fear gripped my heart as my mother approached the lad, chanting spells—and the spells were coming out of her with a force I had never felt before. It almost seemed like fire was coming out from underneath the hood of the cloak.

When she finished, her hand was outstretched over the boy's chest, with the knife facing down. Then the person dressed in red spoke something in a different language briefly.

My mom opened her mouth to speak, but a deeper voice emerged from within.

"For this purpose, you were born."

Then I heard a scream. Still startled by the voice that came out of my mom, I could not register what was really happening. I felt moisture fall atop me, and when I looked up, the boy had been eviscerated above me. My mom tore open the poor boy and used her free hand to rip out his organs. He screamed through it all until the pain was too much for him to bear.

The women to my right and left hurriedly caught the blood that poured from the other child's wounds, grabbing hold of it as though it was crimson gold. They slathered me with the blood then as well, and I was too shocked to fight against the cruel ritual. Everyone in attendance began to chant, and it seemed to resonate with the pounding of my heart.

The demons that flew close to the ceiling descended among the people, and as they neared them, the cultists would vomit on the floor, scream, and gasp. A few of them began to levitate. In some cases, the demons would fly down, scoop them up and perform lewd acts on them as they twirled in the air. After the first few instances of those dark, sexual acts, a lustful aura seemed to take control of everyone. Just about everyone that I could see began taking off their robes, losing themselves to a sex-crazed madness as they intertwined in a violent orgy.

They laid me on the platform, with the remains of the boy all around me. As they held me there, people began to come up and urinate, and defecate on me, one by one. The women that were holding me relinquished their hold, and I was held in place instead by an unseen force. As people came up to me, they began to sodomize me; one by one they would take off their robes—if they hadn't already—and take their turn.

One of the women that previously held me jumped down from the platform and stood right in front of me. She pulled up her robe to expose herself, and as she did, she began to play with herself. I was too young to understand at the time, but her clit began to grow, and grow, both in length and width, until it became a large, throbbing penis. She pulled her hood down, and then completely disrobed.

She grinned as she began to rape me.

When they saw her, with their magic, a lot of the other women also seemed to sprout magical phalluses, and they joined her in her dark, violent, sadistic acts. My mother, grandmother, aunts, teachers, and other people I knew and recognized from everyday life, were there.

My whole body felt like it was on fire. It got to the point that I could not feel it anymore, it felt like it was not my body but someone else's. I felt like swords pierced my soul, and I remember wanting to escape somehow. I was willing it so hard, as one person after the other took turns on me. all I wanted to do was run away, but I couldn't.

And all at once I was out, free from physical pain. My spirit emerged from my body, and I floated to the ceiling of the barn. I levitated to the rafters, and all the demons that I had seen flying up there surrounded me but did not approach me. Instead, they seemed to keep their distance.

I looked down, and I saw people having sex with my body down below. Meanwhile, others were eating the remains of the boy's body.

The man in the red cloak caught my eye as he walked slowly to a group of chairs in the back of the platform, then sat down. His spirit arose from his body, and once he stabilized, he looked around, until he spotted me and flew up to join me. I remember him being a handsome, light-skinned man, with white hair. As he approached me, I realized that the bottom part of his body was smoke, and his eyes glowed red. He reached out to me, and when he touched me, it felt like electricity at first, but then it felt like I had known him for a long time.

He held me by my shoulders and our spirits began to meld together. He took me out of the barn and flew me out into the night sky over the open desert. We did not talk, but he kept looking at me in a way that bothered me.

As he held me, he transformed into a monster, and terror gripped me, he began to bite me, and scratch me, and gnaw at my body, the pain my spirit endured reminding me at once of the agony I felt in my physical body.

He laughed at my screams and bellowed in a deep voice. "Now you're mine forever. I will never let you go!"

Anguish pierced my spirit to its core, making it feel as though my metaphysical presence became corporeal once more. It felt like daggers shredded through my skull. My ethereal body was paralyzed, and excruciating pain ran through my being. I tried to scream, but I could not. His hands were dug into my arms and back, unleashing a great suffering upon me than I could have ever imagined when I was in my own body.

It became too much, and then everything faded to black.

I woke up the next morning in my own bed, in my own room, with everything from the night before still vivid in my mind. Part of me wanted to believe that it was a dream; in my mind I was hoping it was. But all my body and soul were telling me—screaming at me—that it had been real. I tried to move in my bed, but my whole body was sore. I was not cut and couldn't see any bruises or scratches. I did not see any wounds on my body, but I felt like I had been beaten up.

No, it was more like I had been run over by a train.

My mom came into the room smiling. She came to my bed, gave me a kiss on my head, and asked me how I felt, as though everything should have been okay. But I saw in her eyes clear evidence of the previous night. Her eyes looked as if they were glowing black, and with a moving mist of green behind them. As I peered into those dark, sinister orbs, she confirmed to me that everything had been real, but that there was a time and place to talk about it.

They're Everywhere

"So, did your parents work?" the pastor asked. "How were they staying up all night like this, doing these crazy things and keeping a job?"

"Well yeah, they worked," I replied. "Of course they worked. But there is a whole system, a whole underground network of people that work together and support each other in all these practices."

"What do you mean by underground network?" the pastor asked.

"Well, little by little I learned about it. There is a secret network of witches and wizards around the world. It is vast, and it has many faces. As a child—as I grew within this network—I saw that there were many roles that people played in this dark, underground world. There were some roles that varied from coven to coven. The labels may change a little bit from region to region, but their purpose is pretty much the same. They want complete world domination under Satan.

"I learned very quickly that, as a lower ranking member, we had no choice but to serve the elders. We were there to learn from them, and as we received from them the knowledge of our craft, we were bound to protect them from any peril at any cost, even with our lives if necessary.

"We were expected to be one hundred percent dedicated to the cause, always receiving assignments of all different types to further our vision. Sometimes we had to perform rituals to make money, sometimes for an increase in power, while other times we had to fight people spiritually. It seemed endless. When we were tasked to engage in spiritual warfare, sometimes it was with adversaries we knew around us. Sometimes the enemy was in another province, or even in another country altogether. Of course, by completing these special assignments, we were compensated in one way or another: sometimes with more powers, sometimes with special privileges… It varied.

"You mentioned roles earlier," the pastor said. "Were these like different types of jobs, or stations?" the pastor asked.

"Yes, by roles I mean stations within the organization," I replied. "Some of the roles included things like soul trackers, spiritual recruiters, decree enforcers, assassins. There are so many, I don't even know all of them. Some stay in one of these roles for the rest of their lives, while others advance because of their gifts. This is always, of course, with permission from the elders. So, when one proves themselves worthy, they can be considered for a different, or higher role. And there are always politics involved, so it's not always about your abilities—sometimes it's about who you know."

"Interesting," the pastor said, scribbling notes into the book on her desk. When she looked back at me, I could see I had piqued her curiosity once more. "So, what does upward mobility look like?" she asked.

"Under the right circumstances," I began to explain to her, "people can take a more authoritative position. A tracker for example, can become a basic hunter of souls, and from there eventually become an assassin. A caretaker can become a healer…"

"I've heard of this sort of stuff, healing with magic… All you have to do is call on Jesus!" the pastor insisted.

"Well yeah, there's people out there that use magic for healing," I said. "Someone who uses magic to heal, after a while, could work toward becoming a sage, or a priest of some sort. People also became spiritual soldiers, guards, lords, queens, kings, sorcerers, alchemists, assassins, mercenaries, and many other things. Training in one way or another is part of every true occult organization. The larger the cult is, the more opportunity for growth within it. There is more growth in status, power, and rank, but there's also more competition: petty rivalry, jealousy, and everything that comes with that.

"Of course, there's also the privileged folk—those within storied organizations, cults that are hundreds of years old. Those that are born within these cults could be direct descendants of occult members, who have many things handed to them, including generational powers. Those are the ones with a lot of influence in the dark world. Some of those powers and anointing, these generational gifts, include demons handed down through time, one generation to the next, from one family member to another, and are maintained by the repeated sacrifice of fresh souls.

"For the rest of us, however," I continued, "to highly specialize in something, in order to become a master at something, we had to go to a specialized school, or find a master that would be willing to teach us one-on-one. That person or school could be on the other side of the world. Distance is not an issue in the spirit world."

"So, you were born into this occult organization." the pastor said. "How was it for you?"

"I was originally just considered a reward," I said.

"A reward? Is that a good thing?" the pastor asked.

"No, not really," I replied. "Some children are given out to members of the cult as compensation for a task they accomplished. They may be used in any way or form—even sacrificed. There's a whole underground breeding community that makes kids for this sole purpose. A reward, on the other hand, is a young child that is lent out to someone when they accomplished a special mission or a hard task. They are usually used for sex. They cannot be sacrificed, and must always be returned in good shape, and yeah kids are treated like objects—pawns really...

"Because my family was established in the coven, I started as a reward. My parents lent me out to adults for sex, as they were instructed to do so by their superiors. Kids like me took on many evil spirits, as we were passed around from person to person. We acquired attributes from each person's spirit as well.

"For example, a wizard who liked to kill could put the demons that manifested from a murder into a child, as well as part of their own murderous spirit, so that the child would love to kill. A necromancer would put the spirits of death in a child so that they could commune with familiar spirits that were with their ancestors, and a part of their own ability to do so, that the child may begin this practice as well.

"Sometimes, however, this type of practice is used against the child. I've seen it happen that when someone receives a child as a reward, as they have sex, they instill rebellion toward those things that the parents want the child to be a partaker of. They even bind the child in a way that will hinder them from achieving greater powers, or status.

"As a whole, all the kids that I knew…we were all deliberately filled with lust, anger, hatred, pride, deception, and fear. Our hearts became incredibly hardened, all so that we could become the elite of these demonic groups—especially those of us that were enrolled into a school of magic. We were created to become demonic leaders."

Jay and the pastor gazed at me intently when I finished explaining.

I realized then that I had found people that really did care for me.

"Thank you, son, for taking your salvation seriously. I am so glad that you have chosen to believe God," the pastor said. "Did you go to one of these…magic schools you're talking about?" she asked.

I looked at her for a few seconds, hesitating for a moment before I found the courage to speak. "I just… Yes, I did. But I've never really felt power like I have felt in your church."

"It's not the church. It's the power of God that makes the difference. Without Him, we're nothing, just chatterboxes talking about stuff. It's the presence of God, His anointing, that breaks the chains, and He's the one that makes the difference," the pastor said.

"I'd like to hear more about that school," she said, turning the page in her notebook. "The more you reveal, the more access you're giving God to work in your life, son. You see, down through the years, people have come into our church, and talked about the love they feel here, and the presence of God, and how they have never felt so moved by love as when they come to our services. But they never, at least until now, revealed their evil works like you're striving to do, and so they backslide. When the pressure rises, and they need to take a stand against what God delivered them from, they fail. If they had done what you are doing today, they would not have been afraid of the fight.

"You better believe they are going to come after you, son," the pastor said then, the most solemn I had heard her since our meeting. "They may even try to kill you. But just remember: God is right there with you. In your time of trouble, you call on the name of Jesus. Your life is in God's hands."

I rose up from the chair and went over to the pastor to give her a hug. She embraced me dearly, and when I sat back down, she looked at me warmly and smiled.

Driving home, I was thinking over some of the things that the pastor had said, and though I felt some sense of relief, I began to also feel a burden in my chest to continue to talk. I knew something was about to happen. I pulled up to my parents' home and could tell that they had company by the sight of the extra cars in the driveway.

When I opened the door and walked in, everyone suddenly stopped what they were doing to look at me.

"Hi everyone," I said.

I could tell they had been talking about me. Everyone flashed fake smiles at me.

"The prodigal son returns," my dad proclaimed to everyone, holding up a glass of wine.

Everyone cheered and laughed, then resumed their individual conversations. I walked into the kitchen to eat something, and my mom approached me and pulled me aside.

With concern in her voice, she leaned closer to me. "What's been going on with you?"

I shrugged my shoulders.

"Look," she whispered. "You are not your usual self. Things are changing inside you, and they don't like it. Son, what have you been telling those people at that church?" she asked.

"Those are good people. What are you so worried about?" I countered.

"You know what I'm talking about. There's been rumors that someone has been saying things…talking about things. People are beginning to point fingers at you…" she said.

I started to walk away, but she grabbed me by my shoulder.

"I just don't want you to get hurt, and I can see that you're not the same… You're not the son I raised you to be. Everyone can see this, but I'm the only one that's talking to you about it because I love you."

I could tell that she was worried, and I knew that she saw the differences in me especially because she could not control me like she used to.

"Look, those church people are good people. They're friends," I insisted.

"Good people don't separate families!" She grabbed my shoulders and stared at me with an uncomfortable intensity. "You know I will fight for my family. I'm going to do whatever I have to do to keep you by my side. A mother will always protect her children."

"Look, I love you," I said to her. "Those church people are just being nice to me. Please leave them alone."

She looked at me for a moment, her countenance a mixture of sadness and concern, and then she turned and withdrew to the living room.

Though everyone was nice to me, and smiled, I could sense that each one of them had an undercurrent of emotions about me. Some of them felt anger, others rage, and a few were truly concerned about me. They were all focused on my every move. As I ate in the kitchen, one by one the guests and the rest of my family members would come and sit and ask me questions to get a gauge about where I stood. I did not touch on what was going on with me, but they could all tell that something was happening to me. I truly was changing, God was breaking the holds that they had on me, and they did not like it.

But what they felt the most was my spiritual separation from the group. They were just figuring out what they were going to do about me.

I went upstairs to my bedroom to read and fell asleep after a while.

In the middle of the night, I was roused from a dead sleep, and I saw a woman in my room. She was floating in midair, dressed in a long, shiny blue and silver gown. She wore a headdress of the same color, and her hair was long and silver.

I knew she was not there in physical form, but in spirit form, and I saw her clear as day. Her gown and hair moved about as if she was underwater. She descended to the ground and took a step toward me. I could see she was barefooted—but I quickly realized that she held a magic wand in her hand. That was peculiar to me, since I personally never used one. She waved it at me, and suddenly I felt constricted. I was having trouble breathing.

The room filled with her silver light, and as I tried to move, I felt a growing pain in my chest, like daggers piercing my heart.

"You have betrayed us," she hissed. "I know what you've been doing, and I'll make an example out of you. I am the queen of—"

Boom!

Before she could finish her sentence, a large surge of light erupted from the opposite side of the room and slammed the witch away from me before she could say or do anything else to me.

I was flabbergasted. I sat up and looked around, but she was gone.

"Thank you, Jesus…" I whispered.

As a peaceful feeling enveloped me, I lay back down and drifted back to sleep.

I woke up, and the sun was peering through the window. I heard birds chirping outside, and there was a nice breeze that swept through the screen and caressed my face. I couldn't remember the last time I had ever slept through the night like that. That was what it was like to be human, I guessed.

I climbed out of bed, and I got the feeling that a lot had happened through the night, but I wasn't sure what. I wasn't in the dark spiritual loop anymore like I used to be. I realized that all I could hear in my mind were my own thoughts. My ties to the collective spiritual mind of wizards and witches had been severed, and that was why I had such a good night's sleep. I walked up to the window and looked out. I could see the park in front of our house. People were exercising, and some were walking their dogs.

But a noise from downstairs stole my attention.

"Hey!" I heard someone yell.

It was my sister—I would recognize her voice no matter how much time had passed. I swung open the door to my room and spotted her on the second floor.

"I need to talk to you," she said "Like, now."

She walked up the staircase to the attic until she stood right in front of me. Maria was a beautiful girl, with long, dark brown hair, and pale white skin. Dressed in jeans, a sweater, and brown boots, she demanded my attention. She looked at me for a moment and I could see that she was upset about something. As she looked me up and down, I began to see with my spiritual eyes something within her moving about. I looked into her eyes, and there was something else behind her eyes looking at me.

"Mom and dad are not treating you like they should," she said. "They're being too nice to you—too careful."

"What do you mean?" I asked.

"I know exactly what you're doing... You're leaving us!" she cried.

"What are you—" I tried to answer, but she interrupted me.

"We know you've been talking to those people at the church. We know you're not the same. You're…different!" she shouted in frustration.

"Yeah, I *am* different. I found God… He really does have all the power. It's—"

"Shut up!" she cut me off. "After everything, all we've gone through… You promised to be with me. You said you would never leave me!" she screamed.

"I'm right here! I love you. You will always be my sister, no matter what. God is—"

"No!" she interrupted again. "No, I'm not falling for this crap. You have to make a decision quick. You're either with us or against us."

"Maria, I found God, and I wish you would give Him a chance. It's like nothing I have ever experienced. I feel real love, I—"

"We…love you!" she cried, her voice breaking that time. But as she spoke the words, she hurled black daggers at me from her eyes. The daggers hit an invisible force field protecting me, and then all at once, all the magic we summoned disappeared. Surprised, Maria stepped back and looked at me in anger and astonishment.

"We are your family. Our dad puts food on our table," she continued, her voice becoming quieter and more sinister. "I don't care who those people at that church are. I care about my brother. I feel ties between us being cut off, and you're allowing it." Though I saw tears in her eyes, I couldn't help but feel as though she sounded a bit like my mother. "Why don't you love us anymore?"

"But I do love you," I replied.

I leaned over to hug her, but she ducked away and spun around, charging her way back down the stairs. I gave chase and followed her all the way down to the first floor from the attic. I begged for her to stop, but she continued to

run until she reached the kitchen. She fell into my mother's

arms, both standing next to my father then. He had reached

into a cabinet to get a glass. Because of the sudden

emotional outburst, they all looked directly at me, as if I

had completely betrayed them. I stared back at them,

realizing that lines had definitely been crossed. No one said

anything to me, but they didn't have to. Their eyes said it

all. I was no longer one of them—I knew it and they knew

it. I could tell they wanted me to leave the room, so I turned

back around and returned upstairs.

I took a shower and got dressed, and when I came

back downstairs, they were all gone. It looked like they

went out together, but it was no longer my concern.

I made my way out the door and drove to the

church. Once there, I could see that the pastor was coming

out of her car as I entered the parking lot. I parked my car and walked up to the door, hurrying along enough that she waited there for my arrival, holding the door open for me.

"Hi," she said.

"Good morning, pastor," I replied. As I spoke, I realized that my voice broke just the way my sister's had.

"What's troubling you?" she asked. "How are things at home?" she cut right to the point.

"Well, it seems like my whole family is feeling like I'm deserting them. They think I don't love them anymore," I answered.

"They said this to you?" she asked as she led me to the church office. She gestured for me to take a seat.

"They're saying that they can sense changes in me and that I am not one of them. That if the church was really about love, they would not be separating me from them."

"Well of course they are going to see a difference in you," she agreed. "Because as you have been confessing your sins, God has been cleansing you and changing you. And don't feel bad about what they say or do—you must free yourself from the demonic life that you were raised up within. This is where the true tests will come from: your blood…your kin. No one can make you suffer like those closest to you. No one can make you feel bad like your own family.

"That is why when Jesus called His disciples, He told them to forsake everything, and follow Him. The Bible is very clear about this. When you come to Jesus, those that don't believe will not fully understand, and some may persecute you. There is an instance in the Bible where Mary, and Jesus's brothers came to one of His gatherings where He was preaching, and the people saw them and went up to Jesus and said, 'Your mother and brothers are here, and they desire to talk to You.' You know what Jesus said?" the pastor asked me.

"What?" I asked.

"'Who is my mother? And who are my brethren?' Then he stretched out His hand toward all the disciples in front of Him and said 'Behold my mother and my brethren! For whoever shall do the will of my Father which is in Heaven, the same is my mother, and sister, and brother,'" the pastor said.

"When you come to God, He becomes your Father, and His family becomes your family," she went on. "One of the Psalms, twenty-seven I think, also says 'When my mother and my father forsake me, then the Lord will take me up,' so let your determination to free your soul be absolute and let nothing deter you," she said.

We looked at each other for a little bit and then she sat a little taller, arching an eyebrow as she took stock of me.

"Well, are you going to give up or continue this journey of deliverance?" she asked.

"There is no way I can ever turn back now. I mean, if I ever try to go back now, I know they will kill me," I replied.

Enrolling In School

The pastor looked at me as if she knew something. "God is your only protection now. You don't need anything else, just Him." She opened her notebook then, as though that put a pin in our previous topic. "So, let's get to it. What do you want to talk about today?"

I hummed to myself, recalling where we had left off the day before, and remembering that she took an interest in a particular topic. "I think I need to tell you about the school of magic I went to," I said.

"I do remember you saying some people went to school to learn all that dark spiritual stuff," she said, and I couldn't tell if she was pretending to only have a slight memory of that part of my story. She flipped through the notebook back to her previous notes, and I suspected that she could have indeed had too much to remember in her line of her work—even with someone like me having recently come into her flock.

"Yeah," I said, venturing forth to tell more of my tale. "It's not like what you would see in the movies or TV. These places are very dark, and scary."

"All right, go on," she said.

"Well, one night—and this is after I was initiated by blood into the cult. You remember the barn and the man dressed in red that transformed and…" I reminded her.

"Yes, I remember" the pastor confirmed.

"Okay. A few days after that, I was alone in bed."

I remember it was a school night, and when I went to turn around, I felt like my face brushed up against something.

I remembered feeling cold, and when I went reaching for the covers, they were not there. I moved my legs, and the bed was not there either. I opened my eyes and was startled to see where I was. I woke up realizing that I was inches away from the ceiling of my bedroom, curled up in a fetal position in the corner. I looked around and saw my body on the bed below. The room was dark but the blue light from the moon brightened the room as it came through the window.

How did this happen? I thought. I looked around and saw my body still sleeping on my bed below, and I felt an immediate, urgent longing to go back to it, and a sense of danger for being out of it like this. I just wanted to get back into my body, but I did not know how to navigate back to it. I could not go down. I tried to push myself off the ceiling toward my body, but in my spirit form, I could not manage that feat.

I tried to go to sleep, hoping I would wake up in my body, but I could not. Out of the corner of my eye, I thought I spotted something, but perhaps it was just a scared boy's intuition. I turned and looked down the hall and spotted something floating my way. It was silent, and it had a pale, bluish glow. It looked like a cross between a boar, a camel, and something else. I knew at once that it was a demon. It flew toward me—not fast, but steady—until it entered my room and came right up to me. He looked at me with glimmering black eyes, and put his blue hands on my shoulders, spinning me around so that we were both horizontal, face to face in midair.

"You have been chosen," he whispered. "I have been tasked with seeing that you are taken to your designated learning location. I will be your guide for a time, and until that time expires, I have been assigned to you."

I did not know what he was talking about, nor did I ask. I was not able to resist him—he just took me by the arm and led me back down the hall where he had come from. We entered the living room, went out over the balcony, and floated into the night sky. I could see the full moon then, and the stars, and I felt a cold breeze that passed right through my body. Or at least it seemed that way to me.

Aromas washed over me like never before. Everything was magnified, augmented as it were. I saw other spirits floating in the night. Some seemed human, and others were just like shadows moving over water. We floated toward the central town plaza down below, and as we approached the ground, we sped up. I flinched, thinking we would hit the ground, but it suddenly opened like an envelope, and we dove underground.

We traveled down a long passage into the cold, forbidding earth. There were twists, and turns, the walls and ceiling apertures were sometimes circular, then ovoid. We would pass through large cavities, and small passageways. The deeper we went, the more frightened I became, but I did not say anything. Something had a hold of me. There was something that had been keeping me from reacting, and I felt paralyzed—all I could do is yield to the demon. At a certain point, I felt my mouth free up from whatever was keeping me still, so I ventured a question.

"Who are you? What is your name?"

"Morkataan is my name. I have overseen children like you for a very long time. I make sure that your kind gets the proper training you need to serve effectively," he whispered.

"Where are we going?" I asked.

"I've already told you," he answered, and then my mouth became numb again so that I could not speak.

We traveled for what seemed to be an eternity, mostly downward. It was almost pitch black. The only light was the bluish light that the demon emanated. We finally reached the mouth of a colossal opening in the tunnel we were in, and we landed on a cliff. The cliff was the end of a trail. I looked around and saw that it led to another cave, a similar deep blue light radiated from there. We followed the trail and began to walk down into the bluish cave. The ground was black, and the cave was like a large hallway that spilled into an enormous cavity. Only then did I realize that my companion's legs were not like mine. They looked like goat legs—hooves and all. They were hairy, covered in slime, and what looked like feces that continually fell from them.

The larger cave was many stories high, and faintly lit. It looked like the only light was coming from behind rocks all around the cave. I could make out shades of brown and orange on the walls, while the ground looked like fine black gravel. As far as I could see, there were kids everywhere, and each one had a demon companion. There were kids there from many places around the world, and each of their demons looked different. Some had wings like bats, others had what looked like folded flesh. Some were covered in hair, and others were more beastly looking. Some looked more like regular people, like men or women or a combination of the two. Some had tails, some were dressed, some had nothing on.

There was no playing, or laughing, or anything like that. Everyone was just standing until their demons bade them forward. Some demons would talk to each other, or to the kids, but everyone seemed to be very serious. I could sense fear among those my age. It seemed at first that everyone was just waiting for something, but I quickly realized that we were moving toward what looked like a wall of raging fire, with many arches.

The large arches were part of the rock and looked to have been cut out of the cave itself. They seemed ancient, like something out of a Greek temple. But where a door or passageway would be underneath them, there was a wall of fire instead. We began to move very fast, with an unseen force moving us forward, sliding us. I realized that there were many desks up ahead, one in between each arch, and on each desk sat a demon with many books. The demons had living tomes that would open to reveal things about the children. Most of the kids would go through the fire after speaking with the demon at the desks. I saw just a few that were flown away out of that place quickly for some reason.

As we got closer and were able to hear the conversations, I realized that only those that were mentioned in a certain book they held could go in. I would hear the demons scream out things like, "Needs more anger!" and "Not enough faith!" Those kids were denied entry and were quickly flown out of the cave by their demon companion.

When we reached one of those desks, the demon sitting there asked me my name, and Morkataan divulged my identity and where he had brought me from. He insisted that I had proven worthy to be taught there. The lizard-like demon looked at me, as books flew all around him, and he was sitting down on a very large skull. He leaned forward and widened his fiery eyes to get a good look. He then looked down and pointed to a name in the ledger.

"Here you are… Interesting though, because you were not typed in my book, but handwritten in. It seems you were not originally meant to be here."

Without warning, another book jumped into his lap, and opened to a special list. He looked down, and a deviant smile spread over his face.

"It seems…special arrangements have been made for you however, and you are definitely cleared to proceed." He then paused, before looking up at me and blowing smoke out of his nostrils. "Looks like there's something special about you."

He then looked at Morkataan, and they both smiled wickedly at each other. I did not know what that meant, but they clearly knew something I didn't. The demon then held his hand up, catching another book that flew his way. He slammed it down on his desk before flipping through the pages until he got to the end of a list, and then he wrote my name down. The demon looked up at me again. "Go ahead, get in there…"

I was ushered through the wall of fire in order to enter! I walked up to the blazing red flames, wondering what was on the other side. I looked back, and the two demons were just looking at me, then I turned my head to regard the wall of raging fire before me. I looked to my right and there were kids stepping through it, and to my left, and saw even more kids going through it. I mustered up some courage and proceeded forward and as I started to step through it, a powerful force suddenly pulled me and brought me to the other side.

I looked around and found myself in a completely different place. The best way I could describe it was as if it was a park without trees. I looked behind me and there was

no fire, just a solid stone wall—the side of a cave, actually.

The floor was dark brown cobblestone.

There were many strange statues and structures in

the park. There were park benches, and even light posts—

the old ones, from way back. Everything was gray and

brown, and I could see many buildings all around me.

There was a revolting smell in the air, which left me feeling

uneasy, and scared.

It was not a happy place.

There were people of all ages and nationalities

there, and there were demons everywhere, of all different

types. For the first time in a long while, I noticed that there

were a lot of adults present. When we entered the park,

they were going to and fro, talking to the kids that were

arriving. The place looked like it could be found in any city

on Earth at first glance, like any normal park. I thought at first that I was on the surface, but I was wrong. I had arrived at one of the many secret underground cities where the devil trains people, gathers recruits, and conjures evil plans with his servants.

A woman who looked like she belonged in a different era then approached me. She wore a large black hat, a long black skirt, and a dirty white blouse with ruffles. It looked as though she stepped out of the Victorian era.

"Hi there! My name is Wilhelmina, but you can call me Minnie," she said with an almost infectious happy attitude. "And what is your name, you beautiful boy?"

"Nicolas," I answered cautiously.

I was looking around at all the other kids that were being taken away by adults, and diverse creatures. She looked through a little book that whispered things at her as she flipped through the pages, until she struck her finger to a name. She smiled as she looked at me.

"There you are!" She reached out her hand and waited for me to give her mine.

I looked around at the flow of kids coming into this place. It seemed endless.

Seeing that I did not have much of a choice, I took her hand.

"Wonderful!" she cheered. She kissed my forehead, patted me on my bottom and guided me forward. "You're going to love this…"

Holding my hand, she led me out of that place, and into the street. I looked around and saw that the city was far from anything I had ever seen. There were buildings everywhere, and they seemed to be alive. At times I could have sworn that they expanded and contracted like lungs. They moved very slowly from side to side, like seaweed stalks swaying underwater. The buildings were all different shades of brown, maroon, black and purple. There was a brownish hue to everything, almost as if I was seeing things through a coffee filter. Everything seemed to be affected by it.

There was no sky. We were in an enormous cavern. The ceiling was rock, and it was dimly illuminated somehow. After all this time, I'm still not quite sure how. I did see fire bowls in front of some buildings, as well as torches and candles here and there. I saw what looked like flames that arose from natural gas pockets in the cavern, and I sometimes saw a glow that brightened parts of the cave. I could not explain it even if I tried—it must have been magic. The people there were all wizards and witches, from all over the world. I saw monstrous-looking creatures walking around with humans, and what seemed to be dragons flying way above my head.

People and creatures flew all over the place, speedily going from one place to another. The cavern was so big that I would lose sight of them as they flew away from me. There were gargoyles on buildings, but these were real, and they would look at the new arrivals intensely as they passed by. Some would just launch off the buildings with ferocity, only sprouting their wings in the last moments before they would plummet to the ground.

Despite all the people who were present, I felt very alone. I felt like I did not fit there, and there was a knowing inside of me that told me that all of it was very wrong. I felt like leaving. It was all too scary for me, like a live horror show. I did not feel safe.

I looked back and saw some of the children being taken by flying demons. They had bat-like wings, what looked like eagle's feet, and were completely hairless. They were putting the kids into baskets that were filled with a green goo-like substance. These creatures flew away with the kids. Some were taken to the top of some of the buildings, while others were taken out through purple portals that opened in midair. I really did not know what was happening, and it was nearly enough to send my mind spinning.

As I walked closer to the buildings, I could see that what was on them was a substance that was brown, sticky, and thick. It covered just about everything. I thought it was feces. And yet, even though I worried that was what it was, my curiosity compelled me. I touched some of it from a building's wall as we walked along, and it began to spread over my hand, as if it was enchanted. It went up my arm, and onto my shoulder. When Wilhelmina saw it, she snapped her finger, and the excretion began to harden and fall off me as it crumbled.

"Be careful what you touch. I'm sure you already realize that not everything is friendly down here," she said.

As we walked, another very strong, overpowering smell began to fill the air. I would later find it to be the smell of burnt flesh, mixed with sulfur, but I had never smelled that before, and couldn't comprehend such horrors. As the smell grew stronger and stronger, a putrid taste began to fill my mouth. My nostrils felt like they were burning, and my mouth became dry as a desert. I touched my throat with my hand, and Wilhelmina looked at me as if she did not understand why I was reacting this way.

"Can't you smell that?" I asked.

She laughed at the face I was making. "Smell what? Oh, that! You'll get used to that, it comes and goes you know. Soon it will smell like flowers and taste like candy," she winked and smiled wickedly.

"Where is it coming from?" I asked.

"There are many parts of this underground world, and some of those parts are filled with terrors—terrors you could not even begin to imagine. The smell is just a residue of those places that passes by from time to time." Her eyes were fixed on mine at this point.

She wanted to see my reaction. She smiled again, which put me at ease, I had to admit. We turned and continued our trip into the strange underworld. As we walked, I saw that people dressed in many different types of apparel, from all different times in history. Some looked ancient, others like nothing I had ever seen before, and some wore nothing at all. Some people would morph and change their appearance at will. As they walked or flew, they would transform into what looked to be other people, or creatures—or a mixture of both.

There were what looked to be shops all alongside the streets. People and demons entered and exited these shops, and they were bartering and purchasing things. There was a false sense of community that I could not explain. But I do remember liking the fact that people got along like that. Some of the places had windows, while others did not, just a small door from which to enter or leave.

As we walked, we came upon what looked to be a plaza, and it was quite crowded. There were people and demons everywhere who gave into lustful urges and carnal desires. They intertwined on the ground, on small statues, on benches—it was a giant, foul orgy, and I couldn't help but shudder at my memories of what had happened in the barn.

We walked around the edge of the plaza as we journeyed to our destination, and when I looked up at Wilhelmina, she was fixed on what was going on in the plaza as well. I was surprised to see that she was completely naked then as well, the woman running her hands across her body as we walked.

As I took a closer look, I could see some people at the plaza morphing their bodies to change their appearance, and their gender. I could not really tell who was human, or who was a demon anymore—they were all mixed, becoming one large mesh of spirits flying from one to another at lightning speed.

There was a green mist that rose from in between the bodies. It seemed to have a life of its own as it traveled through everyone, and as it did, it jolted them. At times it seemed like someone pressed a fast forward button, because some of the people, together with the creatures, began to move unnaturally fast as the mist touched them. The mist moved upward, above the people, above the buildings, and up toward the top of the cave. As I looked at this spectacle, I realized that there were also demons and people engaging in lewd acts in mid-air, right above us. Way up high they formed orgy clusters that moved from one part of the cave to another. I could see silhouettes going into these large clusters and out of them.

Wilhelmina turned to look at me, a lustful glow apparent on her face. She smiled, licked her upper lip, and looked back into the plaza as we continued to walk. She left a trail of blood that ran down her thighs, and I realized that she had cut herself with one of her long nails while she masturbated. She didn't seem to be in pain, or if she was, it only amplified her pleasure. Her hair had become loose, falling out of the tight style she wore earlier. It floated about as if she were underwater. An almost imperceptible moan of ecstasy escaped her lips.

Almost.

When she saw me looking up, she composed herself a little, but then bit her lower lip. "We are rewarded for doing magic for our master. Sex is one of those rewards," she explained. "There are many places where we gather like this, throughout the world. You'll see."

We walked across the street, away from the plaza, and onto the next block. As we looked at each other, I could see that she had made some spiritual connections with the people back there, without even touching them.

Her clothing began to appear from out of nowhere, and in just a moment, she was fully clothed again in her Victorian attire—hair up and all.

We traveled through the city and Wilhelmina's apparel began to change on its own. Sometimes she had a dress, then it became a skirt and blouse again, then she wore a long white robe with a hood, then back to the 1800's look. Her bare feet looked to be soaked in blood constantly then, leaving a trail of blood as she walked.

"Where are we going? This is so long!" I grumbled.

Wilhelmina stopped, turned around and squatted down in front of me. Her face was right up against mine. She brushed her hands through my hair, and then slid her thumb across my lips.

"I am taking you to a registration center. There seems to have been an issue with your inception paperwork. You were not originally printed into the entrance book" she said. "So, we are going to make a quick stop before I escort you to your school." She started to continue along, but I remained where I was, finally able to show some agency in the strange, scary place.

"Please, I don't want to be here anymore. Please…can you just take me home?"

She paused for a moment, turned around and came back to me, and kneeled right in front of me. "I'm not really supposed to tell you, but I'm a friend of your mother. We went to a similar school together. We were close friends, and I would have done anything for her then, and still would today. And I know she feels the same about me. She asked me to make sure you get a good start here." She paused again, and for the first time, I saw a darker, stronger shade of Wilhelmina. "You may not like it now, but you will. There's no way out of this—you're here now, and there's no going back. So, stop thinking that way, or bad things will begin to happen to you."

As she said that, her face transformed and I saw what she really looked like, an old, rotten corpse of a hag. She gave me a withered smile and then at once her visage returned, and a beautiful face looked at me once again.

As we walked, and she continued to speak with me, I suddenly began to tremble, and terrible pains jolted through my abdomen. I grabbed my belly and felt as if I was going to throw up. Then, what looked like black ink began to spew out of my mouth, and I began to cry out in pain.

Wilhelmina turned around and looked at me, startled. As I cried and the strange substance emerged from my lips, a man wearing only a pair of dirty gray pants from the other side of the street took note and approached us. The man looked concerned, but he did not try to help. They both looked at me very seriously as I gagged and coughed out the black liquid. They would only wait to see what would happen.

I was coughing, and hacking, as the thick black liquid spewed out of me, covering my hands, chest, and legs. Then I felt something crawl up my throat and into my mouth, and my eyes opened wide. One last cough propelled it out of my mouth with force, it was a small black creature with tiny wings. Its body was smooth, and the ink-like liquid kept falling from it. When it ripped out of my mouth, it flew directly to Wilhelmina. It whispered something in the woman's ear. She listened attentively, her prodding eyes sizing me up as she listened. Wilhelmina then turned to the curious man, and he leaned toward her as she whispered something into his ear. At once, they both turned and looked at me with a stone-like stare.

The tiny demon then flew back to me and fluttered toward my ear. I tried to stop it—tried to grab it—but it was too slippery. It felt like a needle pierced my brain when it entered me. I felt so completely helpless at that point, and an overwhelming feeling of loss came over me. I just wanted to go home, but I did not know how. I fell to my knees then. As some of the ink continued to fall from my mouth and onto the ground below, I began to weep. Wilhelmina quickly grabbed my arm and stood me up.

When I looked up at her, I could see that she had changed her appearance to a form completely different than anything I had yet seen from her. She wore a solid brown cloak, she was darker in complexion, her eyes had a red outline, and her pupils were almost completely black. She had no hair, her head covered in reptilian scales instead. Her hands as well as her feet were soaked in blood. She then flew upward, taking me with her. The man that was beside her flew up as well and grabbed me by my right arm. They seemed angry with me for some reason, and I did not know why.

They flew me across the city, past hordes of creatures and people having sex, casting spells, and doing all sorts of strange things.

They brought me to one of the more remote ends of the cave. It was there that I saw a small structure with a curved roof set apart from everything else. We landed on the sidewalk in front of the entrance. It looked like some kind of shop. They hurriedly opened the door, and walked me in, still holding onto my arms, my feet barely touching the floor. We stood there, in the small room of the tiny house that looked to have been there for many years.

The place was claustrophobic. It was dusty and filled with many items from all different places in the world. The room had a dim red glow to it. A small, fat creature came into the room from a door behind a counter filled with magical artifacts that glowed in different colors. The creature looked like a pig mixed with a dog, and it was dressed in turn of last century clothing. It walked toward me and reached out its hand.

"Come here, love."

I thought it was talking to me at first. But the tiny ink-black creature came out of me again, fighting its way back up my throat. It did not hurt as much that time, and it went and rested on the demon's shoulder. The demon kissed it on its head, turned to me and grumbled.

"You were brought to me because you were once heard praying, and it was not to our master. That prayer was indeed answered."

Wilhelmina and the other man looked shocked and scared at the same time. They took a step back from me.

"So, it was with much debate that you were allowed to come here. You could be dangerous," the demon said.

Wilhelmina propped herself up, trying to regain a sense of control over the situation. "I did not know of this before. I would have nev—"

The demon held up his hands and cut her off. He walked up to me, sniffed me and grumbled again. "I need to certify him before he moves on…"

He then snapped his fingers, urging a large tome to materialize out of thin air. He opened it and all the details of my life were projected onto the walls of the room—everything was on display. We could all see scene after scene of my childhood as he turned the pages, until he came to some that were blank.

"Here are some moments in your life that we could not record," he said. "We were being blocked by powers outside of our realm. There is only one that can do this type of thing…and *He* is not our friend."

Everyone cast strange and unsettling glances my way.

"How do you know all this?" And who took these videos?" I asked.

The demon flashed me a grotesque smile with crooked, long and sharp yellow-black teeth. "I am one of many record keepers. And my helpers, like my friend here," he pointed to the little ink creature, "they record events, times, and people—all the affairs of men really."

The demon then turned around. He waved his hand in the air and a tall bookshelf appeared in front of him. He looked up and down the shelves, through hundreds of books, until he found a large one, with a solid wood binding on it. *Amendments* was the title carved on its cover. The book was aged, but the wood grain was still visible. He looked through the book, until he found the place where my name was written, as well as my story. The book began to communicate, and it told us things about my birth, and my life, speaking in unsettling whispers.

"The boy is not one of our chosen seeds. He was offered by his mother. Sacrifices have been made, and the boy has been successfully inducted into our order, long after the appearance of the blank pages. Because of the choices he has made he was allowed to enter, and because we cannot predict his fate, he has been handwritten in."

The book suddenly closed, and it flew back into the shopkeeper's hand.

The demon smiled at Wilhelmina, and then turned to me. "You have chosen a better path, but I still feel a small level of uncertainty with you. Your journey must not be like the others. You will go through a reformation as you train."

"So, he will be ok? He can attend?" Wilhelmina asked.

"Yes, of course. I must, however, first seal my approval upon him," said the demon.

He turned and looked at Wilhelmina, and I could see that she clearly understood what he was saying.

The demon's eyes began to grow bigger and blacker, until that same thick black liquid ink flowed out of his eyes and mouth and flew toward me. It entered my mouth, nose and ears and began to fill me up with a very powerful force. I fell to my knees as the liquid continued to flow into me. I could not look away, as an unseen force held my head, preventing me from turning. Tears began to flow, and I looked at Wilhelmina for help, or at the very least compassion, but she looked on in ecstasy at my pain. She wiped some of my tears with the tips of her fingers, then licked them, savoring my suffering.

It seemed that demonic power in action was a turn-on for Wilhelmina. I, on the other hand, felt like I was drowning. Though it seemed to go on forever, it finally relented. I fell to the floor of the room. Everyone watched as I fell and hit my head on the wooden floorboards, but no one helped me. The room was still, until the silence was broken by Wilhelmina's orgasmic moan.

I looked up at the demon, and I could feel him projecting an understanding of what had happened to me. I realized why the demon had done this: he wanted to have a direct link to me. He attached his spirit to mine, so that he would know exactly what I was doing, always.

Wilhelmina looked at me on the floor as she licked her fingers and her lips. She lowered her dress before walking over to the man that had also brought me there. She thanked him for his help in bringing me there, and then bid him farewell. The man nodded and left, taking to the air before the door could shut once more.

The demon then looked at me, furrowing his brow. "I'll be watching you." He then turned and walked into the back room from whence he came.

Wilhelmina gathered herself and walked over to me. She gave me a gentle kiss on the top of my head and took my hand. She helped me to my feet, and for a moment, I shuddered against the emotional whiplash I experienced. She didn't seem to notice though, and she guided me back out of the building.

"Well, it seems you'll be ok after all," she said as we stood again on the sidewalk. She looked at me and patted my head. "Are you all right?"

I looked down at myself, completely covered in black ink. My stomach felt watery, and my knees felt like they were about to crumble underneath me. I looked up at her and she was smiling at me.

"No, I'm definitely not all right," I replied.

"Great!" she said. "Let's go!"

We began to walk again, toward our original destination. I was naked and covered with stains of ink and fluids from what just happened. My head was spinning, and I could hardly stand. I was embarrassed, but to my surprise, people did not stare at me like I thought they would. Some did look, but I was not ridiculed as I had expected. The weird and unusual was normal there.

We walked through streets and passages. Some were narrow, twisted streets, while others were large avenues. We also walked through what looked like back alleys, where creepy creatures looked at us as we walked by as if we had interrupted them from doing something.

The architecture I saw was diverse as we walked through different sections of the city. I saw buildings that seemed to be from medieval Europe, others from Asia, and yet others from ancient Roman times, with columns and marble faces. And there were others that seemed older than that. The size of the buildings ranged from tall skyscrapers—and indeed, these buildings seemed to scrape against the earthen sky above us—to what looked like clusters of buildings forming large campuses, and even small, narrow buildings. The place was enormous.

We finally approached what looked like a large city library to me, but perhaps it was more like a large museum with towering columns all around and a steep rock staircase leading up to colossal, dusty black metal doors. We walked up the stairs, and as we approached the doors, they opened by themselves, emitting a very loud sucking noise as it drew us into the building. It was as if we were standing on a conveyor belt.

When we were inside, I turned to Wilhelmina, and she had transformed into a younger version of herself. Her feet were no longer covered in blood either, I noticed. She guided me in through an enormous rotunda of yellow marble floors and tall black columns. We walked straight to the back of the rotunda, up a large circular staircase, and then we entered a long hall.

The place had a gothic look to it. There were stained glass windows, and statues of animals and creatures I did not recognize. Some turned to look at us as we walked by. The ceilings were high and vaulted, leaving it looking like a church. There was an old red carpet that guided people from the staircase all the way to a large counter that stood right in front of a wall with tall bookshelves at the end of the hall.

As we approached the counter, a woman suddenly appeared behind it in a puff of red smoke. She was dressed in a long black, gothic-looking dress that went up to her neck with a white collar. It moved as if it were alive, and black dust came out of it as she moved around. She looked to be in her 40s. She was pale white, and her shiny black eyes pierced through her features. She called out my name as we approached.

"Nicolas!" she said loudly.

Wilhelmina and I stopped, looked at each other, then back at the woman. The woman slightly smiled and motioned for us to come closer, so we did. She came out from behind the counter and approached me.

"Hello, Nicolas. I have been waiting for you." She paused and put her hands on my shoulders as she looked at me. "My name is Rose," she said.

As she walked around me, I saw roaches and other insects moving underneath her dress, crawling in and out from under the ruffles. She would leave a small trail of them as she walked, and they would quickly run to return underneath her dress. She continued to look at me up and down, turned me around and back, then began to wipe some of the black stuff off my face with a handkerchief. I had forgotten that the black liquid was still all over me.

She slowly leaned toward me and licked my forehead, whispering something I could not understand. At once, all different types of small creatures came out of the woodwork. They rushed toward me from all over the place—some ran up to me and others with little bat wings flew out of nowhere toward me. They all began to lick me clean, like little dogs would. They were all over me. The creatures were gray, and skinny; some had many legs, others had multiple mouths, and heads like earless bats. Like bees surrounding their queen, the creatures surrounded me. After they cleaned me off, they ran or flew away, some even underneath the administrator's dress. As quickly as they appeared, they disappeared.

The woman walked behind the counter again and smiled at me. Her teeth were rotted away, and the ones that remained were black.

I was frightened. The whole experience was a nightmare, and I just wanted to get home—that was all I could think about.

The women carried on what seemed to be a regular conversation with me. They asked me about my parents, and my experiences with them. They asked me about people in my family, and what I had learned from them so far. I was compelled to tell them the truth. I did not know why at that point—I just did.

"All right, you come over here Nick, and stand right next to me," the administrator said. "We'll get this business done and have you on your way."

I hurriedly went around the counter and stood beside Rose. She then pulled her dress up a little and reached under it with the other hand. I could see hundreds of creatures underneath her dress, just looking at me as she moved her hand around. Finally, she pulled out a large book. The book was unnaturally big and had a gray and black velvet cover on it. She placed the large book on the counter, and it opened by itself. I could see many signatures within as the thin pages by themselves, until to the tome stopped upon a blank page. Rose put her hands on the book and caressed it with both hands. Then she took my finger and placed it on the blank page.

"This is your pen. Sign here and you will be enrolled, and then our business will be complete…"

I looked at my finger on the empty page on the right side and began to sign my name with my finger. As I wrote, some of the ink that was inside me began to pour onto the paper. I could see my name was alive in the book. When I finished, my name moved itself onto the left page, underneath a column where many other names were.

"That was not too bad right?" Mrs. Rose asked. Her eyes sparkled with a green glow.

I walked around to the other side of the counter where Wilhelmina was standing. She placed her hand on my shoulder and smiled.

"How do you feel?" Wilhelmina asked.

"I feel drained, like a part of me left me and poured onto the paper as I was signing," I answered.

"Precisely," Mrs. Rose declared.

Wilhelmina continued, even bubblier than usual. "A part of your spirit was used to register your soul into our school. When you think about it, a part of you will always be here, in this place…forever".

When Wilhelmina said that, the book violently closed itself, grew feathery wings, and flew upward above our heads. We all watched as the book flew up in circles and put itself away onto a very high shelf. The book leaned forward, and I realized then that the book had many eyes on its spine, and it was looking down at us from the high shelf.

The two women smiled at each other and shared a sense of accomplishment, and a look of relief from what I had just done, but I did not share their joy. I just wanted to go home. I felt so tired, my mind gone weary after all the time spent there in that unsettling place. Mrs. Rose then took out what looked to be a gold mat from underneath her dress and placed it against the wall behind the counter.

"Go ahead and step on it. This is your way home," she said.

As I approached the mat, it enlarged and struck ablaze with fire and brimstone upon it. Suddenly the room enlarged itself and expanded away from us with great force. It seemed as if the wall flew away from me, so far that I could hardly see the other end. I was standing in front of a completely different space. I saw all sorts of staircases leading to upper floors, and balconies lined with bookshelves. Everywhere I looked there were many books, shelves, and statues, with places to sit and read. This whole place was where records were kept.

As I took everything in, I saw black smoke, like when you drop black ink into a glass of water. And it moved around in the upper tiers of the library, way up in the distance. It moved violently from one side of the hall to another, having no shape, but it moved constantly to where it almost formed the shape of a man, or woman, or some sort of creature, before it changed again. Mrs. Rose put her hand on my shoulder, pointed to the mat on the floor and assured me that this was the way out. I looked back up to see if I could find that shadow thing. It scared me, after all, and I was hesitant to enter the room.

"Just…follow the path," Mrs. Rose said, pointing again to the mat on the floor that was ablaze.

I approached the burning coals, but they were not hot, and when I put my hand above the flames, they did not burn! I was amazed. I looked back at the women, and they both smiled at me. I stepped onto the flames, and then the mat extended. It suddenly began to stretch out to the other side of the enormous hall, becoming a walkway of fire.

I could not see the other end of the library—it was so far away. I looked up again to see where that shadow was, but I could no longer spot it, so I began to walk on the path of fire. As I walked into the room, the black shadow sensed me, and flew toward me with great force. I could not run away, I was stuck to the path I was standing on, and when it neared my face, frightening sounds erupted from it, like train horns mixed with thunder. I had my arms up to shield my face, and I whispered, almost more to myself than to the creature.

"I just want to go home…please let me by."

The thing stayed in front of me and would not move. It felt like a force that was withstanding me. I heard many voices coming from it as if they were talking at a great distance, but I knew they were coming from within the black shadow. I could not really understand them, but they got a little bit louder every time the thing shifted just a little bit. I had no more strength, and began to fall on the fire below me, but as I was going down, I reached out to the black smoke, and it began to wrap itself around me. My arm looked like a spoon inside gelatin. As I pushed into it, it sucked me up and completely engulfed me.

I realized then that it had wanted me to give in to it. That was what it was after all along. As I surrendered to the blackness, it enveloped me, and entered me, and I could feel the evil of its essence become a part of me. I could feel knowledge and understanding of many different things seeping into my mind. The way I looked at everything was being manipulated and changed forever. I began to see images of people throughout history, those that had been involved in magic, and those that had leveraged an influence on world events, as well as those that worked in the margins and shadows of the past.

Without realizing it, I was being carried through the path of fire by the darkness, until we reached the other side of the room. The dark shadow lifted from me suddenly. I opened my eyes, and I was right in front of a small black wooden door. I looked back, and I could hardly see the two women looking at me in the distance. But I heard Wilhelmina's voice in my mind.

"Go through the door!"

So, I opened the door, and then a force sucked me outside of it. The door closed itself behind me, and I fell down a few stories from the back of the building. In all the time that I spent in the enormous city, I had forgotten that I was in my spirit form. I flinched as I plummeted toward the ground. But I reached it with my eyes closed and felt no pain to land there. When I braved another glance, I found that I was safely on the ground below already.

I found myself on the streets of the city again, by myself that time. I looked up and saw that the door I had gone through slowly disappeared, fading until it was no longer there. I looked around, and suddenly realized that I did not know anyone there, and I did not know where to go.

I looked to see if I could go around the block to the front of

the building that I had just been in. I walked, then ran

around the block, but the building kept changing. The

windows, and even the doors disappeared from where they

used to be. I went around the block several times, but I

could not get to the front of the building. I finally stopped

running and gave up.

I felt awful, and exhausted, and began to walk the

streets. I didn't even care that I was naked, and it seemed

that no one else cared either. I saw people flying above me,

and others walking by me as if they did not see me. I

looked to see if there was anyone with any compassion that

would help me, but I did not know who to trust. As I

walked through the streets, I came across a series of little

shops. Intrigued and desperate, I decided to check it out, so

I walked by and looked in through the windows.

One place sold candies, and it was filled with people and other creatures. They were buying and eating the sweets. The candies would come out of the boxes themselves and fly around the shop trying to get into people's mouths. Chocolates, cotton candy balls, rock candies and more—the place was loaded. There were lot of kids in the shop, running around being chased by flying chocolates and candies.

I kept walking. Another place had magical monsters that looked like little pets, and people would hold them and caress them. But the place was crowded, and I did not want to deal with large crowds. I walked by another shop, and they had body parts hanging on the windows. I was already shaking my head before I started running away from that place.

Then I came across a shop with empty glass jars everywhere. There was no one in there except for the storekeeper behind the counter. I decided to walk in.

I entered, and there were glass jars on shelves all

over the store, and each jar seemed to be empty. The man

behind the counter was almost bald. He had an old, dusty

brown cloak on, and he looked to be in his 30s. He watched

me intently as I entered.

"You're new here, right," he asked.

I ventured a glance at him for a second, and then

looked away, trying to distract myself. I noticed the jars

had labels on the lids.

"I don't know how to get home," I replied.

"I can help you," he whispered, but his voice

sounded creepy.

"What are all these?" I asked as I pointed to the jars.

The man came out from behind the counter and lifts

one of the jars, holding it out to me.

"These are emotions—emotions that can make people feel and do very powerful things."

I looked at the lids more closely and they were labeled with all different types of emotions: anger, hatred, love, remorse, anxiety, rage—every emotion you could think of, had a jar. He opened a small jar, and as he did, pink smoke materialized inside it, he blew it toward me, and it engulfed me. I suddenly felt calm and content. I slowly closed my eyes, smiled, and then opened my eyes. The man held the lid up for me to read, and I could see that it said "Contentment."

The man flashed a crooked smile and nodded his head, but quickly changed his demeanor back to business. "Getting an emotion, that's not why you're here. Sure, I can help you kid. Follow me."

He walked behind the counter toward the back of the room and pushed a large shelving unit out of the way to reveal a hidden door. He opened it and it led to a dimly lit back room.

"This way," he said as he gestured at the door with a deviant look in his eyes.

It did not feel right. I was not about to go through some secret door, as content as I felt. We just stared at each other for a short minute.

"Well, do you want help or not?" he demanded.

I glanced at the little room but turned back toward the exit door.

"It's ok. I'll find my own way," I said, and quickly walked out of the shop.

I made my way down the street, as fast as I could. I did not trust the shopkeeper. He seemed deadly to me for some reason. Before I could get too far though, I felt something grab my arm. The man from the shop had his hand on me, and he was trying to drag me back into his shop! He did not say anything, but he looked furious and stern. He really meant to do something to me, and I began to struggle with him, I was afraid for my life at that point.

He dragged me all the way to the door of his shop—everyone was looking but no one would help me. As he was about to bring me back into his shop, I decided within myself that he was not going to take me. Then something unexpected happened. With all my will and might, I let out a burst of energy. It came from my chest and shocked him loose from me and unto the ground. He was stunned and stared at me for a few seconds.

"Who are you?" he asked.

Then I heard my name being called. I looked around. It was Morkataan, the demon that first brought me down there! He was at one of the ends of the cave, inside a cavern that looked like a doorway. He motioned for me to come to him. I was glad to see someone that I knew, and I ran to him both with relief, and uncertainty. I did not know where my choice was going to lead but I was glad to get away from the storekeeper.

When I arrived before him, Morkataan stepped forward, a question upon his lips. "So how did everything go?"

"It was horrible," I insisted. "Please take me home."

"It wasn't all that bad now, was it?" he asked as he led me into the cave. "From what I could tell, I think you got a good first look at your new home…"

"Wait, you saw everything? You were just looking at me and not helping me?" I asked.

"This is just the beginning," he said, laughing despite my frustration. "You were meant for this. You're already using magic and you don't even realize it."

"What do you mean?" I asked.

He just looked at me and said nothing. We walked into the cave, until the path came to an end. I looked up and there was a long way up, so high I could not see the end of the cavern. He picked me up and flew me up the pitch-black cavern. It was much different than the one I had flown in from—I could barely see a thing. I tried to take comfort in his arms, but there was nothing there. He felt cold and rock-like. I tried going to sleep, but I could not, even though I had never known such fatigue.

After a long while, I could see in the distance up ahead that the cavern was coming to an end. "Hey!" I yelled as I pushed my companion's arm.

He looked down at me, encouragingly. "Trust me."

As it looked like we were about to hit a rock wall, a purple portal magically opened just in front of the rock, and we were suddenly out of the ground. We flew out into the open sky, and came out of the side of a mountain, out into the desert, with the distant city lights visible. The air was freezing, but the cold did not seem to bother him. It was still dark, but in the distance, I could see a bit of sunlight beginning to pierce the night in the east. We flew straight into the heart of the city, and finally got to my parents' apartment. To me it seemed like we had been gone for a week, but the apartment looked like we had never left, and everything that had happened had been a dream. He brought me to my room, and we looked at my body resting on my bed. The only light in the room was the soft blue light that emanated from the demon.

"Get in," he said.

"How?" I asked.

"Imagine yourself in your body and use the power of your will to make it a reality."

I looked again at my body before looking back at him. He just stared back at me without a hint of emotion on his face. I walked over to my body, and reached out to touch my own hand, but I went right through it. I closed my eyes and willed myself to go into it, and then I felt myself being pulled into my body. I flew up, and slowly fell into it.

Once inside, I opened my eyes, and picked my head up. I did not see my companion—the room was completely dark. I looked around, and he was gone. I tried to tell myself I had been dreaming, but I could not convince myself of it. I still felt my insides churning, and aching, and the images of everything that happened kept running through my head. I was so tired though that I put my head down and went to sleep immediately.

I came to a pause and looked at the pastor, noting the intense gaze she sent my way. There was a moment there, where we just looked at each other, eye to eye, not saying a word. It seemed like Jay and the pastor were digesting everything I had just said, processing it. Then the pastor finally broke the silence.

"Thank you for taking your soul's salvation seriously," she said. "I just can't say that enough. You are the only person in my whole congregation, throughout all the years that I've been preaching, that has gone into this type of detail in their confession. But remember, you're not doing this for anyone else but yourself. The only one that's really benefiting here is you. See, God can deliver you from anything. Those papers that you signed and rituals and all of those crazy things you did here on Earth and down in Hell? Jesus can annul it all. There is no such thing as a blood oath, or contract, or covenant of death or anything that can keep God from delivering you. You're confessing so that you can stay free once He delivers you. You're setting yourself free from ever going back that way again..." she looked at me and slightly smiled.

"Let me ask you something," the pastor said. "When you first came into our church, did you really think you were hidden? That we didn't know who you were?"

I hesitated for a second. "Well, yeah. I thought that you did not know who I really was. I mean, I used my powers to hide myself, and really believed that I was hidden, because it had always worked before."

"God revealed you to me even before you stepped foot into this building. He told me you were coming, but I did not know all the details. He left that for you to reveal, for you to confess, so that we can in turn begin to trust you." She reached out, grabbing my hand, and I felt comfort despite her firm grip.

"God knows everything. Nothing is hidden from him—nothing."

You're Out

"Get the hell out of my house. Now!" my dad yelled.

He paced back and forth in the living room. My mom was crying, and my sister was upstairs with her door shut. We had an argument about me going to church, and not spending time with the family, and doing all the things we used to do.

Everything finally came to a head.

"I don't understand. I gave you everything I didn't have when I was growing up. You never wanted for food, or clothing, or a place to lay your head, and this is how you thank me?" he yelled.

"You never loved me," I dared to shout back. "All you really cared about is yourself!"

Then he came right up to me—right up to my face. "Everyone knows you've been talking. You're a fucking traitor! You put the whole family at risk. They're gonna be coming for our heads! And you don't give a shit. You fucking loser—you're the one who only cares about themselves, with your fucking church. Fuck you!" he screamed.

Then he got even closer than before—so close I could see the veins in his eyes. We were nose to nose at that point. "Yeah…you're angry now? Then do something about it: hit me."

"What?" I replied, completely surprised and taken a back.

"I know you want to hit me. Go ahead. Hit me!" he screamed as he grabbed my shirt.

"No… What is wrong with you?" I said as I pulled his hands off me and backed away.

"Get out. Get your shit and get the fuck out of my house! Now!" he boomed.

I didn't have any compunctions about doing what my father said. I went upstairs, and passed my sister's room, noticing the door was still shut. I knew that she had heard everything though. I went to my room, gathered up a duffle bag and began to put clothing in it. I hurried downstairs and found my dad on the couch, with my mom crying next to him. I went to say goodbye to her, and he held out his hand.

"Just leave," he said.

I looked at my mother, but she made no effort to say goodbye or acknowledge me in any way. She was too scared of him. I turned to the door and walked out into the night, and I could see the moon in the distance. I got into my car, throwing my meager belongings into the back, and

I just started to drive. Tears filled my eyes, as I did not know what to do with my life, and I had nowhere to go.

I made my way up to a lookout point where I could see the New York City skyline, and I began to think and pray about everything that just happened. I came to the realization that maybe it was for the best. Maybe it was God's way of delivering me from being under their thumb, and that way I wouldn't be around them when they performed their evil rituals. But where was I going to go?

My phone rang as I considered that question, and when I looked at the screen, I could see my friend Jay's name there.

I told him about all the events of the night. He listened patiently, and I knew he could hear the distress in my voice.

The first thing that he said became my lifeline.

"Hey, don't worry about it man," he said. "You can stay at my place for as long as you need."

"Really?" I asked. "I don't want to be a bother, but I—"

"Listen," he said, "my sister is actually dating a superintendent at an apartment complex, she can help you get an apartment, we'll go there tomorrow. Just…come on over. It's going to be okay."

"Thank you. Thank you so much!" I replied.

Everything worked out. I stayed at Jay's home for that night, and I miraculously got the keys for an apartment the very next day. I realized that I was on my own then, for the first time in my whole life. Things began to settle in, and I firmly believed that all that had recently transpired was for the best. I believed that it was God's plan for me, and that everything seemed to be working out for the moment.

Jay decided to move in with me because he felt bad that I was living alone. He was a good friend.

But of course, things don't always stay that way for long.

One Sunday morning, at church, as we were all sitting down waiting for the service to begin, I felt a sharp pain on the side of my head. The pain was so piercing, that I leaned forward and put both of my hands on my head. The pain spread down to my neck and through my back and I realized then that it was not normal—it was a spiritual attack.

I turned around and spotted a beautiful blond woman sitting in the back, looking straight at me. As I looked at her, her eyes flashed bright red for a quick second, and I realized that she was an agent of hell, and that I was her target. I turned back around, and the pain would not go away, so I began to pray.

The hymnal music started, and everyone stood and began to sing. As I joined them, I began to feel the pain subside. I turned around again to look at the lady, and the woman's appearance had completely changed. She looked bony and her bright red eyes were set back in her head. Her smoky charcoal skin cracked as she smiled again, and green corruption dripped from her lips.

Suddenly, she transformed back to the beautiful young blonde, turned about, and walked out of the sanctuary and into the vestibule.

After church, as everyone was leaving, the pastor came up to me.

"Did you enjoy the service today? Wasn't the message wonderful?" she asked.

"Yes…yes it was great," I replied.

She could see that there was something bothering me. "That lady that came in at the beginning of service?" she asked.

"Yeah," I replied, reflexively bringing my hand to my head. "She was fighting me and—"

"Did you really think that the devil's kingdom was just going to let you go?" the pastor interrupted. "No, they're relentless. They will come after you, over and over. And when they are convinced and see that you truly are a child of God, they'll change their tactics. After that, they will come after you some more, to entice you back to them, to make you afraid. And then they will try to kill you.

"All of these are tests to see your resolve," she went on. "I've seen wizards and witches come to God for help, and He would deliver them. He cast out the demons that were inside of them and broke every dark contract they had made with the devil. But when it came to confessing and telling on the works of the enemy, they would fall short, and not reveal what they had done to the fullest. They would not trust God enough to reveal it all. And it would be fear that kept them back. Fear of the devil and his crew would come against them. With fear, there is torment, and by not revealing the works of darkness, they would become complicit to their past, and eventually backslide to the evil they were involved in.

"Think of it this way," she explained. "When a soldier wants to defect to an opposing side, he is going to need to establish trust with them somehow. They need to know that he or she is sincere. By revealing everything they know, they are doing two things: establishing trust with the side they're going to and creating a breach with the side they're coming from. It's a one-way ticket. Because if they fail to reveal everything, neither side will trust them, nor will they have any friends—only enemies."

"I'm not going back," I insisted. "And I have a lot more to tell."

The pastor smiled and put her hand on my shoulder. "Good. Let's meet here tomorrow at ten in the morning?"

"Okay," I say.

The pastor walked toward other members of the church to greet them, and I felt a bit safer after talking to her. I looked around and took the whole scene in. The church had a very large window by the altar that let in a beautiful light which illuminated the sanctuary. It felt great in there—it felt like home.

It felt…peaceful.

The very next day, I sat in the church office with the pastor and Jay. It was a little cold that morning, and the heat hadn't kicked in, but the smell of the pastor's coffee was comforting. Jay sat on a large reclining chair in the corner, sipping on his tea. The pastor stood by her desk, looking through her briefcase for something. The morning sunlight came in through a large glass brick window in the office and it brightened the whole room.

"So, all the time that that you were coming to church before, you were still doing all of this evil? You were coming out of your body and talking to demons and stuff?" Jay asked.

"Yes," I answered.

"And you would be communicating to people that were outside the church while you were here with us?" the pastor asked.

"Yeah, I was connected to other agents spiritually and I would communicate with them in such a way that they would be able to see and hear what was happening here, through me," I explained. "I was…a conduit for them."

"So, it's like a mental thing?" Jay asked.

"Sometimes it was. That would be telepathy," I said. "There are a lot of different ways in which people can communicate, especially with magic." I hummed to myself then and moved into a familiar position—one I seemed to fall into whenever I was ready to divulge some great secret of my past. "Let me give you an example," I said.

The pastor quickly sat down and put away the briefcase.

It was a weeknight, and I had just returned home from one of the church services. I went straight up to my room and sprawled out on my bed. I was not repentant of anything at this point—still a full-blown operative of evil. But I felt kind of lonely at the time because I was being pulled in two directions. God was pulling at my heart to repent, and the devil was pulling at me and threatening me to stay with him and say nothing.

I wanted to communicate with someone that would understand me. I lifted my hands, and they began to glow purple with magic. In between my hands a viewing portal appeared, and I began to reach out to people to see who wanted to talk.

I tapped into—well you could call it a spiritual network—and I began to communicate with witches and wizards from other places in the world. Their images appeared in my mind and we talked and shared ideas. I talked at length with people from distant cities who I believed I would be working with soon. A very young girl that reached out to me that night I remember in particular.

She asked me for help with her flight training. She felt

alone, had been shunned by her family, and was a complete

outcast. As I talked with her, I became sympathetic to her

because she reminded me of when I was younger. I began

to think back to my early days of training, the times when I

first began to learn magic. When I was learning the craft

myself.

Learning the Craft

On the first day of classes, Morkataan woke me up and carried me out of my parent's apartment just like the first time, and then led me deep down into the earth. That time, it was to a small cave, with a passage that ended in a solid rock wall. The cave was narrow, light brown in color, though in some places it looked almost peachy. The ground was dark brown dirt and covered in small black pebbles, and it felt claustrophobic to be there. As I walked toward the wall in front of me, there was light coming through it. It illuminated the whole cavern in dim yellow. I looked back, to see if Morkataan was still there, and he was.

He had to make sure I went through that wall.

I was still not used to walking through things like that, and as I approached the wall, it transformed into a gel-like substance that reached out to me as if to kiss me. I closed my eyes as it slowly engulfed me. I passed through the wall, opened my eyes, and waited to see if my demon companion would follow, but Morkataan did not join me on the other side. I looked around and saw all the other kids to my right and left, coming in from other locations. All the kids would enter through their drop-off points. Inside there were chaperones and teachers that took us in groups to our classes. I stood at what seemed to be the edge of a park again. Just like the previous time I was there, the place was a large open area with lampposts here and there, park benches, and some odd-looking statues. There was no grass, but scorched earth instead, and I could see the city in the background.

The city looked immense, with towering buildings like I had seen on my first trip to the vast cavern. Even from where I stood, I could see a hue of brown smoke that moved in between the top buildings, as if it was alive.

As I stood there in the park with a whole lot of other arriving kids that were passing through cave walls, posts, coming out of benches and the sort, I saw my first teacher

walk up. It was a man named Charleston. He was dressed

in black attire that looked like a robe, but not like the ones I

had seen before. That one had lots of black ruffles in the

neck area. On top of his robe, he wore a black hooded

cloak. He also had sticky, dirty black gloves on, that looked

to have been involved in a lot of nasty business. But he had

no shoes on. As he walked, I could see his feet. I guess he

was proud of his hairy, wolf-like feet, because it seemed to

me that he would find ways in which to stand so that they

would get maximum exposure.

Charleston was a middle-aged white man, and

though all his inflections and mannerisms would make it

seem as if he cared for us, looking back now, I know he

didn't. He went through the motions and inflections of

someone that cared. He hugged us, patted our heads, and

led us on, but there was no love to be felt in his embrace.

All I felt in my heart was the wary caution that this man was dangerous and would harm us at any moment.

He motioned for us to come to him, and he knew all our names.

"Hello, hello everyone! Welcome, welcome to what's left of the rest of your lives!" he said, as he stood on the arriving platform with us. "My name is Charleston. You can call me Charles if you like. I will make sure that you get into your classes on time, and that you get all your proper equipment. I am so happy that you're here! Please, follow me."

So, we followed him into the city. He walked in front of us, pointing things out as we walked, giving us a guided tour.

"In this building we have spirits that manifest jealousy, all different types," he said as we passed a dark, slimy green building. Then he pointed to another building.

"This is where the enforcers stay. You'll learn all about that later."

We followed him as he pointed to almost every building and gave us a short history of it. Distracted as I was, quite a while passed before I noticed that I was naked. As I looked around, I noticed that all the other kids around me were naked as well—not just the ones that were in my group, but all the other groups around me.

We walked through the streets. The ground below me felt like regular concrete, only a lot warmer than I thought it would be. We went down a narrow street, past some leaning brown buildings that seemed ready to tip onto the sidewalk we were on, and onto the street. It seemed like they could topple at any moment, and I saw creatures and people carrying on inside as if nothing was wrong. We just kept walking.

The whole situation seemed a lot more organized since the last time I was there, and I was happy about that. And for the most part, everyone—all the kids, including me—seemed to be growing accustomed to the weird place rather quickly.

As we walked, Charleston entertained us with magic tricks. He made his hands disappear, and then he made little creatures come out from underneath the sleeves of his cloak. The kids loved it, but I was not amused. All I kept wondering about was when things would get scary for us.

As we drew deeper into the city, the intoxicating smell of death and burnt flesh filled my nostrils, and it sunk deep into my chest where it remained. It seemed to infiltrate me, and somehow, I knew it was becoming a part of me.

There were people everywhere, moving about the city, going in and out of buildings and windows way up in the high-rises. I looked up, and there were people and demons flying across the cavernous skyline. I saw what looked like a dragon feeding on a cluster of people performing sexual acts on each other in the air. They were so entranced by what they were doing, that they did not realize they were being consumed. I could not believe that was happening. I slowed down to look closer and saw the people traveling through the body of the dragon. Eventually the dragon pushed them all the way through his digestive system. When they came out, the people were covered in some green and brown stuff. But they were completely enraged in demon lust and continued in their orgy with intensified energy.

As I stopped and stared, a boy pushed me back in line. I looked at him for a second, upset with him because he had shoved me, but then I realized my class had passed me by. I rushed through the small crowd, and quickly walked toward my group.

We arrived at a ghastly building that was dark brown in color. The doors seemed to be made of glass, but it was a moving substance I did not recognize. We entered a large main reception hall, where the ceilings were high above our heads, and the room was enormous and circular. The walls were decorated with pictures, hanging decorations, tapestries, and metal objects of all different sorts. Things that had been gathered throughout time, it seemed, were everywhere.

The floor looked to be made of some type of marble, interwoven with all sorts of demonic-looking designs that had flashes of light running through them. There was a counter on the wall to the left of the entrance, like the ones you find in hotels. The ceiling was layered almost like the inside of a cathedral. Every circular level had metal spikes going upward, layer after layer, the whole thing forming a conical shape to the top. It was black, and putrid, and it was so high I could not see the end of it, but I could make out some figure flying up there.

The whole building seemed ancient, like it had been there for centuries. There was a green mist that moved inside and out of the walls. It was not like the black mist I saw before. The green mist, it seemed, wanted you to approach it. It moved gently though the ceiling, into the walls, then out again, until it rested upon us, and began to move in and out of us. It would usually go in and out of the mouth or nose. It moved slowly, and it seemed to be alive. When it reached me, it went in through my mouth and out of my nostrils. It felt sickening at first, but when it left me, I immediately desired more of it. As it passed through other kids, it began to levitate some of them, and made others fall on the ground. It moved from child to child, methodically as if it was thinking. Then, after we were all touched by it, it vanished into thin air.

We heard a loud, single clap. All our attention was drawn to a woman who was standing next to Charleston.

"I am Kara, the keeper of this house," she introduced herself as she looked us over.

Ms. Kara was a tall, middle-aged Asian woman. She looked refined and classy. She had thick black hair, streaked with flashes of brilliant red, and it flowed as if she was underwater. She also had red eyes that turned black sometimes, but you could never see her pupils. Her dress was black, with thin red pinstripes, and it also had long sleeves that were connected to gloves, which seemed to be part of her dress. I did not see her feet, as she seemed to float from place to place. She had a presence of old bones, blood, and death.

"I have brought you your novice robes. Please put them on as you receive them," she said.

She lifted her dress, and small black robes began to fly out to all the kids. The robes flew around the room, searching for their new owners, as if they had been preassigned. When they found their master, they put themselves on their predetermined kid, almost against their will.

As I stood there, I felt something grab my ankle. I looked down, and it was one of those black robes. It was underneath me holding my ankle, as if it was looking up at me from the floor.

"Hey! What are you doing? Oh, are you my robe?" I asked.

It slowly moved up my body, and then slid onto me. I looked down on the black robe I was wearing, and the best word I could use to describe it was…nasty. It was raggedy, it had holes in it, it was dirty, stiff, and dusty. It felt old, like it had been passed along from person to person.

"They may not look like much to you, but these very robes have been handed down from one generation to another generation of students, and they are powerful," Mr. Kara explained. "You see, they hold the memories of all those that have worn them before you. They remember the failures. They know the victories. These robes will help you learn and remember what was taught to you. They will become a part of you and will only depart from you if one of two things happen: One, you graduate out of the novice level, or two…you die." She flashed a creepy smile, then licked her upper lip with a forked tongue.

All dressed in filthy black, we were led by Ms. Kara from the reception hall, down a darkened hallway, into another expansive, cylinder-shaped black room. That one's walls stretched high into the air. There was light coming from the top, almost seeming like there was no ceiling—it seemed endless.

As we walked, memories that I did not recognize as my own began to surface in my mind. It was the cloak, and the memories within it. I saw little boys and girls wearing the very robe I wore, doing all kinds of things, like casting spells, flying, fighting with other kids, and some even dying. I opened my eyes and realized that I was not the only one being affected. The other kids were seeing things as well. Ms. Kara just looked on. It took us a minute to compose ourselves again and gather as a group.

"What you are experiencing is normal. Your spirit and mind are being joined with your robe. You are becoming one spirit, one mind, one will. It's ok. Just let it happen," Ms. Kara said.

Slowly we all began to assemble and focus on where we were. I looked up again, and noticed that all around the walls, going way up, were doors.

"These are the doors to your rooms—your safe space in this city. You can spend as much time as you like before and after classes here. Nothing is allowed to enter these walls but you and I," said Ms. Kara. She spent time looking at each of the new students, offering subtle judgments upon them, it seemed. "Each one of you has a predestined room. Your robes will show you which room you belong in. This will be your very first lesson."

"How do we get up there?" one of the kids asked.

"Yeah, where are the stairs?" asked another.

Ms. Kara smiled and opened her arms. "As you feel yourself meld with your robe, let your thoughts become one. Reach into yourself and tap into the robe's memory. Let it lift you up and guide you," she said.

I did not know what she was talking about. I looked around and saw that some of the other kids were puzzled as well. I saw them closing their eyes to concentrate. *What were they doing?* I closed my eyes and tried to do as she said, but I didn't feel anything.

Suddenly, I heard laughter. I opened my eyes and saw some kids begin to levitate. They lifted upward, some faster than others. Doors began to open, and the kids were taken inside their rooms! I didn't want to be left out, so I began to speak to my robe.

"Ok, c'mon robe, lift me up and take me. I'm ready. Let's go!" I said, but nothing happened.

Ms. Kara looked at me, arching her eyebrow as she considered my ineptitude. "You must quiet yourself and listen, not talk to it!"

As I stood there, an understanding came to me. I realized that it was not with my ears, but with my spirit that

I had to listen. I tried to clear my head and yielded my will to the power of the cloak.

And then, I began to levitate.

I opened my eyes in wonder as I flew higher and higher. I looked down at the woman and saw that she was smiling at me.

Up I went, passing doorways where other kids looked curiously around their rooms already, and I also passed others that just stood there in awe. As I was taken up, a bit past the middle of the large cylindrical building, I took a closer look at the walls. They were pure black in color, made of what looked to be obsidian, and they were fully decorated with meticulous silver and gold gothic designs.

The doors on the wall did not seem present in any order, but rather scattered randomly. And though each one of them was black, they changed colors when one of the new students was about to enter. Each child had a different color. I realized then that I had stopped rising, and then a door turned red right in front of me before slowly opening. I floated in, and gently set down in the middle of the room. The first thing that came to my mind was the question of how I was going to get down. Was it in a similar fashion?

The woman seemed to have known what I was thinking.

"When you're ready to come down, your robe will know," she said. Her voice was powerful, yet she did not yell out to her new students. "Yield to its power and you will descend."

I peeked outside and looked down. I had not realized just how high I had risen. I could hardly see the floor below. I looked up and I still could not see the end of the shaft, it was so tall. Children floated upward past me still, and I could also hear them yelling and moving around their rooms. The building, it seemed, was accepting us, almost as if it were alive, with a mind and spirit of its own.

Suddenly, all the doors to the rooms began to close.

I looked around my tiny room. There was no window. The room looked to be something out of the Middle Ages really. The floor, ceiling, and walls were made of dirty gray stone. There was no bed. There was, however, a large antique mirror in the corner, a timeworn desk filled with books, a shelving unit with hundreds more books, and there were even *more* books on the floor. The whole room was dusty and old, and the books looked even worse for wear. I picked some of them up and read out the titles.

"*The Ancient Ways of Babylonian Magic, Flying Assassin from Above, The Secrets of Loving Death, Disappearing in Plain Sight.*" And there were many more like that, too.

I walked over to the full-length mirror in the corner.

I did not really think much of it at first. When I investigated

it, I did not see my reflection, but saw the room instead.

The grayish stone walls, the spider webs, everything was so

very dimly lit. But then I saw a figure begin to appear in the

mirror; it was an older me, wearing a long black robe, and a

head garment that covered my face as if it was a black mist.

There were weapons on my wrists, and waist, and I was

holding what looked to be a spear. I had a broach on my

chest that held what looked like a black cape, and I had

black boots reinforced with some type of metal. The image

moved right along with me. When I waved, it waved; when

I walked around, so did it… And then it slowly vanished. I

sort of understood that it was trying to show me the image

of who I would become—or who they wanted me to

become anyway. It was to give me something to look

forward to.

But that would never be. I turned out to be something completely different, something deadlier than a spiritual soldier. I became something…horrible.

But that is a story for another time.

Before I knew it, I was in the air again, and flying toward the bottom. The garment was taking me back, but I did not have to consciously yield to it. Subconsciously, I was already willing, and that was all it needed. I noticed that the robe no longer looked old and raggedy. It was long and sparkling black and looked new. It even glistened as I moved in it. It looked as if it was filled with stars, and it fit me perfectly. All the other kids' robes looked new as well, and they had magically changed to fit us. As I reached the bottom, I walked over and joined other students down there already. I looked up and saw the rest were coming out of their rooms and floated down to meet us.

The headmaster walked over to a shelf, and picked up a large, old wooden box. She placed it on a small table in front of her and called out to the kids, as she spotted some still descending.

"Everyone, gather round," Ms. Kara said.

She began to hand out what seemed to be candy. The kids were all gathered around her, as she threw the packages to the children. She looked through the box carefully, choosing each one selectively, and then she would scan the children to find who she was looking for, before tossing it to them. Finally, she locked eyes with me and threw a package at me. I reached up and caught it.

I immediately ran out of the crowd and opened my hand to see what I had received. To my surprise, it was a finger wrapped in see-through plastic! It did not seem gross to me for some reason, but I did not like the fact I got a finger. I looked over to my right and saw a boy holding an eye. When he felt me looking in his direction, he passed me a perplexed expression. I motioned for us to trade, and he obliged.

Ms. Kara immediately knew we had traded, however, and she pointed at both of us. "No trading! You were supposed to get a finger; the eye was not meant for you." She walked toward me and then she paused for a second as if she was listening to someone speaking in her ear. She arched her eyebrow again and let out a little hum. "Go ahead. Keep it." Her nasty smirk turned into a creepy smile, then. "Just this once, it's okay."

No longer focused on me, Ms. Kara levitated off the ground, rising above all the new students.

"From this moment on," she said, "you will be separated into smaller groups of classmates. You will study together, learn together, cry, and maybe even die together. And if you do survive, you will be the elite: the most renowned, most powerful witches and wizards of your generation."

And with that, a horde of demons appeared in the cylindrical room, surrounding us. All different types were present. Some were red, with long ears, and others green or gray. The black-and-red ones had wings. Some were partly naked, others were fully dressed, but lust emanated from all their bodies. Some had goat feet with hooves, while others had what to me looked like eagle's talons, while yet others had regular human-like legs. Some had features like horns, and scales on their faces. They all had grotesque appearances, whether they were monstrous or appeared to look more like humans.

The demons called each student in their class and gathered the children to them. When everyone was assembled, the demons took their class of students to different places.

Our green teacher led us to an open field within the underground city, where we sat down and listened to him talk about purpose and the privilege of being there. We were brought there, he said, to be the leaders of our generation, the ones to usher the "great one" into his reign, and so forth. As I sat there listening, I realized that I had begun to feel more comfortable and was not as afraid as I was before. I looked around at the other kids, and the strange but vast place that surrounded us, and I told myself that it was not that bad…

Every night I was ushered by a demon down to the place, and every morning I was taken back to my room by a demon. I was down there so much that after a while, I learned my way around the city well enough to travel on my own. I knew where my classes were, how much time it took to travel from place to place, and how much spare time I had before and after classes.

Time was very important, because we had to get back to our bodies by a certain time, in order to begin our day on Earth. There were no clocks, or watches, but everyone was mentally linked, possessing an understanding of when they had to go back, and how much time they had left. It was like a communal mind that everyone had access to. Intelligence and knowledge could be drawn from it too. Its boundaries depended on each person's rank, and role. As I was talking, Jay made an inquiry.

"So, what sort of things did they teach you to do down there?"

I shifted my position, speaking to both Jay and his mother at that point. "One of the first things we learned was to become shadows, by willing ourselves into darkness."

I began to explain what I learned in that class. It was really the first time that I had used magic to change shape. We had been taken to what looked to be a large, empty medieval dungeon, deep in the bottom of one of the immense buildings in the underground city. The dungeon was bare and dimly lit by what looked to be gas lamps on the walls. Our small class of kids stood halfway down the stairwell leading to the bottom, while our teacher for that class, Mr. Malinda, stood at the bottom of the staircase.

Mr. Malinda had a big personality. He wore what looked like a pirate's shirt, and extra tight black pants. He had long black hair, and tattoos that moved throughout his body in such a way as to enhance what he was saying, reflecting his mood and flamboyant personality. Holding his hand out to showcase the dungeon, he explained that day's lesson.

"What you must know first," he said, "is that in order for you to enter undetected into a fortified destination, and in order for you to leave undetected, hiding in plain sight is one of the best ways to go about doing such a thing.

"Now there are many, many ways one can hide in plain sight, but one of my favorites, and the one that I will teach you today…is shadow-walking," he said as he opened his arms. He levitated upward and then he transformed into a black mist. The black mist looked like a shadow in midair and it began to take on many different shapes of people, animals, and things, and then it flew toward the bottom of the dungeon floor, disappearing as it combined itself to the shadows on the ground.

Then we all heard his voice.

"As you can see, as a shadow, a person can hide in plain sight. You can hunt or track someone, spy, and even get close enough to assassinate someone—and then make a getaway if need be." We heard his voice come from different parts of the dungeon. "You will learn to move on the surface of objects, take on shapes of other shadows, and have deeper and lighter shades of gray. You will learn to connect with each other, to intertwine to form larger shadows. Remember: a shadow is patient, but deadly." He then reappeared amongst the kids. It seemed that he had slipped past us, gone up the stairs as a shadow, and changed again to his human form right in the middle of us without us even knowing, much to everyone's surprise.

"Now you will take the oath of commitment to the prince of shadows and recite the incantation after me. He will give you the power to become a shadow yourself, and lose yourself within him…"

Mr. Malinda held out his hand, and words written in fire began to appear in midair. He told us to read, and everyone did as we were instructed, reading them out loud as they appeared and then vanished, one word after the other.

After that, he told us to invite the shadows of darkness into our lives, and request from them the powers to transform. As we did, kids began to change right then and there. Little shadows began to fly around the staircase. I changed as well and though I did not feel any different, when I looked down at my hands, they certainly looked different. My whole body looked to have been transformed into black smoke. I still held the silhouette of my body, but when I went to walk, my shape changed so that I became like a puff of smoke and instead flew forward.

"So, move out into the room now, will you not?" Mr. Malinda instructed as he walked down the staircase, looking at all the little shadows flying around the room. "There are secrets here for you to discover as you practice. Go and search every corner. Go have fun!" he exclaimed.

We all dispersed and began to take a closer look at the dungeon. As we flew around, we sometimes collided with each other, and when we did, I could feel the essence of the person I collided with, intermingling with them as we became one, and then separating again into two. We spread throughout the corridors and cells within the place, and there was really no one else there it seemed. It was dingy, dirty, and ancient. I could see torture machines in some of the cells I passed by, and as I continued to investigate, I could see that there were traces and evidence that people had indeed been tormented there before. There were scratch marks on the cell walls and floors as if someone had been trying to dig out.

I began to hear faint noises coming from one of the hallways. I flew down the long, dark corridor toward the noises, and as I did, I could hear people's voices. I was even more intrigued, and I continued to fly. I reached the end of the corridor and it split into two: one large corridor to my left, and a smaller one to my right. Both were dimly lit, and as I listened, I could make out the voices coming from the smaller corridor. I looked back and could see other kids in their smoke shape following me. They were a bit far from me, but I could still make out their faces within their shadow forms still.

I looked back at the small, stone, medieval-looking, twisted corridor, and proceeded to journey down. As I did, the voices grew louder and louder. I could make out screaming, and yelling. Sometimes a very deep growling voice would scream at someone and laugh in a cruel, evil way. I neared the end of the corridor and could make out a large, medieval-looking metal door. I was far from it but could still feel heat emanating from it. I began to feel the temperature rise quickly as I drew closer to the door, and the screaming became excruciatingly loud, to the point where I could hear multitudes of voices screaming with gut-wrenching pain. I turned back into my normal shape, and cautiously approached the door. I looked back and the three kids that followed me were standing right beside me, sharing looks of terrible fear.

"Is this what I think it is?" I asked them.

"We should not be here. Let's get back now," one said.

"That would be very wise," our teacher said, startling all of us as he pulled away from the shadows in the corner of the corridor and manifested himself in front of us.

"What is that…beyond that door?" I asked.

"That is where the disobedient go—those that do not do what they are told," he said as he looked at us and smiled wickedly. He lifted his hand and suddenly the walls and door magically disappeared and gave way to a horrific scene of people being eaten by demons of every sort. They would excrete them like refuse from their digestive systems, and eat them again and again, chewing them up over and over. Fire would come out of the burnt cave floor, and out of the demons' mouths, flowing through what seemed like endless canals of lava. We hid behind our teacher in horror, until he waved his hand back down and the scene disappeared. We looked at the large door again, relieved that the horrors we had seen were gone.

"I come here sometimes when I need to feel better about myself," Mr. Malinda said. "Is it not wonderful to hear that pain—all those souls being torn apart…over and over again?" He closed his eyes and listened as if he heard beautiful music. We all looked at each other in horror as we continued to hear the very loud screams.

"Ah. I almost forgot to tell you," he continued. "Never open that door, because the force behind it will suck you in and you will never get out—ever." He looked at us and his eyes began to glow. "Let's get back to the others now. Come on." He motioned for us to go back, and we quickly did.

Terrifying incidents like that became so commonplace for us that we became numb to them after a while. Over time, I learned to enjoy my life in the spirit world more than my real life on Earth. On Earth I was just a little kid—constantly abused, molested, raped, and I did not feel loved. In the spiritual world, there under the Earth, I had powers, and could call on demons to help me if someone tried to hurt me. Over time, little by little, I learned to translate those abilities to the physical world.

"Ok, hold on a minute," Jay interrupted me. "Are you saying that you were also doing this stuff in the natural world? Like…physically?"

"Yeah," I replied.

I continued by explaining that my growth in the knowledge of the dark arts didn't just come from the underground school. It also came through tasks that I did physically because everything is connected. The physical deeds opened doors for the spiritual world, and the spiritual things I did helped me accomplish evil things in the physical realm. The cult met regularly, and I was made to be a participant in all their rituals. There were ceremonies specifically performed to corrupt its members in order to obtain power, stature, and ranking under Satan's rule, and to gain influence over others, among countless other things.

All the kids in the cult, after being inducted, were first made to take part in sacrificial rituals that were meant to bring people in the area under Satan's dominion. They were made to say chants that released demons into the earth and create chaos and havoc on the world.

"Nick, with God, it's very simple," the pastor said. "All you must do is believe in Him and yield to Him. He is good and means us to be good too, because He loves us. As a real believer in Christ, you will suffer in many ways, but He is always there to help, heal, and comfort you.

"I'm sorry," she said. "I just felt the need to tell you that. Please continue."

"No, that's ok," I replied.

"Maybe you can elaborate a little bit more on what you guys did in the natural world," Jay said. "You know, some of those rituals."

I paused for a second to think but began nodding my head. "Sure. Well, not long after the barn incident I told you about before, where the elder took me out of the barn and out to the open sky, remember that?"

"Of course," said the pastor.

"Well…"

I went on to tell them the story of another large gathering that took place in the physical realm. We were in our Volkswagen Beetle, driving down an open road.

The sun almost completely set in the distance behind the city, as we headed directly into the darkness of the empty road. I remember my mom and dad talking. They sat in the front of the car, and my dad was driving. From the back seat, my little sister interjected into our parents'

conversation, but I couldn't. I was just sitting quietly beside

her, looking out the window. I was dreading the things they

were about to do to me. My eyes filled with tears, but I

quickly wiped them away before any of them could fall.

My parents had been carrying on as if everything

was ok, and as if the stuff that had happened to me in that

barn was no big deal.

But it was a very big deal to me. I had not forgotten

anything.

They made simple conversation in the car, all the

way to the outskirts of the city. We approached what

looked like a small village out in the middle of nowhere.

Looking around, I saw that everything looked abandoned. It

was night, and a little cold when we got out of the car in

front of a large warehouse surrounded by desert. We

hurried inside, walked past a small office, up a flight of

stairs, and entered the main part of the warehouse through an open walkway. Looking down into the center of the place I saw there was a large group of people gathered in a main area below me, all dressed in black robes. They encircled some naked men, women and children strapped onto poles with ropes.

There were also a few people with purple robes—and of course the red one—standing in front of the bound naked people. They all looked up at us as we entered the area and moved toward another office on the upper floor.

The warehouse looked like it used to be a place for shipping, or storage; it was made from concrete and steel, with storage shelves in many different places, and a great many boxes stacked on top of each other all over the place. The floors were bare concrete, and I could see smaller rooms off to the sides that looked like large open shower areas, which were tiled all the way up to the walls.

My parents left me in the care of three women who were up there with a few more kids. The women were dressed in black robes, the hood of their cloaks hung behind them and they were barefoot. I did not recognize the women, but they somehow seemed familiar to me. I felt like I had seen them before or something.

One of them came up to me and took me by the hand. She led me to a desk that had been cleared out. To my surprise, a dead naked baby sat upon it, stretched out on a shiny silver tray. A large lamp shone on the boy. They gathered us around the body, and we could see that his chest had been opened, and that a lot of organs were already missing from the carcass. Blood stained the tray and the desk. She asked us to touch him—and pet him—so we did. Two of the women began to undress us, as the third explained their purpose.

"You are privileged because we have been chosen. Today you will feel the power of our master. Today, you will learn to use the power you will be given."

She recited spells as she moved her left hand throughout the child's body. As I stared at her, I realized she had a knife in her other hand. She finished what she was saying and looked right at me with wild and crazy eyes and cut a piece of flesh from the carcass and ate it. She then cut small pieces for every one of us and began to hand them out. The other women finished undressing us, and we were left completely naked. As the kids and I stood there holding the pieces of flesh, the other two women went around and wrapped a red cloth around each child, covering our privates.

"Eat…" the woman said.

I put the flesh in my mouth and chewed. When I swallowed, I felt very confused for a minute, but then suddenly, an overwhelming hunger to eat the rest of the baby came over us all—it was uncontrollable. The woman looked at us gathered around and began to cut more pieces of flesh and we ate. As we consumed the flesh, electric power rushed through our bodies, charging us with supernatural strength and altering the way we thought and perceived. It seemed like a new intellect was taking over me, as if my mind had expanded to do more than it was supposed to.

Taking the blood then, the women began writing spells all over our bodies. They prepared us for what was to come. The women cleaned all the blood off themselves, lined us up single file, and walked us down the stairs.

A large crowd had gathered, and it seemed like a lot more people had arrived. We walked through the sea of black cloaks, the cultists quickly making a way for us as we approached. With our bodies painted in blood, it was clear we were there to do something important. We were led right into the middle of the circle. The atmosphere was thick with evil desires, with no sin being off the table.

There was an anticipation of something. It was evident in the air. The electricity there was almost tangible. All the adults wore hoods, leaving their features obscured, but from time to time, I saw a flash of a face or two underneath the robes. Some looked human with glowing eyes, while others looked like monsters.

I shivered, and fear took hold of me. I did not know what was going to happen. The ground was covered in blood, urine, and feces. I looked at everyone that was tied to the poles and saw that they were not hurt in any way. Everything on the ground must have been from other people, I thought. Then my presumption was verified when I saw the trails of blood leading from where we were standing to a back room. It was during these meetings that I grew fearful for my life, because I did not know if I was going to be killed or not. The people that were tied up begged for their lives, crying and screaming. Some yelled frantically, others were in shock, with their mouths open as spittle cascaded from their lips.

"Let the chosen be given the instrument to sacrifice," someone said.

The red-hooded figure then faced us as we approached. "Power through sacrifice," he said.

Suddenly everyone in the room began to chant something in another language. I could not understand what they were saying but it was creepy. As they chanted, the atmosphere in the room began to intensify even more. The kids and I suddenly felt an invisible force hit us, and flood us with even more supernatural strength. The surge took away all forms of normal thought that were left in me. I felt a drive to do evil with no remorse like never before, a rage sweeping over me.

Everything in the room began to fade away. All I could focus on was a gold knife the man in the red robe offered to us. He pointed to one of the kids and then held out the blade directly to him. The child approached him, took the knife from his hand, and with it, he walked over to one of the men that was strapped onto the pole.

The one in red bellowed. "Do not hesitate. Surrender yourself completely. Whatever you are led to do, do it!"

The boy slowly put his bare hand on the man's belly and looked up at him. The man sobbed and pleaded with the child, who stared at him unblinking, even as the man's tears fell on the boy's face. The boy smiled for a few seconds, then violently stabbed the man in the right side of his body. When he withdrew the blade, blood gushed out like a water balloon had just been pierced. The man screamed at the top of his lungs, and an uncontrollable urge caused him to relieve himself, urine and excrement staining his legs a moment later. The boy began to stab him repeatedly throughout his chest, until the child was completely covered in blood. The man hung from the post, no longer able to even groan in protest. His stomach was eviscerated, and intestines hung from the wound, only obscured by the blood from the countless stab wounds inflicted on his chest.

The boy turned around then, and I could see his eyes had turned completely black. Even the skin around his eyes darkened, as well as the flesh from his forehead and down to his mouth. I knew it was a demon looking out through him.

The man on the pole gasped for air, the only sound he could produce. The boy—or whatever controlled him—heard it, and he turned around at once, and put the knife right into his neck. The grotesque scene grew worse, then. Barely reaching while on the tip of his toes the boy opened his mouth and drank the blood that poured down the man's neck. The boy pulled the knife out and stood there as blood covered his face. Once there was no more blood dripping from the man's wound, the boy turned around and wiped some blood from his eyes.

Handing the knife back to the elder, the boy came back to the group. His features were hideous to look upon. His eyes were glossy black and the skin around them had turned a green hue. It looked like there were many eyes looking out through his own. His expression would change from one monstrous look to another, continually morphing underneath his face.

Child after child went up to murder one of the captives. Everyone came back with similar haunting features upon their faces. They had been transformed by the ritual.

Then it was my turn. I was led up to the middle of the room by an unseen force, and at that point there were only two women and a man left alive on the poles. I was afraid at first. I did not know if I would be able to perform such a vile act, despite all the rage and power I had felt before. The man in red saw my hesitation and grabbed my hand. He placed it on the knife and held his hand over mine.

"All you have to do is yield to the power," he said.

When he said this, I began to yield, and that strength came over me again. That time I was filled with a great bloodlust. I could taste copper undertones in my mouth, as though I was already feasting on the life force of my victim.

The man stood aside when he felt this emanating from me.

I looked at the people, and they began to scream. But I could not hear them. All I heard were the insults my mother and her friends hurled at me. I saw their faces in my head, and flashes of the rapes I had endured. They came back to my mind, and I was filled with rage.

I took the knife and ran toward one of the women, stabbing her in her lower abdomen and cutting her open. I reached into her bowels and ripped out her insides, screaming at her even though I could not hear my own voice. I stabbed her countless times in her legs, taking vengeance, I felt, for what had been done to me. The pain and suffering I had gone through rushed into my heart and mind, and I went to the other woman and did the same to her.

When I was going to the third, the man, an invisible force stopped me cold. Someone wearing a purple cloak approached me, and grabbed my right arm, steadying the hand that held the knife. As soon as they put their hands on me, all those feelings vanished, and I was left with fear, and the reality of what I had just done.

Someone from the audience guided me out of the circle. The one in red robes stared at me with folded arms. His glower went right through me. I did not know if I had done well in their eyes or not.

I looked back and the women were screaming in pain, and as they cried, the red-hooded priest walked up and sliced their throats, then glared at me as I was quickly taken away.

I was taken upstairs in a rush. The person that led me up, the one in the purple robe, shoved me into the office I was in before and closed the door. She squatted in front of me and pulled her hood off, and I was surprised to see that it was my grandmother. She looked at me intensely, up and down, but did not say a word to me. I was in a daze, my ears were ringing, and the whole scene seemed like a dream. My grandmother sent a stoic gaze my way for a few seconds, then got up and left the room.

With the door shut, I walked over to the mirror. I was horrified at what I saw. My face was horribly changed, worse than the other kids. I saw my eyes had enlarged and almost looked like those of a fly. They had turned completely black. Dark red and black bags sat under my eyes, stretching all the way down my cheeks. Most of the skin on my face was gray.

I felt awful. I did not want to look that way, but I could not even cry when I saw myself. I did not even know how or if I could become normal again. Rage crawled its way back into my heart at that point, then it blew up inside me like a volcano. I could not help but clench my fists and scream. My head felt like it was going to blow up.

I don't know how much time went by, but I know I was in that room for a while. I cycled through emotions—anger, sadness, loss, and self-pity. Then a woman walked into the room, and as she drew closer to me, I realized it was my mother. She took me by the hand and led me downstairs to the main room. It was empty then, except for three people dressed like janitors that cleaned the bloody mess that was left behind. They stared at me. One of the women shivered and looked away. I knew I looked like a monster, but I felt like one even more. As I walked by her, I screamed at her, and though I could still only hear ringing in my ears, my scream felt like fire coming out of my mouth. She averted her gaze and continued to work.

My mom led me down a long hallway. It was dark and gloomy, but I could see an orange-yellow light coming from a doorway up ahead. She led me to a large, carpeted room, where I saw a multitude of people having sex, far too many for me to count. My mom brought me to the edge of the orgy and left me there standing. She ran toward a group in the middle, and I lost sight of her a few moments later.

I stood there for a while, and then a young woman walked up to me and held out her hand to me. I was hesitant at first, but when she smiled, she seemed like she meant me no harm, so I took her hand, and she led me into a group.

The rage in me began to subside, and my face began to slowly turn back to normal, I learned that day that sex and lust worked well at masking pain.

At that point the pastor interrupted me to ask a question.

"So, what happened? It sounds like you did not do what they were expecting or something."

"Well, I was later told that I did not react to 'the surge,' as they call it, the way that they had intended me to. I did not kill any of the women—I did not offer a sacrifice to the devil—but mutilated them both instead," I answered.

"Oh, I see. So did you get in trouble for that?" she asked.

"Well, some people's previous hesitation to accept me truly being one of them seemed to have been justified.

It was like they now knew that I was somehow different and did not really fit into their fold all the way. Some of them treated me as if they knew something about me and were just nasty to me. Others were afraid of being friendly, and the rest kept their distance..." I replied.

The pastor looked at me confidently though. "Well, you are here with us now, and we love you son. I'm so sorry for all these things that you've suffered. Only God could've kept you alive. It's a miracle that you're here, and I'm glad that you are allowing Him to help you."

I looked at her, and she smiled at me and nodded for me to continue, and so I went on to tell them what happened next. After some hours went by and I had lost myself in the orgy, I could not think at all. My mind felt broken, and all I could do was live in the moment—sex was the only outlet I was given. I learned to accept that was my life. I drowned my pain in carnal desires. I had lost track of time, but after what seemed like forever my mom came and got me from underneath a woman that was smothering me. She walked me to a bathroom that had showers and cleaned me up, dressing me before bringing me to the car to go home.

As we walked out of the large warehouse, the sun was breaking through the mountains in the distance. It was morning. Cars drove away from the place, and we got into our car and headed off. We were there all night.

I sat up in the back seat and looked at my face in the car's rearview mirror. My features had returned to normal, though I could still see a wild blackness in the pupils of my eyes as I stared at myself. I sat back and wondered about what had happened. Again, it was so surreal, it was almost like it had never happened, almost like a dream in my mind. Yet my body could still feel all the dark desire. I was so tired, I drifted off to sleep, and did not wake up until later that afternoon in my own bed.

A Look Behind the Veil

I cannot count the times that I have woken up after a crazy blood-filled night and have tried to forget all that had happened. I could hardly function sometimes, thinking of all the stuff I had done. Everything seemed like a horrible nightmare, and that's what I would tell myself, even though my heart would be heavy with guilt, sorrow, regret, and anger.

I felt like I could not get out of that lifestyle. I did not see any way that I could find salvation from the evil powers around me—and within me. I felt bottled up inside. I hated my life, everything, everyone, and myself. I went through the days sad, and mostly stayed to myself. I would not play with other kids at school.

Sometimes I would begin to talk about cult rituals with teachers at school, and to other kids, and when my parents got wind of that, they acted quickly. My parents took me to specialized psychologists that would hypnotize me in order to keep my mouth closed and control me. They could not afford to have me talking out in the open about cult rituals, and the like.

Everything needed to be kept secret, otherwise it would bring unwanted attention to our practices. Even though a lot of people were in some type of occult practice, everyone was to keep a code of silence. Things could only be spoken of at certain times and with certain people.

"So, they had you hypnotized?" Jay asked.

"Yeah, but it had some unexpected side effects that they did not anticipate," I replied. "I developed multiple personalities. One of them was the 'normal' boy. Another was the wizard that loves spell craft, and another later would become a destroyer—the one my family would really fear.

"They took me to people who specialized in mind control. I did not know it then, but I now know that they put mental triggers in me so that my parents could control my moods by saying code words, and even whistling.

"My God, what did these people do to you?" the pastor asked. "Do you remember any of that?

"Actually, I do remember one of those sessions," I replied.

I elaborated on one of the first times I went to one of the mind control people. My mom opened a large door, and I entered the room. It was cozy, though it was mostly brown in color. The large leather couches were brown, and so was the wooden fireplace. There were plants everywhere, and frames with paintings and pictures on every wall.

There was a man behind a large wooden desk, and he asked me to sit down on the couch. He came out from behind the desk and sat on the couch opposite me and asked me to close my eyes and think about one of my favorite memories.

He then began to ask me questions about my life, my likes, and dislikes. He made me feel so comfortable with him that I told him everything about my life that I could remember. I told him about the devil and the cult during the night traveling out of my body. He listened to me for a long time, and then when I stopped, he told me to open my eyes and listen to him very carefully. He told me the reason why I was sad was because I believed that God would punish me for these things I had done, and that I was wrong for believing that. He said that what he would do was to separate my conscious being from knowing or remembering those things that hurt me, but he needed me to allow him access to my mind.

So, I said yes!

To me this was excellent. It was like he was going to perform magic on me. I would not have to deal with the pain, the regret, or anything else that came with it.

He took out a metronome and told me to look at it as it moved. His soft voice counting down was all I remembered, nothing else after that.

They mentally manipulated me in order to separate my day-to-day life from my life in the cult, so that I could not remember the awful things that I did, unless I was triggered to. This is where I suspect I first became two different people, with different sets of emotions, reactions, and desires. And from there, I began to develop more personalities.

During the day, I would no longer remember anything evil that I had done, but after I went to sleep, I would wake again, or be "activated" by my parents—or even demons. It was then that I would understand my past, and everything that went on in the cult.

My parents would soon find out that they would never be able to control me completely though, because deep within me I developed a particular personality that was completely rebellious to all their conditioning. There was one personality that wanted vengeance—that wanted them all dead. And this personality began to say "They want me to be a monster? I will be the worst of them all! I will make them regret all that they have done to me."

Yeah, I was truly insane. I had personalities inside of me at war with each other…

"So, how do you know now that you're not like this still?" the pastor asked.

"I know I'm better because I can remember so much now. There are no whispers in my mind—no blank spots in my memory, at least not like before, I know I'm a work in progress. Even though I came to your church as an enemy, God really has touched me here. I know that He is real. He has broken a lot of holds that my parents had on me, and He has given me enough clarity to see where He has brought me from, at least thus far anyway," I replied.

I went on and told the pastor that because I saw everyone around me was involved in an unholy diabolical mess, I thought that was how everyone in the world was. I would go to cult meetings, and see my teachers, family members, neighbors, my doctor, the local priests, and even police officers partake. I thought to myself that this was the way the world worked, and this is what they led me to believe.

I remember saying to myself over and over, "Where is God?"

I saw men, women and children die almost every week, without any repercussions to us. I mean, these poor souls were picked up off the streets, or born and raised just for this purpose, and then killed.

"You said some were born and raised, just to be sacrificed?" asked the pastor.

"Yes, there are people who never see the light of day," I replied.

I went on to elaborate on their underground black market for human sacrificing, at least what I had seen. Every year thousands of women are impregnated, so that they can bear children just to be sacrificed. A lot of the children that are conceived in cult orgies are also used for this purpose. Some of these women were allowed to breed under close watch, while others who were kidnapped or enslaved were kept in chains—in bedrooms, warehouses, basements, closets, all sort of places. And eventually, they became sacrifices themselves.

I've seen locations that were filled with people in cages, kept like animals, for the sole purpose of human sacrifice. The men would be sacrificed first. Women were screened to be breeders, and if they were not picked, they were put on the list to be sacrificed. If they were picked as a breeder, they were taken to one of the holding locations, where men that were handpicked by the elders would impregnate them.

Their children would never see daylight. They were kept from going to school, and from the outside world.

Some would be sacrificed at birth, some as toddlers. Others were used for sex for many years then killed as teens. But only a few made it that far, and they hardly ever became adults. They only reached adulthood if someone within the cult would be willing to "sponsor" them, per se, and take them into their family as a servant of some sort. It rarely happened, and even then, they were treated very badly.

Because the children were used for sex, the little girls kept in captivity usually gave birth to other children, as soon as their bodies were capable of it. Kids born of kids were thought to be more "pure"—extra special—and were used as bargaining chips, and gifts. Many babies never made it though. The innocence of these babes is what made them most valuable, and they were one of the most precious types of sacrifices.

Homeless people are usually the main prey of kidnappings because they usually have no means to fight back. The authorities would make money by selling people to cults. I saw many trucks filled with people brought to holding facilities where they were screened, separated, and put into portable cells made of steel. There are warehouses filled with enslaved people. Most were from other provinces, some from other countries even, travelers and tourists just passing through. Once captured, those poor people have no hope of ever returning to their former life.

I've seen this as the end of some cult members as well. Becoming a slave or human sacrifice were some of the harsher punishments for people that were caught trying to escape the cult, or that were disobedient in a very grievous way.

I continued to tell the pastor and Jay that as time went by, and I did everything that I was being told to do, the elders put me through test after test in order for me to prove myself to them. I eventually did make them feel confident enough for them to give me a small thread of trust.

Slowly, people started coming around in their perception of me after that night. They started seeing that I was doing everything that was required of me. After a while, everyone around me seemed to approve of me, somewhat. I felt a little more accepted, but I still felt others had some reservations.

At least it was not like before when I felt like a complete outcast.

I continued to go to the school of magic at night, taken by different types of spirits—either demons, or other witches or wizards—until I was doing it by myself. I learned many evil spells, incantations, and skills that elevated me within the ranks of Satan's kingdom.

"I can understand what you're saying. The spiritual world is directly tied to the natural one," the pastor said. "It makes me so sad to hear about all these people out there, being used in such an awful way."

"Honestly, leaving my body and going to that school of dark magic was my only way to cope," I explained.

"Can you tell us more about the school, and that underground city?" Jay asked.

"Yeah, of course…" I answered.

I proceeded to tell Jay and the pastor about a particular night that my class was gathered on the very top of the highest building of the underground city. It was the first time that we had been allowed to go there, and we were all excited. I could clearly see from there that the top of the cave was a lighter shade of brown, and it seemed to be smooth and luminous somehow. We could see that the building was almost right in the middle of the whole city. Dragons flew by us, almost grazing us, and an energy like lightning emanated from them. Some had more than one set of wings, others had many tails, and some had many heads. All these dragons varied in color. Some had scales, others skin, but they all had blazing, fiery eyes.

There were naked people floating in clusters, having sex on many sides of the cave ceiling, but they were not moving in a normal way that I had previously perceived when I saw them from the ground. They moved violently,

almost as if someone had pressed the fast forward button.
They joined each other and then went from person to
person like lightning, and there were other sexual creatures
in there with them. Some were made up of only sexual
parts, others I could not even begin to describe. There were
some that had human forms, but many different sexual
body parts on different places in their bodies, and yet others
resembled animals.

From time to time the dragons would blow fire into
these orgy clusters, and everyone moved even faster, being
charged by the fire. That sight scared some of us, but we
tried the best we could to avoid showing it.

So, there we were in our black robes, on top of the
gothic-looking tower, when our teacher appeared. It was a
demon, with solid green eyes. He was bald and had no ears,
but multiple little holes where the ears should have been.
His face was gray, and he had a mouth that looked like that
of a bat. He was tall and slender, and at first glance you

could not really tell if it was male or female because it had no sexual organs. I forgot his name, but I do remember that he moved slowly and deliberately, almost as if he was waiting for instructions to radio into his head, or as if he was waiting for permission to make a move. He was dressed in a long white see-through robe that seemed too large for him, and inappropriate.

Before long, he told us about what we could expect during that class.

"Today you are going to learn how to link to something that you have never seen the location to. You will learn to be guided to it by the power within you. In order to find it, you must be drawn to it." He walked in circles around us, measuring us up as he inspected each of us.

"When you arrived, you received a gift, remember?" he asked. "And each one of you should have it still. It is now time to take it out. Go on. Hold it in your hand.”

I reached into the little pocket at my waist and removed the eye I had received.

“Find the body of that member you hold in your hand” he said. “You must find it first in your mind. Reach out with the power within you and feel for it. When you get a lock on it then go find out where the piece you hold came from. Let the desire to discover that grow within you. Let it become the only thing that matters, the only thing that drives you, the only thing you want to see.”

The demon’s black eyes began to glow green as he stared at us. I looked around and some of the kids closed their eyes, so I closed mine.

I began by allowing the desire for knowledge to grow in me. I didn’t just want to know about the body that the eye came from—I needed to. As I gave into that desire, a picture began to appear in my mind. I began to see cave patterns, underground hills, a pit, and then I saw a black figure in a hole reaching out to me.

When I opened my eyes, some of the kids had already taken off. I surrendered to the powers of evil and willed myself to fly. At once, I levitated and began to glide. It was as if the black figure was calling out to me, and as I flew down the side of the building, past other structures and into one of the openings on the side of the cave, I began to see the patterns that I had seen in my mind. I flew past hills, small openings, larger caves, and then straight down a pit that grew darker and darker. As I went further, I became adamant about finding my prize.

I went through a large opening and saw that I was at the ceiling of an immense cave. It seemed different than others I had seen. The ground was completely black, and the walls and ceiling presented strange patterns of black and dark brown. I saw many fires in the distance, and as I flew lower, I saw thousands upon thousands of figures moving amidst the black ground, anchored in chains. I was led to one of the sides of the cave and landed on what seemed like scorched gravel.

Before me, there was a sea of thousands, maybe millions of people—charred, black, burnt people. Screaming and whimpering in pain as I walked past them, some hopelessly tried to pull on the chains that anchored them to the ground, but to no avail. I walked toward the location the force led me to, avoiding all the arms that reached out to me. When I neared my destination, I stopped right in front of one of the charred figures. The people were so burnt that they had no features left and were completely black. The nearest one was hunched over and wept uncontrollably. As I looked on, I crouched down to take a closer look. I was going to say something, but suddenly they turned around, looked at me and screamed with a violent, horrific scream, like nothing I had ever heard before.

Lava began to seep upward through the ground, engulfing the person's legs. They reached out to me in a desperate attempt to stave off their agony, but I flew upward, quickly pulling away. I looked around and there was lava coming up throughout the whole cave, covering the sorrowful people and burning them as they all screamed in horror.

I then heard a wind-like sound coming from one side of the cave. I looked and saw a wave of fire approaching me. The wave, almost like a wall of fire, covered the cave from top to bottom, and it moved directly toward me. I felt my heart thumping, my fear palpable.

I flew up the first hole I found in the cave ceiling and fled as fast as I could. I traveled so fast, through tunnels and underground cavities, that I did not take note of where I was going. I soon realized that I was lost. I did not recognize anything around me, and I started to panic.

That was Hell, I remember thinking to myself. I knew it was—that was actually a place in Hell. The screams resonated in my mind, and then the shaking bodies as the lava rose in the chamber. It was all too much, and I dropped to a ledge at the mouth of a large cavern.

I tried to gather myself. I closed my eyes, and I concentrated on seeing the tower's top, and soon found myself floating. Then I was flying again, but that time, in another direction.

I was returning to the city, I knew. I flew for a little while, then I began to see formations that I recognized. Soon I was flying into the city cave, up toward the citadel. As I approached the top of the structure, I could see our teacher looking directly at me as I approached. I landed right in front of him, and I could tell that he was pleased. I looked around and realized that I was the first one to make it back. I approached our teacher, and he flashed his eyes at me.

"Very good. So, tell me, what did you find?" he asked.

I hesitated for a few seconds, but I knew that I had succeeded in the lesson, and that gave me confidence. "I saw thousands of people—charred, burnt beyond belief. Fire… There was fire everywhere. I almost did not make it out," I explained.

The teacher's expression changed, and he seemed to glow as I told him of my experience.

"I would like the token please," my teacher said, holding out his enormous hand. I placed the eye in his palm. Then, to my surprise, he put it in his mouth and ate it. "Well, congratulations," he said as he chewed down on the eyeball. "You are the very first to finish this task, returning so quickly and all." He smiled at me with a devious look in his glowing eyes.

"The cave I saw, with all of those people, what was that place?" I asked him.

The smile left his face, and his eyes began to glow brighter as he closed in on me, getting right up in my face.

"You know exactly what the answer to your question is, don't you?" he asked. "You know what that is. We train here because we absorb the power from there. We train here because we become part of it. All you need to know is that if you are disobedient you will end up there as well. Another shit in that cesspool of fire. You already know the answer. You know.

"But, if you do as you're told, if you're obedient till the end, our master has provided us with cities, just like this one, where we can spend eternity with him," he explained.

It sounded like a lie, it felt like a lie, but I did not say anything to him.

But the pastor interrupted me.

"That is a complete lie!" she cried, even as I nodded in agreement. "When you die, you go to Heaven if you believe in Jesus and asked for forgiveness. Otherwise, you go to Hell if you so choose to reject Him. That's it."

"I know," I told her. "I know."

I had never seen her so shaken before, enraged by what I conferred with her. The demon's words had affected her, and even her son seemed surprised by her outburst. She settled herself though, taking a sip of water as if to cool herself off.

"I'm sorry," she said, her voice seeming more tempered then. "Please continue."

I went on to explain to her that I knew that false salvation was one of the many lies that the devil promises his people.

And when it comes to lies, the ones that get it the worst are those that once knew God but renounced Him in order to serve Satan. They are consistently being "reformed", brainwashed, so that their minds will be so twisted with lies, and half-truths, that they will never be able to believe God.

I saw one child after another return to the dark rooftop. They all seemed to have had an experience like mine. I could tell by the looks on their faces that they were in shock at what they had seen. One by one they returned, and were asked for their tokens, and the demon ate each one.

There were some kids that never made it back that day. Only the ones that returned remained in my class.

Some kids I saw later in other places, some I never saw again.

Every task we were given was a test that was used to classify us. We would do this sort of thing all the time, and each test would become harder in different ways. Sometimes the distances we would have to travel were exceedingly long. Other times we would have to retrieve an object from a certain place, or in someone's possession, but we had to figure out how to do it.

On one occasion, we were standing at the side of the sea. It was night and we were going to be sent on a retrieval mission. The stars twinkled in the sky, and I could hear the waves crashing beside me. The cool breeze went right through me, literally because we were all in spirit form, and not present in the flesh. I could feel every bit of it, and I loved it.

Dalvian was our teacher that night. She told us that we had to retrieve a small golden ring that was at the bottom of the sea, just offshore. She was a mix of both sexes. She looked altogether human, but I was not sure if she was. She would change some of her features back and forth from male to female. I remember feeling attracted to her—she reminded me of someone from ages past, like from ancient Greece or Rome.

As we listened to her talk, her face would sometimes take a slight masculine shape, and then go back to a feminine shape. Her long black hair moved with the wind, and she wore a sheer, almost see-through white robe. Her stature remained the same regardless of how she presented, and all her mannerisms were always feminine. There was a light, like a moving glow, that moved through her body. It went through her face, and down her neck and slowly traveled through every body part. I did not understand it.

She explained to us that we needed to get the ring, and she held up a red handkerchief, and said that this was our only lead. We all looked at it, studying it and trying to make sense of it. The key to finding the ring was not to think naturally, but to understand where it had been.

I closed my eyes and began to reach out with my senses. I quickly began to receive images in my head of the ocean, a ship, a cave, an underground passageway—and this was enough to get me going. As I flew into the ocean, images continued to come to me of an underground seashore inside a large cave. I allowed the powers of darkness within me to guide me through the sea.

Through many miles of underwater terrain, I traveled through the waters. There were fish everywhere, but the other kids and I were moving so fast that things around us became a blur. Finally, we arrived at what looked like an underground cave opening. It was pitch black in there. We could see no light, but we entered, all of us driven to get the ring without hesitation. As we moved through the cave, shimmers of a faint light began to appear in the distance, and everything I saw was exactly as I previously envisioned. It was almost déjà vu.

We drew closer to the source of light, and finally saw an opening in the ceiling of the underground passage. We traveled upward and broke through the surface of the water.

We were in an expansive cave. Much of the length of the cave floor was covered in water, but we found ourselves in a large, air-filled cavity. On the far right, there appeared to be a pile of rocks stacked all the way up to the ceiling. The place had caved in and been sealed up long ago.

At the far end of it I saw a small shoreline, with what looked like a shipwreck. The cave ceiling was mostly made of very sharp rock formations with a luminous, glittery rock that set the cave aglow somehow. I realized that was the light we saw from below.

We flew out of the water and toward the shore, and as we landed, we saw that there were unlit torches sticking out of the sand. One of the kids pointed to one of them, and fire burst from his finger to ignite the old material. The fire spread to the other torches, lighting them as well, giving us a clearer view of the cave and the wreck.

We felt the presence of the ring then, knowing it to be somewhere inside the wreck. Without saying a word, we took our first step toward the ship, when suddenly, we heard a noise that startled us.

From behind the wreckage came a slithering creature. It had the upper torso of a man, but the lower half looked what I thought first to be a snake, but as he came closer, I realized it was an eel—a half-man, half-eel creature. He had long, webbed hands, with long and sharp fingernails. He was bald, and he looked to have boils all over his body. The human part of him seemed to have pale green skin, but the eel part of his body was jet black. He wore what looked to be a torn shirt, but nothing else. His shiny dark green eyes looked at us, and he seemed to hiss before he spoke to us.

"I know why you are here," he said in a soft voice. "My ring. Every few months that damned school sends their kids to retrieve something of mine." He pointed toward the wreckage, and we could all see a large pile of gold and treasure spilling out of the side of the broken ship. "Sometimes it's a golden coin, sometimes a necklace. Today, it's a ring. Well, you can have it!" He slithered toward us, and reflexively, we all moved back a step. "But only on one condition: there must be a blood sacrifice. I would very much like to eat one of you, so choose amongst yourselves," he said. "And then, you can have the ring." He smiled then, showing rows of razor-sharp teeth inside his unsettlingly wide mouth.

Everyone remained quiet, and we all began to look at each other.

It was crazy I thought. As the remaining kids arrived at the undersea shore, we told them what was going on.

"You can't really be serious," one kid said. "This is supposed to just be training!"

"The reality of things—seeing how things are in real life—that is the best training you will ever get," the eel man hissed.

"There's got to be something else we can give you. Name it!" one of the girls yelled at him.

But the eel man just looked at us, licking his lips.

We tried reasoning with him, but he would not budge, regardless of what we offered. Some of the kids tried to enter the shipwreck anyway but the monster would move so quickly that he would always grab them before they could enter. Even when a lot of us would try at the same time, he would get to each of us somehow, grab us and throw us out to the water. After a while, the kids began to argue and fight amongst themselves about what we were going to do.

I thought that maybe this was some sort of riddle. Maybe there was something we were supposed to do here. I went over to the water's edge and began to ponder our situation. There we were, unable get to the ring, and we could not go back empty handed. One of us would have to die to get what we wanted. I just could not see a way to solve this.

I was so caught up in my thoughts that I did not realize that everything was quiet until I looked up at the group and saw everyone looking at me. Even the creature standing close to the shipwreck looked intensely at me. I felt unsettled, and I quickly gathered that somehow, *I* had become the sacrifice for this creature and had not realized it.

As I looked at them, the creature placed a small golden diamond ring into the hand of one of the kids, but it kept its eyes transfixed on me. Kids began to fly off into the waters of the cave, back to shore, but I was frozen solid with fear—I could not move. I looked down and realized that the eel part of this creature had already wrapped itself around my lower body, immobilizing me. The creature came up to me and wrapped itself around me further. I thought that I was going to die, as its long eel part squeezed me. I fell to the ground, and he put his face right up to mine. He kept looking at me almost stone-faced.

I was so scared that I could not make a sound. He smelled like rotten fish and was sticky all over. We stayed there for a while, but I did not understand why he did nothing else, I thought that he was going to kill me, but he then released me and moved away from me, looking at the water, as if trying to find something. Dalvian slowly emerged from the waters, and the creature was clearly excited at her arrival. Dalvian walked toward us, and the creature made its way toward her.

When my teacher reached the creature, she embraced it and passionately kissed it for a long while. When she finally separated from it, she looked at me and smiled, her face covered in the creature's slime. She walked closer to me and placed her hand on my head and grabbed me by my hair. Without notice, slung me right into the water, leading me back to shore.

I realized then that it had been an exercise after all.

We reached the other kids that were waiting for us by the seashore, and she placed me down among them.

"The lesson here was not in getting the ring," she said. "Sometimes you will find yourself in a situation where a sacrifice—the shedding of blood—is the only option. You all did well tonight." She looked over the children and smiled wide, showing sharp yellow teeth. She then turned to me. "Don't feel bad, it could have been anyone."

She flew up and gestured for us to follow. We did, and then we all traveled together back to the underground city.

The pastor and Jay listened intently as I spoke, but I could see they both looked tired. The night sky was clearly visible through the office window and the light from the fading streetlamp gathered bugs around it outside.

The pastor climbed out of her seat, stretching her weary body. "I think we should call it a night," she said, a weak smile stretching across her face.

We all nodded in agreement. It was getting a bit late. We gathered and began to make our way out the door. The pastor couldn't take her eyes off me for some reason, and she finally spoke up as I was getting ready to leave.

"Son!" she called out.

Jay and I both turn around at the same time to look at her. She motioned for us to come back, and she put her hands on both of us as she began to pray.

"Lord, I thank you for all your mercy and goodness! Thank you for your Spirit of revelation, and for your precious son Jesus. Without him we would be lost but are alive and have eternal life because of Him. Thank you. I pray you protect us and most of all that you protect Nick as he goes out and comes in. Please put a special shield round about him, and give your angels charge over his soul. He's Your son now. He has been striving to enter as you told us to do. Keep us in the hallow of your hand, send your warriors, and your flames of fire to protect us. Keep us close to you, I pray… Amen."

"Amen!" Jay and I replied. We each looked at each other for a moment before we made our way home.

As we drove away in separate cars, a large white van began to follow me down the street. I did not notice the van behind me at first.

And what I also didn't know was that inside the van was a hit team in full tactical gear ready to assassinate me.

I barely crossed a yellow traffic light turning red, and the white van was not too far behind. They ran the red light trying to catch up. I came to a stop sign and tapped the brakes, then proceeded slowly. I spotted the van coming up right behind me and watched as it suddenly lost power and came to a sudden stop in the middle of the street.

I drove on, completely leaving them behind, and they were left stranded. There was no one around, and it was late at night.

Some men exited the van, while the driver kept trying to turn the van's engine over, but it just wouldn't start.

"I don't know what happened sir. We are dead in the water," one of the men said over his radio. He listened to the other end of the conversation through a headset, and then he nodded. "Yes, we'll need to be picked up… I don't know, we lost him."

A mystic emerged from the van, dressed in a long black cloak. He cast his gaze over the area, narrowing his eyes. His face was marked with unusual tattoos, resembling spell runes.

"There is supernatural intervention here," the mystic said. He looked up to the sky and nodded at an unseen force that was invisible to the others around him. "Understood. We will not stop," the mystic said. "Of course, he's revealed too much—and he needs to die!" The Mystic put his head down, then looked over to the man in charge of the team.

The officer barked his orders. "All right, you heard the man. We need to continue the pursuit until we're satisfied! Get on that radio and notify the other team immediately! And get transportation here now!"

Suddenly, out of nowhere, a twenty-foot angel comprised of pure white fire appeared in front of them. The area was illuminated in light as bright as though the sun had descended on that part of the city. He held a gigantic flaming sword, and his eyes were made of pure light. The men screamed as the angel swung his sword. He cut through them all in one blow. The men burst into flames, and the van exploded.

In an instant, there was nothing left but burning, charred bodies and the melting chassis of a burning van.

The angel stood erect and then vanished.

One of Us

The following morning, I was sitting on the office chair again, looking down at the water bottle in my hand as I talked to the pastor and Jay again about my past.

"One of the most important things we learned, aside from the tracking exercises, was to read behavioral patterns that people displayed. Emotions, facial expressions, body movements, speech tones and changes in the person's spirit—these were all things that gave us clues as to what a person was going to do next, and how they would react in certain situations. By putting the patterns together, we were able to create profiles that we could all identify and recognize."

"How did they teach you these things?" Jay asked.

I went on to tell them how we had classes on that sort of thing.

During that part of training, we would gather in the main hallway by our dorms. Our teacher for those lessons was a demon called Ista. He met us by opening a purple portal in midair that he would just drop in from. He was light in skin tone, and he had red eyes, small black horns like a bull, and a long tail that ended in what looked like a finger with a long black claw. His legs were like the hind legs of a deer, but he had large toes for feet, and he had dark brown spots all over his body. Some of those spots were small, but others covered a body part whole. He was almost completely nude, except for a belt that held a raggedy piece of cloth, and jewelry that he wore on his face and hands. The demon would change from male to female, and when he did, all his sexual organs would change as well. Sometimes, he would keep some parts unchanged, so that he would look like a man with female genitalia, and then a woman with male genitalia. Every change also changed his voice slightly. And it looked like his body would become water in the middle of changing, ripples of emanating magical desire moving through his body.

As we all gathered for the class, the demon introduced itself.

"Gather around, gather round. You all look so yummy," it said, waving us closer toward it. "My name is Ista, and I will be your teacher for today."

There was something incredibly enticing about Ista. It had a magical, magnetic appeal that just drew you in—so much so that kids including myself gathered very close to it and could not help but touch and caress it like some kind of pet.

"Yes, yes I understand," it said as it opened its arms and began to place its hands on our heads as we continued to caress it. Sparkles and pink puffy smoke, like cotton candy, would flow out of his hands and onto us as he touched us.

As we caressed its silky, watery skin, we felt an overwhelming feeling of desire. It was a primal feeling, as though we were having sex with the demon by just touching it. It was an engulfing, and absorbing feeling that made me disregard everything I had been thinking about. As the feeling intensified, we saw a large ball of light begin to grow within the demon, until suddenly it emerged from its chest and burst out onto all of us with a climatic burst of energy that pushed us back all at once. I remember thinking that it was like an orgasmic experience, but without engaging too much. It was like a sex bomb. It was very bizarre.

We all stood there for a minute, just taking in what had just happened. When I looked up, Ista was smiling wickedly at us, as all our eyes were shining red just like the demon's. It felt like he had put something in us, like a seed—a part of himself. I remember feeling odd after that.

"Well, that was unexpected for you, but delicious, no?" Ista asked. "Now we go to work. Follow me please."

He led us to a doorway made of stone located toward the end of the hallway. We walked down a long corridor made of what appeared to be black glass, with all different types of human faces and busts hanging from the ceiling. I noticed that the pieces of glass on the ceiling moved about, arranging themselves to form gestures. All the busts, hands, and other body parts would move to resemble emotions like anger, fear, and excitement. They would take on a shape, and then arrange themselves to form another.

The walls were made of many different broken pieces of dark mirrors. I would see myself floating down the hallway with the other kids, and then I would see my reflection—or someone that looked like me—looking back at me angrily, then sad, then screaming, then laughing, I knew I was not doing any of that, but as I saw my image change, I felt the emotions inside me changing slightly even just to see them. And it was as if my confusion drained me.

We arrived at a door, stopping a little less than halfway down the corridor. As I waited behind the other kids to proceed in, I turned to look further down the hall, out of curiosity. I found myself staring at the only other door at the very end of the hallway. The other door had a large frame, which had points on the top left and right corners, which were shaped like horns. The door and the frame were both a dark, deep red, while the wall around it was completely black, and dusty. The door itself looked ancient and unused.

Some of my classmates had already descended a flight of stairs leading right from our door's threshold. I looked back at the glass hallway I came from and saw all the images of me mockingly laughing at me. I took another glance at the red door, spotting smoke that slowly came out of the bottom. I was the only one left standing in the hallway then. The red door began to shake like it was about to burst open, so I quickly followed my classmates down the staircase. Our door shut behind me.

I descended what seemed to be an endless, twirling staircase made of pure black stone. The tall stone walls leading downward were solid matte black. After a little while, we could see light coming from the bottom of the stairs. As we descended, some of the kids in the front decided to float down rather than walk down. It was a lot faster, and everyone followed suit. Floating down as a group, we landed in front of a series of completely empty black open rooms.

It looked like a set right out of a TV show, but it was completely empty. The rooms were connected through doorways and hallways, and from our viewpoint, we could see into every room, as if the walls facing us were missing. As we stood there wondering what we were looking at, the rooms came alive, and people began to appear within them. They looked like everyday people, doing regular, everyday things.

Suddenly one of the black rooms lit up, and we could see someone's kitchen. It looked like an apartment, and it was dirty, run down, and old. There was a man sitting at the kitchen table, and he slowly stood up.

"Now pay close attention to this man," our teacher said as we saw the fellow walk up to the kitchen fridge. "On first look, you would see nothing in particular. But use your spiritual eye to look into this man's spirit. What can you see?" Ista asked.

"I see pain," one student said.

"Good. What else?" our teacher asked.

"The man lost someone—someone dear to him," another said.

"Yes!" Ista excitedly returned. "Now...who did he lose?"

Everyone grew quiet for a moment. I personally could not garner more from what I was looking at. We saw the man get a water bottle out of the fridge, and then he sat down on the kitchen chair and began to weep. He sobbed slowly at first, then it got to the point where he began to cry, looking down at his hands, beginning to shake.

"He lost someone, but he also lost part of himself," Ista said. "Look closer: this man has done something that has changed him forever."

We saw the man peer into an adjacent room, and then the other room lit up before us. There was a little boy on the floor, lifeless, unmoving.

Ista then walked into the room where the man was crying and walked right through him. "What where the clues you missed?" Ista asked. "By the way, this image is live, this is happening right now in Akron Ohio, USA—on South Maple Street, north of the Glendale Cemetery. It should be 2:45 a.m. there right now." Ista looked at all of us and pointed at the scene again. "Now take another look and call out what you see!" Ista shouted.

"The open toy boxes on the floor," a boy yelled out.

"Yes," Ista replied. "That was the lure."

"There's a box of condoms on this pile of garbage," another boy said.

"That is one of this man's vices. Good, good," Ista replied.

"When he opened the fridge, it was empty. This is not his place," one of the girls said.

"It's not." Ista confirmed.

"Look at this corner: a backpack, garbage bags, packing tape and a saw…" another girl yelled.

"Very good. So, what is it that you're really looking at?" Ista asked.

Everyone stayed quiet for a few seconds, and then one of the boys stepped forward.

"Death and birth," he said.

"Please explain," the demon said.

"The death is the boy, and it's also the man's innocence. And birth is also the man. This is obviously the first time he's killed…" the boy said.

Ista quickly replied. "And it won't be his last. We'll make sure of that."

We were taught to study people's behavior, and how to read their every move, but we also had to look beyond the obvious. We were made to analyze hundreds of human emotions, reactions, microexpressions, and even the sleep patterns of people so that we could understand and then manipulate them.

The rooms themselves were receivers for what spy demons would look at on Earth's surface. All the images they saw on Earth were immediately sent to these rooms.

We became capable of deciphering people's innermost feelings by divining their experiences and then piecing together the things we observed.

On some of our other training sessions we were brought into rooms where demons would simulate scenarios on Earth, taking on human forms to train us to deceive, manipulate, and overcome people's psychological obstructions. We were literally taught in Hell how to entrap people by manipulating emotions, conversations, situations, and even people's minds into wanting to do what we wanted them to do, without them realizing it until it was too late.

Learning how to manipulate a situation is most important to an agent. It's what makes them deadly, and this is why it was taught at a very young age, so that it would be instilled in us, and become a part of us. This is how many people were convinced to do things they would normally never do. An agent of Hell befriends them, manipulates them into thinking they only want what is best for them, and before they know it, they become a puppet in the agent's hand.

The pastor interrupted me, then. "Thank you for telling us that. It explains the behavior of a lot of these people that have come and gone from the church."

"I was one of them," I reminded her.

"I know," the pastor said. She looked down at her notebook, but I could tell she wasn't truly studying her words. She looked up at me again, curiosity etched on her face. "Did you ever befriend any of those kids in your class? You never really mentioned any of them specifically. Were you always alone during all this?" she asked.

"I really didn't have any friends down there," I said. "Well…let me take that back. In the very beginning—in the first year or so—I did spend some time with a few kids, but it did not really last.

I went on to explain how for a brief period, it seemed like I was going to become friends with a few of the other students, but it all fell apart. It was usually after classes that I took the time to look around the city, as we were encouraged to do by our teachers.

As I walked and explored, I saw three kids coming down the street, wearing their black cloaks. I knew they were from school. I waved at them, and they waved back. They seemed friendly.

"Hi, we were going to check out these shops down the street, want to come?" one of the girls, Dana, asked.

"C'mon it'll be fun," another student, Dave, said.

I shrugged and nodded, and we began to walk together down the street. As we walked, I learned a lot about them.

The girl was Dana, but her real name was somewhat longer. I could never remember it, but we called her Dana for short. She had black hair, light brown eyes, and was from the Middle East somewhere. She was a really pretty girl, and because of that she was learning to be a "bait" at the time. Then she would move up to seductress, then to assassin.

Children can be used as "bait" on an assignment to murder someone, or to get information from someone. The child is taught to connive, and even to subtly seduce an adult, to disarm them. Then they lure them to a place where someone else will kill them or capture them.

Dana was not the quiet type, and from what she told us, she had come from a long line of high-ranking witches. They had destroyed the lives of high-powered men through sex, murder, and seduction, and she was following in their footsteps.

She never stopped practicing her calling. Whenever I saw her, she was working on her craft. Dana was beyond persistent and would find so many ways to come at you, until she was able to find a way into your heart. She could hardly help herself—she was driven, but always seemed to treat it all like a game.

Dave was another student that joined us that night. I remember having seen him in some of my classes. He was from Czechoslovakia. He had blond hair, and blue eyes. He looked big for his age, and hardly ever smiled. He was already a hunter when I met him, and he said he wanted to be an assassin, but he was being made into an assault or infiltrator agent. He came across as being the quiet type and loved to listen to our conversations. It was rare, but every now and then he would put pipe up, offering his own opinion, if the topic deserved it.

He was learning to get into places that other people would not be able to get into, both in the spirit realm, and the physical realm as well. He was not too happy about his lot in life when I met him. As time went by, I believe he realized that he was talented at that sort of thing, and I think he learned to like it.

The last kid was Chris. He was a taller kid from London with short brown hair and blue eyes, and—

especially compared to Dave—he was a talker. He was extremely opinionated about everything, and would lie, just for fun, even though he did not really need to. He said he was being made into a charismatic figure like his father. He insinuated that later he would be getting into politics just like his dad. But he had to first learn how to master being a "persuader." Being persuasive is a natural ability that some people have, but the devil enhances it with his powers of lying, deceiving, divination, and mind control.

Beyond the ability to observe details, the agent uses divination to obtain information about the target. It's usually likes, dislikes, ways of thinking in different situations. Then, mind control is used to manipulate the target into listening, agreeing, and then accepting what the agent is saying. Ultimately the target is made to do things they normally would never have done.

Personally, I thought that was boring, I could never see myself in that role. Chris would say that he did not like it, but we could all see in his eyes he loved it. I did not spend much time with him, but I knew of him, and he knew who I was, and he would look at me from time to time as if he knew something about me that I had not told him.

As for me, by the time I met the other students, I had already achieved the rank of tracker. I was learning to be a hunter and was going to become a punisher. That would be the first of my masteries. I was not too happy when I was given this role, but quickly learned to like the qualities I was given.

A punisher was used for many different purposes. The first was to intimidate people into doing the devil's will. Second was to inflict pain on them—even death—if they got out of line. Third was to carry out the punishments if needed. A punisher was given more authority, and power, at a faster rate—and especially over those he was watching. He or she can immediately obtain more power to overcome retaliations. They were part of Satan's muscle and were given special secret powers of pain not available to anyone else. Punishers were greatly feared, and never really liked. There comes a point in every punisher's life when they only associate with others like themselves, or simply work on their own. This was one of the reasons why I was never allowed to have friends…or so my teachers told me.

As we walked down the street, we came across a shop that had a suit of talking samurai armor beside its front door.

"Come on in and see what we have!" the armor said, motioning toward the shop's door. "You will surely need what we have to offer…"

We entered the shop through its little door, and when we walked through, we found ourselves in a large, open store. It seemed tiny from the outside, but inside it was enormous. There was clothing, and armor of all different types, and from all different eras in history, it seemed. There were things there that I had never seen before—not even in history books.

As we split up and began to explore the place, I saw armor that seemed ancient and others that looked to be futuristic. I passed by a vest hanging on the wall, and it looked like it was made from a transparent liquid. I got closer, and as I reached out and touched it, it rippled just like water would. There was a sign above it that read, "when you need to go for a while." I reached out to put it on, and it became a liquid, flowing up my arm, down my torso and then it became a vest again. I could reach into it as if it was a body of water, and as did so, I could feel something in there. When I pulled it out, I saw that it was a small seashell. I was admiring it when I heard Dana.

"Guys, come here!"

We all rushed to her and saw her completely covered, like a mummy, in what looked like pieces of light blue cloth. She was wrapped all the way up to her neck, and the scraps looked like they waved in the wind—even though there wasn't a breeze in the shop. Chris went to touch her arm, and pieces of the cloth smacked his hand away. Dana levitated then, and the scraps of cloth extended outward as if they had a mind of their own.

"I think I'll take this!" she yelled out loud.

A box flew off the shelf and landed right in front of Dana, and in an instant, the strips of cloth flew off her body and right into the box. The lid flew up and shut the box perfectly.

"Let's see what other shops are around here," Chris said.

"Guys, I think I saw a bakery across the street…" I suggested.

We all looked at each other for a moment and then ran out of there looking for the bakery. It was right across the street, and the aromas pouring out of it were enough to catch all our attention. The place looked quaint, a dark brown wooden storefront with a small window showing some pastries.

We entered through a glass door, with a sign above it that read "Wicked Treats." When we walked in, there were plates of pastries and treats floating all around the shop. Some of the treats flew up and tried to get into our mouths on their own. On reflex, I tried to avoid them, but they were so fast. A few of them flew into my mouth and as soon as I bit down, I knew I was in trouble, because they tasted so good. It was complete ecstasy. The taste affected me throughout my body. As I ate the goodies, we began to feel bloated—so heavy that we all sat down right on the floor.

"I don't feel so good," Dana said.

"Me neither," I agreed. "I feel really dizzy."

"Kids. Kids! What have you done?" we heard someone say.

Out of the back of the store, a small man dressed in white came out, looking like a baker.

"Guys, everyone knows that you have to say the magic words when you enter the shop, otherwise my treats will attack you! They are wicked… Wicked treats!" he said. He walked over to the entrance and pointed to a sign on the wall. "See right there?" He pointed to the wooden sign right next to the door "Wicked treats to thee I plea, let me be as I enter in. See? It says it right there!"

We all held our stomachs. The baker walked behind the counter and pulled out a small flask and began to make us drink from it.

"Here. Take this," the shopkeeper said.

I thought it was tea, but it tasted like dirt. I almost spit it out, but he held my mouth shut until I swallowed it.

As we sat on the floor, customer after customer would come into the shop, say the magic words on the wall, and then laugh or get a small chuckle as they saw us on the floor.

"First time here?" some would say.

Others snickered at us. "Forgot the magic words, eh?"

We began to feel better after a little while and slowly climbed to our feet. We were done with that place, and we thanked the shopkeeper for his help. He nodded his head and ushered us out the door as he attended to other customers.

We continued to walk for a while, and we saw a whole lot of different types of shops. There were some that appeared to be from different times in history and from all different places on Earth. Some shops were filled with books, explaining any subject you could think of. Some books were alive, and told you what was in them, rather than you having to read them. Some played out like a movie, while others looked completely blank to us, because to read them, certain incantations and spells had to be performed before the contents would appear.

All these places had the same old, dusty, ancient feel to them—some more than others. The walls were usually brown, but each one was decorated differently.

One place that I will never forget was a shop that sold body parts. When we walked in, the first thing that hit you was the smell. But it wasn't from dead limbs or organs. It was the strong smell of roses, and it was intoxicating. The walls were lined with naked arms, legs, and torsos, while the heads were placed on shelves in a section all by themselves. There was a counter in front of the wall, and it surrounded the whole store. Inside the glass counter I could see that it was filled with eyeballs, tongues, noses, ears, and a huge assortment of penises and vaginas, among many other things.

When I drew closer to the counter, I saw that all the body parts were alive! The eyes looked at me; the arms and legs began to move slowly; the torsos moved too. I was astonished and could not believe my eyes.

The storekeeper came out from behind a curtain with a smile on her face. "You want to try some of them on?" she asked.

The lady was beautiful. She was tall and bronze-skinned, with long black hair, and bright green eyes. One look at her made you think she looked almost too perfect. She wore a very thin piece of purple cloth, which covered her private parts and wrapped around different places of her body. Her hair and the cloth seemed to move on their own, as if an invisible wind moved them.

"What do you mean? I asked.

"No one's ever explained this to you?" she asked us. "Unlike your body on Earth, here you can become anyone you like…"

She suddenly changed into a young man, then to an older woman, and finally into a middle-aged man that was fully dressed in a long black robe. The man was bald and had a lot of wrinkles, along with blotches that looked like bruises all over his face. His dark brown eyes looked like they were full of pain and regret.

"My name is Cameron," he told us.

"So, this is what you really look like?" Dana asked.

"Yes…sometimes," the storekeeper replied as he changed back to the pretty girl. "This woman you see now is someone I fell in love with a long time ago. She is a goddess. I was never able to…" She shook her head and flashed us an excited look then as she waved off her memories of a time long before. "Anyway, let me show you how this works."

She took a hand off the shelf and brought it to us. The hand looked like it was from an old man. She looked at Chris and explained the witchcraft to him.

"Concentrate on absorbing the hand into your own body. See it as your hand now. Will it to be, and it will become your own."

As Chris concentrated, the hand disappeared, and then Chris's hand transformed into that hand.

"Excellent," Cameron said. "This is how you change your spirit shape, and when you change your spirit shape, your physical body can't help but change with it!" She gestured broadly to the rest of the shop, an ever-brightening smile crossing her face. "Look around and see what interests you."

She watched as we looked around the shop, and then saw that Dana was looking into the penis display. Cameron joined her there, took a large phallus from the display, and held it in front of Dana.

"Yes, you can try these on too if you'd like," Cameron said.

Dana smiled, and closed her eyes as she made it disappear. She opened her eyes wide right after that, stepped away from the counter and looked down at herself. The penis protruded from between her legs, and it was so big, it hardly fit underneath her robe. She lifted her robe to expose it, and it looked out of proportion to the rest of her body.

Everyone stared at her. We took turns touching and inspecting her. There was no seam or anything—it had become a part of her body.

"I… I love this!" Dana said.

"You can disguise yourself to be anyone and anything you need to be, especially when you're going on assignments," Cameron said. Then she then looked at Chris aside and spoke to him again. "With your will, release the hand, and I will take it back."

Chris closed his eyes, and his hand returned to normal. The old man's hand reappeared on the counter. Cameron looked over at Dana, and she also closed her eyes, willing the penis to reappear on the counter.

Dana pointed to the penis, a grin on her face. "I'll take one of those, please."

"Me too," said Chris.

"Me as well," I agreed.

Cameron looked over at Dave, and without hesitation Dave nodded.

"Yup."

We looked at all the different body parts in the room. There were so many different types and colors, it seemed endless. We tried on all different types of body parts and changed ourselves into different women and men—so much so that we lost track of time that night. As the hour grew late, and we had to say goodbye to Cameron, we put all the body parts back where they belonged and hugged our new friend goodbye. I saw her wave from the door of her shop as we flew away together.

As we neared the top of the cave, we said goodbye to each other. I somehow knew that we would never really spend time like this again. I looked at their eyes, and I could tell that they were feeling the same thing about me.

What was it that set me apart from all the kids? I just did not understand it.

I saw them, one by one, take leave through one of the passages on the top of the cave, and then I made my own exit.

As I traveled up the passageway, I reached out to feel where the location of my body on Earth was, and sure enough, I could not only feel it, but I could see it in my mind.

It was time to go back.

We had learned to make our bodies on Earth a beacon for our spirit forms. Just like we learned to track different things down in Hell, we learned to go back to our bodies from anywhere on Earth, by following their individual signature. We were drawn to our bodies by the powers of darkness, through our wills.

I flew up a long, narrow cave, at blinding speeds, through different passageways. Then I made a turn and saw something that I had not seen before. It was a little structure that looked like a house, way in the distance of a very large cave I was flying through. I saw it briefly, on the side of a cliff, and I could see a light inside it. I also thought I could see some movement.

I made note of it in my mind, turned my head, and continued to fly back home.

I flew out of a statue in the main plaza, and then up to my apartment. When I came into my room, I saw my dad in my room doing a power ritual on me. He poured blood on my motionless body as he chanted demonic incantations.

I got so angry at him. He sensed me in the room the moment I entered. His spirit within his body turned to look at me and he smiled wickedly, forcing me with his power to rejoin my spirit to my body.

I hated the fact that I had no control, and I felt violated by what he was doing. It was my body, after all—

not his to do with whatever he wanted… But he was stronger than me and forced me to yield to his will.

A force pulled me into my body, and he continued performing witchcraft on me. Once inside my flesh, I felt powerless, so tired, and drained, like he was sucking everything out of me. Back then, my parents had complete control over me, even my emotions. I was like a little puppet to them, and I hated that.

Jay interrupted me then.

"So do your parents still have this type of control over you?"

"No," I replied.

"Why not?" the pastor asked. "How can you be so sure?"

"Well, since I started coming to church, even though I meant it for evil, in the services, I felt things. The dark spiritual things broke their hold on me. I can actually stand up for myself now.”

“I know God has been watching over you,” the pastor said. “He wants to help you, and revealing the things you’ve done, the things you’ve gone through, guarantees that you will remain free. Maybe one day you can help others as well.

“It’s horrific to hear that youths like yourself have gone through so much at such an early age,” she continued. “There are laws to protect children from this sort of thing, but our system has failed. We must look to God.”

I nodded. “When the ones that make the laws are the perpetrators, what can you do?”

“You look to God,” she affirmed. “God is your protector, and He will avenge you. There is no escaping His judgement.”

Bloody Vengeance

It was a very clear autumn day. There was a nice breeze in the air that picked up all the golden and red leaves on the ground and swirled them up onto the sidewalk as I walked by. I heard a bird chirping on the trees above me as I passed, then another bird answered his call a few trees down.

Everyone seemed to be going somewhere that morning. People walked their kids to school or went to work. I didn't think they realized how beautiful all the trees were. And the sky…

What was happening to me?

I looked at a mother struggling with her kids as they walked, and I felt pity. It was almost…love?

I never felt that before. It seemed like I was seeing the world in a different light. Perhaps my eyes were being opened for the very first time.

I nodded, thinking that had to be the case. They were some of the changes that Jay and the pastor told me would happen. I was feeling human emotions and becoming normal, perhaps.

As I went on my way, I felt a strange sensation, as if I was being watched. I turned around and caught a glimpse of a white van behind me in the distance, inching toward me. I began to walk faster, and when I reached the corner, I turned to speed along. I looked back and noticed the van turn as well.

I knew it then. I was being followed.

I slowed to a walk again, trying to determine my next course of action, and in hopes that my stalkers weren't aware that I was onto them. When I arrived at the next corner, I turned down a side street, and the van followed me, speeding up. As it drew near, the sliding side door opened, and I could see someone inside ready to jump out.

I ran onto someone's property and jumped the fence into their backyard. I jumped over their neighbors' fences too, until I arrived at the opposite side of the block, and from there, I charged forth in a blur. I kept looking back, but I didn't see the van following me. I didn't know who they were, but I knew what they were trying to do.

I didn't stop until I made it back to my apartment. I never went up to my unit. I just got into my car and drove.

I was paranoid then. I kept looking back through my rear-view mirror, driving erratically as I made my way to the church to meet the pastor and Jay.

It hit me then. I had a sense that it was not over.

I went to a red traffic light and stopped. I looked around and didn't see anything strange, just the regular flow of traffic. The light turned green, and I was still looking around, not realizing that it was my time to go.

The car behind me honked its horn, and I nearly leapt out of the window of my car. I began to make my left turn as I was in the middle of the intersection, when a large, red truck came at me from the direction where I was heading. They swerved, and when I caught a glimpse of them, I realized they were distracted, not targeting me. They had not paid attention, and they were about to fly through their red light.

Even though it was an accident, I could see that they were about to hit the back of my car.

"Jesus!" I screamed out loud, wincing as I prepared to take the brunt of the car crash.

My car was suddenly pushed out of the way of the oncoming truck, and then completely straightened out. The truck breezed by me, missing me by a hair.

I was shaken at that point, but I realized what transpired was a miracle.

But one miracle did not save me from my pursuers.

I spotted the white van then and noticed it driving toward

me on the opposite side of the street. It passed me before

the driver realized who I was. I sped up, making the next

right turn I could. I look back, watching the van make a U-

turn before speeding up to pursue me once more.

I made a left turn into the church parking lot, and

parked my car as close to the door as I could.

The van slowly passed by the parking lot entrance,

and I was sure the driver looked at me straight in the eyes.

But they finally sped away, giving me a faint glimmer of

relief.

Once I was out of my car, I sprinted to the building.

I was quick to ring the doorbell, and luckily, Jay was quick

to answer the door.

"Hey," he greeted me.

"Hi," I spat out, pushing past him to get into the building.

"You…ok?" he asked.

"I've just been through something," I said. "I'll tell you inside."

"Alright, come on in," he said, detecting my urgency. "My mom is waiting for you in the office."

I walked into the office, greeted my pastor, and sat down. Just sitting there talking to them made me feel better. I realized that I was more at ease there than anywhere else in the world. As I told them of the morning's incidents, they both listened attentively, and when I finished, the pastor reached out and grabbed my hand.

"Well thank God that He kept you," she said. "Don't you be afraid of them. This means that you have made true progress. Now we know they want to shut you up for good. You trust God and continue to call on His name. This is where you must be determined that no matter what happens, you will stay true to God."

Then Jay chimed in as well. "Even if God allows them to catch you, and torture you…and kill you. Remember that they did the same to our Lord Jesus, but he stayed true to His Father until the end. And so must you if you want to make Heaven. You cannot go back now. Cherish what God has done in your life. You are fighting for your eternal soul..."

I listened to the pastor speak, and even then, I realized I was scared regardless of what she said. But I knew I had to put my trust in God. I knew the kind of stuff that we used to do to people that betrayed us, and it was horrible. As she continued to talk, my fear dissipated. There was something inside me that gave me confidence, like a certainty that I would make it, that I could do what they asked of me. I found courage within me, and I could feel it. Past the fear, and the worry, it was there.

"So, last time you were talking about some friends that you had made at that magic school. Did the four of you stick together from then on?" Jay asked, taking my mind away from what I was thinking.

"Well, not exactly," I replied.

I went on to explain that after that night, Dana, Dave, Chris and I would meet just a few more times. We would talk about the different things we had learned and the different powers we obtained when we saw each other in our comings and goings, but it would not go much further than that. I did think at one point that we were going to become close friends, but it never turned out that way. Because in that life, happy endings don't happen, and things don't always turn out the way you think they will.

We were all pulled in different directions due to the different types of curriculums we were in. As the months and years went by, I saw them less and less until I completely lost touch with them.

One night, many years later from when I met those kids—and about a year and a half before I met the pastor—I did see Chris again. I had just arrived in the underground city, and I saw Chris on the side of a street by our school building, sitting, and crying. I walked up to him, interested in understanding what had caused him such grief.

"Chris, is that you? Chris, what's wrong?"

Chris looked up and could not believe that it was me. He looked at me for a second then finally answered. "Dave's been taken..."

"What do you mean?" I asked.

"He's been taken by his parents. He was thrown out," Chris cried.

"Why?" I asked as I sat on the curb beside him.

"He killed Dana without approval!" he sobbed.

I paused there for a moment and could not believe it. Dana was gone, and I would never see her again. My heart clenched inside me.

"What happened?" I finally asked.

"He tracked her back to her body, back to her house where she lives. Her brothers saw him coming and told her dad. They accused her of compromising their home and sacrificed her the same day. She didn't even know Dave was following her…" he continued to cry.

I could not say anything at the time. I went to put my arm around him to comfort him, but someone called his name. I looked up, and it was a man and a woman who looked older. Chris ran to them and hugged them, looked back at me briefly and then, they just flew away together.

I assumed they were his parents, but never found out for sure.

I got up from the curb, and just as I was about to walk away, I glanced through a nearby doorway and saw a dark figure smiling wickedly back at me. It smiled like my dad, but it did not hit me at the time that it really could have been him. I simply thought it was someone else.

Creatures, and vague moving figures are commonplace down there, so I did not give it much thought as I walked away. I know now that my family did not want me to have friends. The lonelier I was—the more pain I felt—the better I would be at my job.

I walked and walked through the city that night. Something inside me told me that there was more to what Chris had been telling me. I just felt that something did not add up.

As I made my way, I decided to go see for myself. I wanted to know whether what he told me was the truth. I flew up past the buildings, and through a hole in the roof of the cave, and I began to link spiritually with demons, trying to find where Dana's body really was. I received whispers from different places on Earth. Most of them would deny that they knew anything, but then I received one—one that told me she was not dead, but alive still. I even sensed a signature of her body heat, and that was all I needed.

I knew then that I was going to be able to track her. I homed in on her body signature, until I could feel her. She was behind me. I turned around and immediately flew through a series of tunnels, cavities, and cave systems that led me directly to her location. I broke the surface of the Earth like a bat out of hell and sensed her not too far from where I was.

But something was off. I quickly realized that there was something wrong and sensed it immediately.

I looked around and I found myself at the edge of a sandy desert. It was night, the sky was full of stars, and the

Milky Way was clearly visible—better than any picture I had ever seen. I looked all around, and in the distance, I could see a lot of tents with fires burning in different locations of what looked like a camp.

I knew she was there. I could feel her.

I realized that what I saw was some type of gathering. I approached slowly, as arriving uninvited to certain "spiritual" events can be deadly. Taking caution, I proceeded to send a demon ahead of me to ask for permission, to see whether I could approach.

I waited a few seconds, then the telepathic answer suddenly came to me with force. I could enter the camp and look, but not take part in anything. I slowly approached and looked around as I traveled slowly through the desert. The sky turned darker and darker the closer I came to the camp, as if the stars disappeared into an abyss and there was nothing but a void. A desert breeze passed right through me, and as it did, many diverse smells from the camp began to reach me: incense, various perfumes, burning flesh, and burning wood. I saw hordes of demons circling the camp, marching around it, and flying above it in circles. There was a great expectation in the air. I could feel it and knew then what it was all about. It was a celebration in honor of someone, and there were a lot of human sacrifices going on.

I drew closer still to the camp, and when I touched down at the edge of it, I could clearly hear screams, yelling, and a lot of laughter. It was certainly a feast.

I looked back to the desert I came from, but the view was blocked by the demons walking and skipping around the camp. I began to walk toward the center of camp, closer to the main bonfire. As I strode forward, I saw the tents around me, and noticed that they were all adorned in many different colors, tapestries, and metal hanging decorations. I did not know what they all meant, but I recognized some of them as major family insignias belonging to very prominent dynasties in the devil's kingdom.

Demons from different tents would poke their heads out and look at me. Spirits ran past me, and some would fly down and swoop beside me. I began to see a mixture of physical people in their Earthly bodies, and spiritual people in their ghostly form, like me. As I walked past a large burning fire to my right, I saw dead bodies skewered into metal posts above the flames. They were roasting people, and it looked like they had been burned alive, their jaws open as if they had been screaming. All around the fire, there was an orgy of people, demons, and animals. Sometimes one or two of them would stop, go right up to the burned cadavers, rip pieces of flesh off them, and eat the chunks.

I turned toward my left and continued to approach the main fire in the middle of the camp. I sensed Dana, then, an almost overpowering feeling coming over me. I felt her toward a smaller campfire a little bit further down. I walked closer, and knew she was in one of the tents up ahead. Before long, I stood in front of an enormous red tent, knowing she was inside.

As I glanced at the tent, a foreboding feeling washed over me. I looked around, to verify no one was looking at me, and I walked into the tent.

It was beautiful inside. Expensive and glamorous decorations of all different types adorned each room. I saw lavish rugs and tapestries with antique furniture everywhere as I made my way toward the back. I walked through a small corridor before I reached a back room of the tent…and there I saw Dana.

She was not dead, but she was in deep trouble. Her hands and feet were spread out and tied to the frame of a large wooden bed. Her mouth was gagged, and no one cared about her muffled screams. Demons surrounded her, going in and out of her body, ravishing every part of her soul.

She was being tortured.

I recognized the type of demons that were around her: the demons of death. They were black, adorned with skulls of dead souls, and their bodies were almost pure skeleton, reeking of putrid flesh. I realized then that she was going to be sacrificed.

I went to approach her, but an invisible force pushed me back. It would not let me get close to her, and I was left unable to venture further. Suddenly, a mob of men ran into the room, and rushed up to Dana, forming a circle around the bed. The men started to chant and wave their hands upward into the air. The demons jumped into the men, and they became enraged, their faces changing shape to resemble the demons that inhabited them. Those demons helped the men beat up the young girl. They slammed her, punched her, and beat her bloody.

I wanted to help her, as she screamed, and offered up muffled cries for help, but I knew I would be putting my own life in jeopardy. I made a small move toward her, and one of the demons popped his head out a man's body, and immediately turned his head toward me, locking eyes with me. I moved back slowly.

I continued to look, and just hoped that it would end, but it was not to be. I had not realized that there were more demons that I had not seen before standing in the back corners of the space we were in the whole time. They had been patiently watching. But without warning they jumped into the men and possessed them as well.

The men's hands transformed right before my eyes. They grew massively long razor-sharp fingernails. Their teeth became like needles. The men began to rip Dana apart. They bit into her with their teeth and cut her open limb by limb. There was blood everywhere, and pieces of her quickly spread all over the floor of the tent.

I wept as I watched her disappear before me. I quickly flew out of the room and traveled toward the opposite side of the camp. I touched down near some tents at the edge of the perimeter, still stunned. Then I heard a familiar laugh.

It couldn't be, I thought. In disgust I walked around the tent and took a stealthy peek. I could not believe my eyes. Chris was there, speaking to an elder of the group. He was laughing and carrying on, just enjoying himself.

The elder put his mouth very close to Chris's, and a black smoke flowed into Chris's mouth. The elder gave Chris demons of his own, bringing the boy into his fold and empowering him with a strong alliance. I realized then that he had made some type of deal with the elder and made Dana some sort of sacrifice.

The knowledge of it flew into my mind. It was his fault she was dead. Why else would he have told me that she was already dead otherwise?

I sent out spiritual telepathic inquiries to verify my suspicions, and they all came back confirming what I had perceived. I swore then that I would take vengeance on him.

He was going to pay for this!

I flew up into the sky, and back the way that I had approached the camp. The anger inside me was like a fire out of control. As I flew back home, all I could think about was how much I wanted Chris to suffer. I swore to myself that I was going to kill him, no matter how long it took, or what it was I had to do.

I flew all the way home, clouds of darkness covering me as the desire for retribution filled me completely. I was so angry I could feel it like a tangible thing encompassing me. I burst into my bedroom and screamed so loud that everything within vibrated with the energy I was pushing. I couldn't contain myself, repeating the action several times, sending the items in my room scattering. Even my resting body was moved slightly.

I sat down at the head of my bed and looked at my body resting there, as if it was someone else. I slowly rejoined my spirit to my body, and then sat up. I climbed out of bed, walked over to my door, and looked down the hallway. I saw my dad. He was standing at the top of the stairs, naked, looking at me. His chest and arms were covered in blood, and I could see that he held a knife in his hand.

"You coming down?" he asked.

I looked at him and did not answer. After he turned around, I followed him downstairs. There was a gathering of cult members in the living room, right in the middle of a sacrificial ritual. Every eye was on me when I walked down the stairs. I felt a little bit out of place, but as my dad got back into the circle they had formed, I joined them there.

I could not stop thinking about what I had seen that night, I could not let go of the anger I felt for Chris. We went through with the ritual, but my mind was elsewhere throughout the event.

After we were done and everyone had gone home, as I was cleaning up, I realized that vengeance had completely consumed me. I had to act upon it, or I would lose my mind.

I went upstairs, showered, and headed to bed again. There were a few hours left in the night, and though it had been a long one for me, it was not over yet. I sat on my bed for a few minutes, gathering my thoughts, and I thought about what I was going to do.

A quick glance at my alarm clock showed me it was almost three thirty in the morning. I had not realized that it was so late. I knew I had to hurry. I laid down and turned off the light. A second later, I walked out of my body.

I floated to the center of the room and looked at my body lying down resting. Everything was so vivid and clear. I could think better when I was separated from my body.

The demon protecting my body looked over at me as though he knew what I was about to do. I transformed into a shadow and flew out of my bedroom window. As a shadow, I traveled through the sky out of the city and toward the ocean.

I ascended high into the sky, above the clouds, so high that the city lights became like distant stars. I began sending demons out to search and find where Chris was and what he was doing. Whispers began to return of a meeting taking place on the side of a cliff, in a cave.

Chris was there. I could see him then!

I flew through the night sky as fast as I could toward that cave. I was hidden, camouflaged as a shadow so that no one would recognize me. As I drew closer to the shore where I was certain Chris was, I slowed down to see if I could locate where the meeting was taking place. The air was brisk, and I could smell the salt in it, even felt it all around me. I saw a cliff with a lighthouse above it in the distance, and I knew that was the place. I flew down to the sand and swiftly traveled through the darkness toward the lighthouse.

I reached the rocky cliff, looking up to see spirits enter a cave above me.

Chris was one of them.

I became smoke on the side of the cliff as I traveled upward and rested behind a boulder just outside the mouth of the cave, where I could hear them talking inside. Chris was coming up in the ranks and had some say in a lot of regional spiritual matters. I heard him talk with other wizards and regional demons about all kinds of strategies regarding people in the government, as well as people in regular businesses. He had his hands in a lot of things.

But it would not be like that for long.

All I had to do was wait.

As time passed, I mused on what his final expression would be as he lay dying. Would he cry? Would he be angry? Besides our meeting in the city, we had not seen each other in years, so I was sure he would not expect me. Would his final expression be one of surprise?

The talking inside began to slow down, and they finally started to exit the cave. The spirits within burst out into the sky. I saw Chris as he flew out with them, and then separated from everyone to head down to the sea.

Still exercising caution, I followed from a distance.

As I flew, I looked back to the cave they were in, and I noticed that it was empty then. It seemed to grow smaller as I bolted through the sky after Chris.

He followed a typical flight pattern. As I expected, he had not changed his routine. He dipped into the water, catching me off guard, and I followed him. I knew he would go to the underground city where we studied, probably for another meeting.

As we traveled through the water, it became very dark. But I wasn't concerned. I knew exactly where he was—I could feel him. He, on the other hand, had no idea I was in pursuit.

He entered a cave at the bottom of the ocean, and he traveled through a rift in the Earth. I followed a bit closer then.

We traveled through caves, funnels, and openings, leaving the ocean water behind us. We went deeper underground, and as we did, we began to travel faster and faster. I was right behind him then, until we finally reached his destination.

I knew exactly where we were.

Chris floated down a long, wide, stone corridor, and I could see the bright orange glow from where I was standing. The smell engulfed us at once, and I could hear the cries and moans from there. We were at one of the entrances of Hell. I knew he would make his way to that exact entrance. He always went there after one of his meetings.

Chris traveled past the opening and disappeared into the red and orange glow. I quickly followed, and watched as he made his way onto the cliff where I had set my trap. He approached the edge and suddenly his smile turned to horror as he was immobilized. He stumbled forward, falling over the cliff, straight down to the bottom, as if being pulled by a powerful unseen force.

I floated up to the cliff's edge and looked down. Seeing him struggling to move, I smiled and slowly levitated down to where he was. I landed several feet from Chris and walked toward him. He was paralyzed, part of his body buried in the black burnt earth, his face covered in fear.

Chris heard someone approaching him. "Please, help me!" were the first words out of his mouth when he saw me through blurry eyes.

He did not yet know it was me. I saw the large green and black snake wrapped around his body, going in and out of his chest, wrapping itself around his throat. I dispelled the shadow that hid my identity with a wave of my hand, and he gasped when he saw my face.

I slowly walked toward him, my long black cloak trailing behind me. I walked around him, looking at him as he struggled to move. I shouldn't have dragged on the torture on, but I enjoyed it too much, like scratching a blister begging to pop.

"Nick, help me…please!" Chris cried.

But then he realized that I was not going to help him.

His expression changed to one of betrayal, and anger. "Why?" he shouted, as much as his crumpled form would allow.

"Dana was our friend…" I said.

"What is it with you? Why don't you get it?" he snapped.

"Friends don't kill each other, Chris!" I shouted.

"So what? How many people have you sacrificed?" he screamed.

"This is not the same, Chris. You know that!" I boomed.

"You would have done the sa—" he began to speak. But I never gave him the chance to finish. I thrust my hand into his torso, and his chest opened like a blooming flower. An instant later, I held his heart in my hand.

He looked down, surprised that I could perform such a maneuver, but he grew further shocked a second later. The snake jumped into his mouth, slithering down his throat until I could see it emerge into his shattered chest cavity. It bit his heart as I held it, and all at once, the snake disappeared, and I relinquished my hold on Chris's withered, bloody heart.

I stood up and walked back a few steps. Chris looked at himself, then slowly climbed to his feet.

"Really? That's it? You came all the way out here just to give me a little chest pain?" he mocked. "You're going to regret this!"

But then he stopped, taking another curious glance at himself.

I know he felt it. There was a change, and he knew it too.

"What did you do?" he asked in fear. Then, he spotted the demons flying toward him with chains. "What did you do?" he screamed.

"Well, Chris," I said, "You just had a—well, your body just had a heart attack. You just died."

"It's not possible!" he screamed "No…how?"

There was nothing he could do.

In an instant he was overwhelmed by a horde of demons that chained him and began to bite him, and rip at his spiritual flesh. They dragged him away, Chris screaming hysterically all the while. He looked back at me, but his eyes had already been feasted upon, and his stare was bloody and terrorized.

I stood there listening as his screams faded away from me.

Dana's family had not agreed to her death. He stole her. He sacrificed her for his own gain, without permission. I liked to think that I took revenge on their behalf, and that they gave me their blessing, and helped me harness the power I needed to take him down.

Of course, I enjoyed it.

Just like he enjoyed Dana's death.

I looked around then. I was surrounded by fire, lava, and nasty dirt. An overwhelming feeling of loss came over me. I felt lost, and hopeless, like I was buried in darkness, and could not get out. I heard the faint screams and an occasional deep demonic voice that would scream and taunt the lost. I slowly began to fly upward, and as I did, I wondered what it would be like to never be able to leave a place like that…

Jay put his hand up and shook his head as I was speaking. "So, this is the result of that magic skull serpent spell thing you were telling us at the beginning?"

"Yes," I replied.

"Such hatred—from you and from that boy Chris," the pastor said. "Only God can transform a heart like that…"

Children of the Night

I looked into my pastor's eyes, and I could see real love. I don't know how to explain it, but it was the kind of love that goes beyond just caring about someone. I could tell that she loved me like her own son, but also that she loved my soul.

It left me feeling sure that I could find redemption, despite all the things that had been done to me—and that I had done—in my past.

"Son you should know by now that the relationships that you had with your family were not normal," the pastor said. "Your parents could not have possibly loved you when they put you through all these things. Love works no ill; when you truly love someone, you don't hurt them willingly."

"I've been hesitant to tell you what I'm about to tell you…" I began to explain.

"After all of the things you've revealed?" the pastor asked.

"Well, I guess you're right," I tentatively replied. "My relationship with my mom was not normal. It was also sexual…"

The pastor's face contorted into a painful expression then. "You know, despite everything you've already shared, I was hoping that someone in your family at least was not touching you that way. But it's nothing new for me to hear. A lot of people have been abused by their parents. You're not alone, son," she said.

"It started when I was a little kid, and it continued into my teenage years," I admitted.

"I get it," Jay said. "When you're a kid, you're small, and don't know things as they should be. How did it continue though? How did she keep it going as you got older?" As he finished asking his previous questions, he hunched over, as though he believed he had stepped over a line.

I was done feeling sorry for myself though. "My parents had control over me. They had power over me and could make me do things that I did not want to do. They had been grooming me for a long time. And I learned to like the sex. So, when I became a teenager, I did not see it as abuse anymore," I said.

I went ahead and gave them an example from about ten months before, when I hadn't even considered coming to church.

One night, when I finally returned home from traveling in the spirit world, I was surprised to see my mom waiting for me, sitting on my bed.

I flew into the room through the window, and she looked up. She knew I was there, immediately feeling my spirit. I hovered close to her, and she smiled. So, I flew into my body, and she reclined back on the bed to hug me, so I hugged her back. She drew closer to me, and then slowly kissed me on my lips, and I realized then why she was there. She began to undress, and as she did, her lustful energy hit me like a wave. I felt a surge of desire—mixed with resentment and anger at the same time.

I just…I couldn't resist her, and I had sex with her…

I knew she owned me, and I felt powerless. After a while—after she had her "special" time with me, she sat forward, leaned over, and kissed me on my forehead.

"You know I love you right?" she asked.

"I know," I replied.

But it took a lot to keep myself from biting her damn throat out and letting her bleed in front of me. I felt anger, resentment, and love all at the same time.

She climbed from the bed and left as if nothing happened, and I sat up, grabbing hold of my knees.

She wanted me to believe that she loved me, but I really didn't believe it for a second. She had a selfish lustful desire for me that she called love, but I'd seen times where she would be perfectly fine with me being taken out.

My eyes swelled with tears, and they began to fall onto my lap. The pastor rose from her chair and walked around her desk to place her hand on mine as it trembled uncontrollably.

She looked at me, an almost pleading look upon her face. "Your mom tried to kill you?" I could see the pain in her eyes.

"Yeah," I said, looking down at my lap. "There were several times in my life where I could have died, and I think that she would have been completely fine with it."

The pastor gently lifted my head up to meet her eyes. "Can you tell me a little bit about that?"

I nodded trepidatiously. "Yes, I think I can…"

I proceeded to tell her about the first time she tried, and it was again, when I was a small child, maybe seven years old, I think.

I don't quite remember how I got there, but I knew the place. I was at my town's community pool, and it was nighttime. I looked up to the sky and I saw stars everywhere, and the full moon, so big and white, with not a cloud in sight.

It was a warm summer night. A light breeze hit my face, and the smell of flowers caught my nose. I stood close to the pool.

There was a mischievous feeling in the air. I heard kids running around, chasing each other, but I did not see any adults. I looked around, and everyone was wearing white see-through cloaks. I felt the breeze again, and I looked down to see that I was wearing one as well. I saw right through it to my bare skin.

I smiled as I heard the kids laugh in the distance. I saw them running past the trees. I turned around as I watched them and saw the back of a woman standing a few feet away from me. She also wore a white cloak.

I did not recognize her at first. She stood underneath a light post near the pool. She had long blond hair, and it moved slightly as the wind would catch it.

I slowly approached her, and I could tell she was holding something up to her face, but I could not see what it was from my angle. I drew closer toward her, and I heard something wet fall on the ground in front of her. I continued approaching her, intrigued. I went a little bit closer still and saw a small toddler standing in front of her. The baby wore a white garment as well. He bent down and picked up what she dropped, and then stood back up, holding it up to her.

I finally reached her side and saw that she was holding a newborn baby's body. She pushed her face right into its chest cavity, tearing the insides out with her teeth. Her face, arms, chest and belly were covered in blood, and the toddler at her feet was eating the piece of flesh that had fallen. I looked on in shock, and then she turned to look at me.

"Hi Honey!"

It was my mother.

She looked at me with a sadistic, yet satisfied look, and she licked her lips. She turned again to look at the baby in her hands, completely compelled to continue eating. She took another bite, her eyes turning red and glossing over. When she turned to look at me again, it was a fierce presence of desire that I felt coming from her. She looked at me with an overflowing rage that consumed her eyes. She ripped a piece of flesh from the carcass with her teeth, then handed it to me. Absolute disgust took hold of me.

"Eat her…now," she said.

Suddenly, I felt a cannibalistic urge come out of her hand, and into my chest. The spirit that was in her—that depraved craving for flesh and blood—took me completely over. I took the meat from her hand and devoured it, greedily awaiting another piece. As she ate, she fed the other child and I the baby flesh.

We walked over to a grassy area, sat down on the ground and finished our meal. I remembered being full but still wanting more. Then, as we sat there and looked at what was left of the carcass, we heard music in the air. I looked at my mom and she smiled. She looked more like herself then, and not like a crazy banshee.

As the distant music played on, I noticed that a lot of the kids began to come out of the woods. Kids of all ages came to where we were sitting. Some were just babies, and others young teens. They looked at us, gawked at the spectacle before them, and began to ask my mom what had happened, and what was going on with the music.

She did not answer their questions. She just smiled at us. "Let's go. I have a nice surprise for all of you." She walked away, leaving a bloody mess on the ground behind, and we followed.

My mom led us barefooted through the woods toward the music. She held the toddler she had fed in one hand and the remains of the carcass in the other. We walked deep into the back of the property, and by then, I could make out a building that was all lit up.

As we approached the building the music seemed to grow louder and louder. I saw people in through the windows, dancing and singing. They were drinking, and some were kissing. I finally was able to make out the music. It was a soft classical piece that seemed to carry the cheerful mood of the place into the night. It was mystical.

The house itself was luring us closer, urging us to enter. We followed my mom as she walked around the building. There were gardens with gorgeous flowers adjacent to the building, and beautifully decorated trees were adorned with lights all around. We heard many voices coming from inside the house, laughing and cheering.

We walked through the wet grass lawn, and finally arrived at the front of the property. I looked at it closer, and it was a Spanish style house—old, but well-kept, it seemed. It was a colonial design, with a clay roof, and I remember there were flowers outside the second story windows. I could smell them from downstairs. The moon shone directly on the front of the house, and my mom turned to us, her bloody garment now almost dry, and her face and hands stained in dried up blood.

"Wait here for just a minute," she said.

She walked up the white steps to the house, and when she reached the door, a tall, grizzly, naked man suddenly opened the way and greeted her. He stood right in the doorway, and she talked to him for a little bit, before she turned and pointed to us. She handed the carcass of the dead baby to the man, who wickedly smiled and snatched it from her. I did not know what was going on, but it seemed like she was trying to get permission to go in. Mom finally walked down the stairs to address us.

"I'm going to bring you inside. They're ready for you."

She smiled, the blood still staining her face. Her eyes seemed to be glowing again. We didn't know what she meant by "ready for you," but we followed her up the steps anyway.

Slowly, we entered the house, one by one. I smelled beer, wine, and cigarette smoke the moment I passed the threshold. It was a completely different atmosphere in there than what I thought it was. I looked to my right and there was a hallway filled with naked people talking, flirting, kissing and laughing. I turned to my left and there was a group of men and women having sex with a pony and a goat, laughing and falling all over the place. There was fecal matter everywhere.

I looked straight ahead and saw my mom had stopped and was looking back at me. It was creepy because her eyes had become black, as though oily liquid had coated them completely. The smirk on her face was not human. She turned again and led us deeper into the house.

As we walked, I could hear moans, and laughter everywhere. We passed a doorway, and there was a group of people gathered around a few dead bodies. They were chanting and pouring blood on each other. In the corner one woman was eating a hand.

We continued to walk down the hall, and we arrived at what looked to be a large living room, I saw that a busy orgy was already in full swing. There were so many people present that we could not see the floor. We were shocked at all of this; the kids and I were unable to reel back our surprise.

As I looked around, in a remote corner beside a mantelpiece, and behind the whole scene of bodies moving, I noticed a large-framed man looking straight at me. He was fully dressed and seemed to be completely out of place. I looked at the group of kids I was with, but nobody seemed to notice him. He just stared at me. He had black hair, and olive skin, and he seemed concerned about something. He looked at me intensely, like he had been waiting for me or something. I looked back at the kids again, to see if they finally noticed the man, but when I turned back in his direction, he was gone.

My mom led us out into a courtyard at the back of the house. The backyard was loaded with people partying and carrying on. The party must have grown since we first arrived, as they didn't seem to be there during our approach. Right in the middle, there was a massive orgy of people and animals of all types. There were lights up in the trees, and string lights over the courtyard and the sides of the house. The smell of incense, blood, and burning wood from a large bonfire burning in the back of the courtyard filled my nostrils. Everyone seemed to be in a cheerful mood. They got drunk, high, or both.

My mom turned around and faced us, opening her arms. "Enjoy!" she exclaimed.

The kids and I spread out and began to go our separate ways. I walked around the perimeter of the festivities and looked around. During all the laughing and noise, I faintly heard sobbing, and whimpering coming from somewhere. I looked around and did not see where it was coming from. I looked at my mom, and she was distracted by an older woman that was holding her while she licked the blood off mom's face.

The kids had already started to mingle, and were blending into the party, so I continued to look around. As I explored, some adults reached out to me and tried to pull me into the orgy, but I quickly skittered away from them. I carefully walked over the blood and feces that were all over the floor, stepping over body parts scattered here and there, while avoiding the people who were having sex all over the place.

I walked along the perimeter of the yard and made my way toward the back behind the big fire. It was there, behind the bonfire, that I saw a large metal cage. It looked like a cage to hold animals in, but there were six people inside. One man, two women and three kids. I looked carefully, but I did not recognize any of them. Their terrified eyes stared back at me, and I started to feel bad for them as they cried there, trembling, and barely dressed.

As I drew close to the cage, the man inside reached out to grab me, but I pulled away. He kept reaching for me through the bars, as he begged for his life,

"Please let us go. Please don't hurt any more of us. We won't tell anyone about this… Please!" He cried as he continued to whisper to me. I could see that he was very scared.

Someone hit his hands with a large stick, and he pulled them back into the cage as a painful reflex. I looked up and saw a tall and broad, bearded man looking down at me. He was naked, covered in blood, and had a sinister smile on his face.

"Throw her in the fire," he shouted.

I looked past him and another towering bald man, standing in front of the bonfire, threw the remains of what appeared to be a woman into the large fire. He looked at her burn for a second then turned his head and saw me. He walked to the cage and stood right beside me.

I looked back at the bearded man, and he was looking straight at me as well. He then unlocked the cage, and walked in. Everyone inside started to scream, each of them running toward the back of the cage. He punched the man in the face, bursting his lip open. The caged fellow dropped to the floor, shaking in fear. One of the women stood in front of the children, but the large, bearded man slapped her out of the way with one stroke. The giant grabbed a little boy, dragged him out and handed him to the other man, who was covered in blood. As he locked the cage, the fire seemed to come alive, and dance on its own.

The boy cried frantically, and the man that held him handed him back to the bearded fellow. With one hand, the giant held the boy by the neck and began to lick him like a fleshy popsicle. Then he started beating him without mercy with the stick.

As the boy screamed, people looked up, and they cheered when they saw what occurred. The man continued to beat the boy over the head until it split open, and the onlookers rushed to the boy to drink his blood. They began to eat him alive as he was beaten. They ripped the boy apart, pieces of him handed out to the crowd, who did all kinds of things to them.

As I watched the mutilation, an older lady I did not recognize grabbed me by my head and pushed me to her groin.

I was now part of this blood orgy.

One after another they took turns with me and passed me around the courtyard. Sometimes they would gang up on some of us kids at the same time because they were amused by it or try to cause us pain. They enjoyed that sort of thing.

Some of us kids were already used to it, others cried or asked for them to stop, never finding reprieve.

I was at the bottom of a pile of people, and I saw that one man again. And he stayed in the background, still dressed, and was still looking straight at me. I moved slightly out of the group I was in, and I kneeled to get a better look, but he was gone again. I didn't know who he was, but it was strange that he was not joining in, I thought. I tried to remember if I had ever seen him before, but I could not recall.

I looked up from time to time and I would see one of the two large men go and get someone from the cage, bring them out, and maim another of the prisoners. Sometimes the poor souls would be stabbed; sometimes they would be ripped apart slowly. But in the end, they would all end up in the fire. These were sacrifices—mass sacrifices done to honor the devil—and there was no one to stop this from happening. The whole town was there participating, from teachers and grocers, to lawyers, judges, and even police.

The night carried on slowly, and people went about through the house. Animals were passed around the group, another type of forbidden pleasure.

As soon as I found my chance, I pulled away, and climbed to my feet. I was able to make my way to the cage again, but there was no one in it then. It was unlocked and the door was open. My curiosity won me over, and I walked in to get a better look. The smell of urine was overwhelming, and it didn't take long for me to find a puddle of it toward the rear of the cage. Someone had lost control of their bladder as fear took them over. I would have too.

I began to think about the people that were just in there, and about what they must have thought while they were living their last moments, seeing their companions die, one after the other. I kneeled to get a better look at the puddle of urine, and I put my finger in it. As I brought it back to my mouth to taste it, someone grabbed my arm and pulled me up. A big, heavy man grabbed me, and began to drag me out of the cage.

"Hey!" I cried, but he did not reply. "I'm not one of them, let me go!"

The man smiled at me but did not say a word. He began to drag me to where the other captives had been killed. I don't know if he thought that I was a sacrifice, or if he didn't care and just wanted to give in to his dark desires. But fear gripped my heart—I truly believed that he was going to kill me. I screamed for help, but no one responded. No one paid attention to what transpired. I tried to escape, but his grip was too strong for me to break.

He was almost completely covered in blood, and as he dragged me along the blood and feces-stained ground, I was soon covered in it as well.

"I'm not a sacrifice! I'm a member just like you! Stop!" I begged, but he did not listen.

We arrived at the spot in front of the fire, and he turned to look at me. By then he did not look human. His eyes were completely black, and his nose seemed to be almost gone, with only two holes in his face where his nose should have been. I screamed out for my mom, scanning for her in the crowd. I finally saw her amid the crowd of people on the floor, but she would not turn to look at me. As I stared at her, I saw her pass a glance my way, before she turned back.

She knew.

I spun about to look back at the man that held me, and he smiled at me, knowing that what I had just seen devastated me. His teeth were yellow, long and sharp. I saw him lift a bloody knife up above his head, and at that moment I thought I was destined to die. He head butted me in my face, and I fell to my knees with a bloody nose, surrendering at his feet. I looked up at him, and terror took hold of me as I saw the knife come down toward my face. The blood from it splattered my cheeks, and everything seemed to move in slow motion.

As the knife closed in on me, to my surprise, I saw another hand grab the man's arm. The mysterious man pushed the knife into the large man's chest, and the knife was dragged down to his belly, opening his abdomen, spilling his guts onto the ground. The stranger picked the large man up and cast him into the fire. The mysterious man—the one I realized had been watching me—grabbed hold of me then. I felt a comforting warmth come out from him.

"I never left you," he said.

Sharing an uplifting smile with me, he placed me gently upon the ground. I looked around, noting that everyone was still preoccupied, oblivious to whatever happened. I saw my mom leaving the courtyard, and I rushed into the house.

I turned to look back at the man that had saved me, but just as before, he was gone. I did not see him anywhere. It was like he had vanished into thin air.

I never found out who he was, and I never saw him again.

I ran into the house, past a group of people that were passed out, naked on the kitchen floor. A lonely little boy, clinging to his sleeping mom, looked at me as I ran past him. I ran upstairs, past a group of girls making out on the staircase landing and arrived at the upstairs hallway. A squealing pig ran past me and into one of the rooms. I saw an open door and entered it. The room was trashed, but empty. I found a closet there, so I entered and hid behind a pile of clothes in a corner.

I stayed there the rest of the night and waited for many hours to pass by—it seemed like forever. I didn't care about the wait though, as I was still shaken up by the fact that I had almost become a sacrifice. Even so, eventually I succumbed to exhaustion.

After a long while, I woke up to loud footsteps. They stormed back and forth outside the closet door. The closet door opened, and I saw my mom peering in, a stern look upon her face.

"Let's go!" she grumbled. "C'mon we're leaving!"

She was curt with me. She seemed angry, and somewhat disappointed. Something inside me told me that she had expected me to die that night. We walked way back to the car, where my dad had been waiting with my younger sister, who was asleep in the back seat. I saw my mom get into the front passenger seat, so I jumped in the back seat. No one said a word.

My dad drove slowly from the building, and as I looked out the window, I saw rays of sunlight coming through the top of the trees.

"I never did find out who that man was that saved me," I said to the pastor.

"It seems to me that God sent an angel to the pit of hell to save you," she replied.

"An angel?" I asked.

"Of course… Only God could have saved you at that point. Wow, God was looking out for you, even back then."

I sat there amazed, as the realization hit me that the man who rescued me had been an angel. It was the only explanation.

"So, what happened next?" Jay asked.

"Well…" I began.

I went on to tell them that the days that followed were filled with an expectant silent excitement of the manifestation of an upcoming event. No one spoke of it, but everyone that I saw had that look in their eyes, and I knew that there was something coming up. There had been a lot of blood spilled, a lot of sacrifices made, and it was for something. I could feel it, but no one would say anything.

Then, little by little, people started getting money, as if out of thin air. My dad started a new business, my uncle hit the lottery, another one of my relatives was able to sell his business and got rich. It had all been done for money.

They spilled blood…for money.

"Well, they will have to pay an eternity in Hell if they don't repent to God for such an atrocity," the pastor said. "I've encountered people like this here in America, and overseas. When the Lord sent me to Africa to evangelize, he set many people free that had been bound to darkness in the way that you just explained. People forget that God is above everything. He created it all, and all power comes from Him. He is in control. Let me explain.

"I was with a pastor friend in Africa. He was from Nigeria, and some of his congregation had joined us. We were walking away from a village I had just preached at, but I didn't know where we were walking to. I had been preaching for several days already, and had gone to several towns with him, so I assumed we were doing the same that day.

"This time however, we were walking into the jungle—or the bush as they called it. Everyone was singing praise songs as we walked, and I joined in. Their songs are so beautiful.

"After a while, I felt God in my spirit, sobering me up. I started feeling the powers of darkness in the air, and I began to pray. I could see a clearing up ahead and we were walking toward it when suddenly, the Holy Ghost took hold of me and I jumped up in the air, speaking in tongues. I reached out and grabbed a devil from the air, and when I came down, I threw him under my feet, and continued to speak in tongues as I stomped him.

"The singing stopped, and I knew all eyes were on me. But I continued to pray to the Holy Spirit for a few moments until I felt compelled to stop. When I finally opened my eyes, we were at an opening in the jungle, in front of a village, and everyone was looking at me.

"Out of the village, a woman came toward us, accompanied by a very large man. She was saying something that I could not understand, but I saw the devil within her, watching me beneath her countenance. As she approached us, she held out a little dish, and began to blow dust at us. I knew what she was trying to do, but it wasn't going to work.

"I pointed at her with the finger of God and backed her up all the way toward one of the huts. I bound up and cast the devil out of her in Jesus's name. She fell back toward the hut, and fainted, and the man that was with her ran off.

"The pastor that was with me and his congregation were jumping up and down, praising the Lord out loud in front of everyone, but I did not understand. The pastor came up to me and pointed to the young woman that was passed out. She was a young, good-looking woman, but the paint she wore was for witchcraft, and it made her look sinister indeed.

"'That woman right there, is a very powerful witch,' the other pastor said. 'She had taken over the minds of everyone in this town, and whenever anyone came to try to tell them about Jesus, she would get the men in the village to drive them away. These villagers have been her slaves, doing everything she told them to. We are praising God today, as He has destroyed her power over the people.'

"I then felt the unction to preach. As the pastor translated for me, I told them about the true power of God, Jesus our savior, and how they needed to repent of the mess they'd been practicing. As I preached, more and more people came out of their houses. The whole village stood before me. I told them that if they truly wanted to be free, they needed to burn all their idols—all the things they used witchcraft for—and to confess.

"They began to run back into their houses. It was a sight to see, I tell you. They began to throw their artifacts in front of me, and the pile grew before me. I could not believe it.

"Then they lit in on fire, and as it burned, they began to repent before God. I preached throughout, leading them to Christ. They dropped to their knees—the whole village, Nick—and they confessed to all the things they had been doing in the devil's kingdom.

"The anointing of God was there. People were liberated, with spiritual chains being broken off the people. They truly did come to the Lord that day.

"That witch? She was passed out the whole time. There is no bondage, no contract, and no covenant of death that Jesus can't deliver from. I know He can do it. I have seen it, and He can do it for you.

"I went back to that village years later, and they had established a church there. The streets were paved. There were actual houses and businesses that had been established. They had brought in electricity, and water. God was blessing them, because they had come to Him."

"I love hearing that one," Jay said.

"Well, I'm so glad they were unshackled, because I know all about having forces of darkness control me," I said.

"What do you mean?" Jay asked.

"I'm sure you have a good explanation, son," the pastor responded.

"Yeah, I'll give you an example of how we were mentally controlled, even as kids," I said.

I began to tell them of the way mass mind control was used in my little town back in Argentina. I must have been about eight years old by then.

One night as I lay in bed sleeping, I remember hearing a faint, soft melody. I don't remember what I was dreaming, but I do know that in my dream the melody was there, and when I opened my eyes, the melody still played in my head. I sat up and listened. It was something I had never heard before, and it was extremely catchy—

seductively alluring… I felt it all through my head and spine, and it tingled down to my fingertips and toes. I heard someone moving in the room next door, then footsteps on the floor, and then I heard my sister's voice. She was humming the melody I was hearing.

We were staying at my grandmother's house at the time. She lived at the edge of the city, and the open desert was just about a block away. My sister usually slept with my grandmother, and I slept in my uncle's bedroom when we stayed over. When I heard her get up, I immediately looked over at my uncle, to see if he would say something, but he was still asleep. My uncle was young. He must have been about fourteen at the time.

I looked back at the wall from where I had heard my sister humming. It was so catchy that I started humming it too. My uncle woke up, and I smiled at him, but he just looked back at me confused. He didn't seem to know what was happening. I climbed out of bed, opened the bedroom door, and my sister, in her pajamas, was already walking down the long hallway toward the front of the house.

The tall, dark hallway was covered with old pictures that were lit by the moonlight coming from the front living room windows. I followed my sister down that corridor, and when we reached the sitting room, we both jumped on a chair there to look out of the window. We saw all the kids from the neighborhood coming out of their houses, singing the same melody we still heard.

I could not control myself. It was as if something was controlling my motor functions, like someone else was driving in my head, and I was just watching. I opened the front door and began to sing out loud with the rest of them.

It was an alluring, spiritual desire to join them all as they walked down the street, singing the melody. My sister and I ran out and joined them. I looked back, and my uncle just stood there at the front of the house, watching all the kids pass by.

As we walked down the street together, kids ran down to join us from all over. We walked to the edge of the city, and into the open desert—a massive group of kids. Parents and teens just watched as their kids or siblings would leave them, and they themselves were caught in some type of trance that prevented them from moving or reacting. I just felt an irresistible desire to be in the group, and my grandparents were not coming after us, and I was at peace with that.

I looked around and there were so many kids from all over the city that were walking with us that it seemed like everyone had joined us. As we all marched down the desert road of the city I looked up and the stars seemed to be moving. The night air was cool and refreshing, and in the distance, I could see a blinding white glow coming from the side of a mountain.

We walked all the way down the long road into the middle of nowhere. I could still hear the music in my mind. We walked until we arrived at a crossroads, and then we all turned left, as if we knew where we were going. We turned onto a road that led to the bright light in the mountain. As we drew closer to the light, I could see in the distance what looked like an entrance into the mountain, and that was where the radiant glow was coming from, so bright that it illuminated the whole road, and the night sky above it.

We began to walk up the mountain, and the road turned from pavement into golden brickwork. I could see a wall of fire at the entrance of a large, golden entrance on the side of the mountain. Everything looked to be fashioned from gold.

How was it that this was here? I thought.

As we drew closer to the wall of fire, I could hear the melody that we were all singing, almost like crystals chiming. They came from the cavern, and the fire danced along with it. I felt a stronger urge to continue inside, and I gave in to that urge.

All the kids began to laugh hysterically. We were drawn in as if it was a dream. Not seeing any danger in the fire, we walked right into the dancing flames.

We were not burned though. We walked through them, and into the cave.

As we walked inside, our appearances changed. We glowed slightly green, and our skin had a golden hue to it.

I felt like I was in a mystical world.

Inside, the cave was enormous. The whole top of the cave was covered and lit with a moving green and golden fire. There was a golden road leading all the way to a pyramid-shaped structure made of pure white rock. The pyramid looked ancient—a hybrid of different types of architecture.

On the top of the pyramid, I could see someone standing, but I could not make out who it was. The pyramid and the walls of the cave were adorned with many golden fixtures, emblems, and symbols I did not recognize. I looked around, and it was so bright in there that it seemed like daylight, enhanced by the fire on the ceiling.

As the multitude of kids gathered inside the cave, we continued to sing out the haunting melody, and as we did, it resonated throughout the cave, making it even louder.

The person on top of the pyramid came forward. Better able to see him, I noticed he was a handsome, black-haired and olive-skinned man. He wore white pants, and a long-sleeved white shirt. He did not speak, instead connecting with us telepathically. He raised his hands, and immediately everyone quieted down. I could hear his voice inside my head, resounding and echoing within my mind.

"You are the chosen ones. You are privileged to be here and witness the birth of a new era—the birth of a new generation. Surrender to your calling. This is why you were born, and why you are here tonight," he said.

And with that, he looked to his left, and a woman wearing an all-white robe brought him a newborn baby. He held it up, and two other men came up and held the baby for him—one on his left, the other on his right. He took out a golden dagger, and cut the baby's throat, the blood spilling over the front side of the pyramid. As soon as the blood spilled, we all heard a rumble, and then as more blood fell, we saw a portal appear from the spilled blood.

Tremendous demons entered the cave, and they began to fly about. The man looked down at the blood, and handed the baby to a woman as another baby was brought up.

Baby after baby, sacrifice after sacrifice, the portal became bigger and bigger, and the demons grew larger and larger. They flew all over the cave. Some continued flying close to the ceiling, but some descended, joining spiritually with the children below. As they were possessed, they screamed in monstrous voices.

Then, we saw men come out of the sides of the pyramid with silver knives, and they began to go through the crowd of kids. The demons above them would point out kids to them, and they would kill that child immediately. The demons would grab the child's soul and hand it to a smaller demon who would take the soul back through the portal. The men walked through the crowd of kids slowly, and deliberately, but for some reason, fear was not present. We felt like it was a gift to be sacrificed.

One of the men walked close by me, a large demon hovering right above him. The demon pointed to a girl right next to me, and the man sliced her throat. She fell at once.

With one swoop of his tail, the demon grabbed the soul of the girl and handed it to a demon standing right next to the gate, and as soon as the smaller demon grabbed the screaming soul, he withdrew through the portal.

As the men walked, they left a trail of children's bodies and blood.

During this time the man on top of the pyramid continually killed baby after baby, each handed to him by a new woman. Then, without warning, he stopped, and when he did, the men walking around us also stopped in conjunction with him. The demons that guided the men on the ground still hovered above them, as the rest of their cruel, wicked flock flew about farther above. The men walked back toward the pyramid, and stood in line, right in front of it.

Then, the demons that were above those men entered them, causing them to fall to the ground. I looked up, and the demons that flew above the cave descended on all of us children below and possessed us. I remember yelling something out loud, then I blacked out completely after that.

I don't know how much time had passed until I opened my eyes. As I came to and looked around, everyone was getting up. The cave was not bright like it was before. In fact, it was dimly lit, and I could barely see around me. The kids from the town were scattered everywhere. Some were still unconscious, while others stood, holding their heads. We were all confused and stunned.

The men that I saw walk through the crowd of kids before wore regular clothes then. They picked the kids up and helped to usher us back to the mouth of the cave.

I did not see any bodies on the floor, or blood on the pyramid, or fire on the ceiling.

The mouth of the cave was wide open, and there was no wall of fire either. I wondered then if it had all been a dream. I looked back and saw the man standing on top of the pyramid looking straight at me. He watched me as I walked out, as if he was just discovering me or something. I turned around, and in a daze, I walked away.

All the kids and I walked back to town together, no one saying a word. It was still dark, but the night was far spent, I was sure. It seemed like it took forever to get back, for some reason. It had not seemed like we had traveled that far earlier.

Finally, I arrived back at my grandmother's house. I walked up to the entrance and the door was open. I walked to the back, passing my grandparents' room. They were not there. And when I entered my uncle's room, I realized there was nobody there either. The place was empty.

I crawled into bed and stared at the wall. Everything that night seemed right out of a movie—or a nightmare. I looked at the dirty wall until I went to sleep, my curiosity about what happened that night overwhelming me until it gave way to fatigue.

The next morning, it felt like some type of dream. Little by little, the memory of it completely faded from my mind until it was gone.

"It wasn't until I decided to confess my sins that these memories began to come back to my mind. At first, it almost felt as if they belonged to someone else. But my heart would always tell me that these were my memories."

There was a small moment of silence in the church office. The pastor scribbled notes in her book for a moment, and then she looked back up at me.

"So, the whole city was under the influence of the devil," the pastor said.

"The whole city," I confirmed.

"Such wickedness… Son I am so glad you have decided to surrender to God. Remember, as you confess your sins, you ask Jesus to cleanse you with His blood. It's very important." The pastor reclined in her seat, and I could see that though she was intrigued about the information I had divulged, she was beginning to grow weary.

"Thank you for caring enough about your soul to reveal the devil's works, son," she said. "I know I've told you before, but it's important for you to know. It's the only way to not get blackmailed back to darkness."

She rose from her chair then, and her son rose from his spot in the corner of the room then as well.

"If you don't mind, son, I think I'm going to go home and go to bed," she said. "That will be all for today."

"Of course," I reply.

"We'll meet again, okay?" she asked.

I nodded in approval.

We gathered up our things, headed outside toward the parking lot, and said our goodbyes.

It was a cloudy night. I could see the moonlight peering through the clouds, and as I drove away, I could hear the wind whistling through the tree leaves. It was nice out.

I drove out of the driveway and into an industrial side street, and as I headed down the street, I saw something on fire way up ahead. As I drew close, I could make out that it was some kind of vehicle. There was no one around.

As I neared the blaze, I realized that it was a van, and that it was partly up on the sidewalk. The front of it was engulfed in flames, like it had been hit suddenly by something big.

There were bodies on the ground all around it, each of them burnt to a crisp. I stopped the car and got out to take a better look. I made my way to the back of the van, the only part not yet reached by the fire. It was one of those white vans, looking just like the one that was following me.

I tried to peek inside, but I was afraid of the fire. I didn't want to be near the thing if it blew up.

I continued to peer in through the windows, and I saw all sorts of electrical equipment. It was a surveillance van.

I looked around, and I could see there was no one close by. I walked back past the bodies on the ground, and they seemed to have been wearing tactical gear, barely discernible by the burned body armor.

I grew scared and realized that what I saw was not normal.

I rushed into my car and quickly drove away.

I wondered what could have done something like that.

Slide and Recover

It was a beautiful Sunday morning. I was at church helping to get the sound system up and running, as we were having visitors from another church set to join us that day. I ran to and from the studio, trying to get rid of the feedback we heard. People came in and out of the church studio, saying hello, and there were a lot of distractions. Out of nowhere, one of the parishioners that I was familiar with came into the studio, a confused look upon their face.

"There's a lady at the door that says she wants to talk to you," she said. "She says she's your mom."

I turned around and looked at Jay. My friend shared a concerned expression, but my curiosity was already overtaking me.

"Really?" I asked.

I walked out of the studio, through the hallway, and reached the vestibule. I saw her outside the building, close to the front door.

It was indeed my mom. She was standing there by herself, in a red flower dress, looking innocent, as though she hadn't inflicted years of torture on me. I walked outside, and she flashed a bright smile at me before she jumped at me to give me a kiss and a tight embrace. I tried to pull away but couldn't. She finally released her hold on me, and I took a step back to talk to her.

I could see that the visiting church members were arriving, so I pulled her aside from the front entrance, and into the parking lot.

"What's going on?" I asked. "Why are you here?"

"I haven't seen you in such a long time," she replied. "You don't come to visit, so I figured I would come here to see you."

As she spoke, I began to feel something I had not felt in a very long time. Her magical, carnal hunger—a dark allure—exuded from her.

"All you had to do was call," I said. "You have my number."

"Yeah, but that's not the same as seeing you. I miss you," she replied as the allure cast out from her intensified. "How have you been?"

"I'm fine," I curtly returned. "Look, you shouldn't have come. Next time, just call."

Her magic was trying to find a way inside me and was pressing my spirit. I should have walked away. I should have just run. And though I felt that I could resist it, I chose not to.

I accepted it and her lustful magic ran through my body, filling me up with a powerful sexual desire.

"I've got to go…" I said, already ashamed that I yielded to her in my spirit.

"Don't you miss me?" she asked.

I knew what she meant. She was talking about all the sex we used to have, and the orgies we were involved in. At once, I begin to see images of her and I. Explicit images, one after the other, played in my mind. That onrush happened so quickly that I couldn't shake them off. I looked directly into her eyes, and saw that they were blood red. She flashed another smile, that one devilish and wicked.

"Look I'm needed inside, I…"

I tried to finish my sentence, but I couldn't. I was overwhelmed by the memories of primal, carnal intertwining. They flooded my mind and heart, and my body began to respond.

She came up to me slowly and puts her hands on my shoulders. From between her legs, a strong surge of magical desire expanded, and like a wave of fog, it washed over me.

"I miss you," she said, her voice a raspy, seductive thing. "Please, come home."

"We need you inside!" Jay yelled out at me from the door.

I looked at Jay and then back at my mom, and I yielded to her charming magic again. It electrified me and permeated through all my being.

But I was able to wrench myself away.

I began to walk back toward the building, and when I looked over my shoulder, she blew me a kiss.

"I love you," she said. "Come back home."

I skittered away, like an animal that knew they had just escaped from a trap. When I entered the church, Jay sensed that something was wrong, but I hurried past him. I walked back inside to the studio, and I felt awful. Though nothing had happened, I felt as though I had given in to old desires and committed something sinful with my mother. Everything about me felt off somehow.

As I resumed my work on the sound system, I looked over at Jay. I knew he noticed a difference in me—something had changed for the worse.

"What were you doing out there so long with your mom?" Jay asked.

"Just talking… She wanted me to come back home with her," I said.

"You were out there locking horns with the devil!" the pastor said.

I turned around and did not realize she was standing right behind me. "I was talking to my—"

"No, you were not just talking. You went back!" she snapped, conflicting expressions of anger and disappointment etched upon her face.

"I was in my office, and the Lord let me know what was happening. You went out there and fell for their trap!" she said.

"I was just talking to her…" I said.

"No. Whatever she was offering you, you bought it, and received it, didn't you?" she asked.

I realized then that there was no way I could hide it. I had slid back and accepted what I used to have with her. I desired it and received it back into my heart. It was like a part of my soul was being revealed to me in that very moment. I realized it was God showing me my own heart.

"Yes, I did," I admitted.

"You cannot go back like this. You must make your choice to stand with God a sure thing. They are trying to pull you from God's grace and His protection. Once they do, they will kill you," she grumbled. She shook her head, and I could see how much she felt I had betrayed her and all she stood for. "How can you treat God like this, after all the love He showed you—all of the mercy and forgiveness He's given you for the things you've done?"

I felt horrible and could no longer look her in the eyes. Tears began to swell in my eyes, and I could see them drop from my face to fall onto the floor.

"This is what I was talking about," she said. "They will come after you in many different ways."

"Are we still going to meet later today?" I asked, trepidation shaking my voice.

"No," she replied. "You must make up your mind on who you're going to serve. Right now, your heart is full of…whatever it was you were doing out there. You make up your mind. If you want to come the Lord's way, I will know it. Then…then we can talk." Her anger had not abated, and she stomped into the sanctuary of the church.

I looked out into the sanctuary, and it was full. There were people from other churches there as well as our members, and the service was about to start. I looked over at Jay, and he motioned for me to get to work.

It was a rough week for me. I felt completely out of place, and even though I had asked God for forgiveness. and repented for what I did, I felt like I had something to prove. I didn't meet with the pastor at all that week, and it felt unusual after seeing her so often all those weeks prior. I considered that I probably just needed some time to heal the rift between us, even though I knew the door was open for me to talk to her. It just didn't feel right for me to jump back in.

I started noticing black trucks and cars with tinted windows following me wherever I went. I knew it wasn't the cult I used to be with. The new people seemed more organized. Everywhere I went, there was a vehicle tailing me, and when I would enter an establishment, the place would grow busier than when I had arrived. I knew I was being followed, and everything about it seemed like it was the government.

I met with Jay toward the end of the week, after I got off work, and we went to a diner to get something to eat. He met me inside, in a booth by a window. The diner was a bit dingy. It had a has-been vibe and gave us the sense that its glory days were in the past. It was as though they were trying to hold on to some kind of fame from earlier days.

The food was good though, and it kept us coming back.

We sat down and ordered. Somehow, our conversation led to other people that had been thrown out of church for practicing witchcraft.

"Look, there have been so many people that have been sent against my family and me," Jay said.

"Like, to spy on you guys?" I asked.

"Not just to spy, but to take us out—to kill my mom and those that are helping her," he revealed. "We've met people from all over the world that would just come and tell us that they had been fighting us spiritually".

"Why would they tell you this?" I asked.

"God would put them in such a place where they would be compelled to reveal themselves. Their lives would be in jeopardy somehow, family members kept dying—all sorts of stuff. But they would only go so far… Just enough to stave off God's anger. You know, some of them would want to be free, but they would not fully reveal the works of the devil in their lives. I mean over, and over, and over, down through the years. You're not the only one we've heard from, but so far, you're the one that's revealed the most, and that says a lot about you."

"So, did any of these people get delivered?" I asked. "I mean, did any of them really make it out?"

"Yeah, some of them did get out," Jay said. "But not many. There's been a few people that trusted God enough to reveal all they needed to stay free. They're just living normal lives now—at least, as normal as they can. When you come out of all that spiritual activity and enter God's kingdom, you become a target, and it's a challenge. It's a fight on a daily basis. Every day, someone or something will come against you, and you must persevere, through the power of God. Your determination to live for God must be renewed each day."

"So even after they find salvation, they're still going to come after you…" I mused.

The waitress brought us our hamburgers and smiled at us. We returned the gesture and waited for her to leave before we continued our conversation.

"Thanks for ordering for me," Jay said. He nodded a bit more enthusiastically though as we returned to the topic at hand. "Yeah, it's a daily battle."

I took a moment to consider what he was saying, and then I blew out a nervous sigh before I let my friend in on one of my revelations. "I've noticed that there have been cars and people following me."

Jay took a bite out of his burger and looked out the window into the parking lot. He took a sip of his soda before he gestured to the rows of cars there. "It was only a matter of time. This is where you need to believe that God will keep you."

"Who are they?" I asked.

"The government," he said. "They follow us."

"What?" I asked. "Why?"

"They keep tabs on churches that have the true power of God," Jay replied.

"But we're such a small church," I said.

"They don't care about how many members you have. They care about who has the power of God. They want to know where the Holy Spirit is moving, and what He is doing. They can't control Him, or manipulate Him, so they watch," he said.

We finished up and headed out to the parking lot, and I sat with him outside in his car, as we continued to talk. Out of the corner of my eye, I caught a glimpse of a looming dark figure standing toward the back of the building. I turned to look and there it was, moving back and forth from one side of the parking lot to the other.

I looked at Jay and saw that he had already spotted it.

It wasn't human. He looked like a giant old man, covered by a willowy black cloak and hood. and he was walking back and forth from one side of the parking lot behind the building toward the other side. He held tight to a large walking stick that looked to be fashioned out of someone's spine, and it was decayed and crooked.

He was agitated, and turned to me, opening his mouth as if to scream, but I couldn't hear anything. He tried several times to make his way toward us, but he couldn't. It was as if he was corralled by some type of invisible forcefield, so he continued to pace back and forth, pointing the stick at me, and screaming. Every time he turned to look at me his black eyes with red pupils flared up.

"God's keeping the devil at bay for you," Jay said. "He is so angry about the things you've been revealing…"

"What?" I asked.

"You've got to come all the way now. There's no turning back for you. You go back to the mess you were in, and they will certainly kill you."

We continued to look at the strange being. Finally, realizing that it would not be able to pierce the veil that kept it from me, it disappeared. I just sat there for a moment stunned.

Jay tapped me on the shoulder, and when I looked at him, he gave me an assuring nod. "All the way now…" he said.

"Yeah. All the way," I replied.

The week came to an end, and I had a new resolve within me to continue revealing all the things that I had experienced. I had yet to contact the pastor again, however.

I had not heard anything from my mother either. And I did not want to. I avoided her with all the composure I could gather.

It was Sunday again, early on, and Jay and I had picked up some breakfast and were sitting in the studio of the church eating our food. One of the church members popped her head into the studio, and I already had a pit in my stomach before she spoke.

"Your mom is outside looking for you."

I looked at Jay, and he flashed his eyebrows. I couldn't believe she was there again. I immediately began to pray for God to give me courage, even though I was quite afraid.

I walked up to the entrance of the church, and I saw her through the window in the door. She sent another falsely innocent smile my way. There were a few members of the church behind me when I opened the door. But I would no longer allow shame to cow me.

"I know why you're here and it's not going to work," I yelled. "Just go and leave me alone!"

"What?" my mother asked. "No, I just want you to come home."

I looked at her straight in the eyes, and her skin began to shift to a green color.

"You belong with us," she almost seemed to hiss. Almost looking like a snake, she began to saunter toward me.

"I bind you, devil!" I shouted, pointing my finger at her.

She looked at me in disbelief, and her smile was switched with a sinister scowl. She continued to head in my direction, but I noticed she had slowed.

"I bind you in the name of Jesus! I don't want anything to do with you anymore! You no longer have power over me!"

The power of God had her bound then. She could not move, nor speak a word to me. Black smoke began to emerge from her mouth, and her eyes turned completely black.

"Get out of here…now!" I demanded.

She continued to look at me with anger, and I caught another countenance protruding out of her face, looking out at me from behind her eyes with rage. As I continued to bind the devil out loud, she stomped her foot on the concrete sidewalk and retreated to her car as if something was dragging her. She walked backward all the way to the parked car waiting for her, almost appearing to slide. The whole while she looked right into my eyes, mouthing something I could not understand. The car door opened for her. She was pulled into the vehicle, and then I watched as it drove away. I looked at the car as it headed down the street, realizing that I felt joy.

I was not afraid of them anymore.

I turned around and saw that all the church members were looking at me. Some didn't understand, but others knew exactly what sort of battle I had just endured, and they offered warm and welcoming smiles to me.

We went inside and I felt as though a gigantic weight had been lifted off me. It was one of the best services ever for me. After the pastor delivered her sermon, she stood in front of the podium, closed the bible, and looked at me.

"You stood up against the powers of darkness that were coming after you today, and you succeeded because Jesus stood with you! You keep on standing, and God will stand with you! No matter what comes after you, remember, God is greater!"

I was so happy. I knew that day that the connection to my family had been severed, finally. I could feel its absence inside. There was hope in my heart again—hope for the future. I did not know what was ahead for me, but I knew that it was nothing that had been designed for me by the evil forces of the world. After the service ended, the pastor came to me and wrapped me in a warm embrace.

"I have been praying for you, son, and have been expecting your call all week. Did it take you this long to make up your mind?" the pastor asked.

"No, I just…didn't know how to," I said. Steadying myself, I looked at the pastor, a new conviction in me.

"Well, can we meet tomorrow? I have a lot more I need to talk to you about."

"Of course," she said as a smile stretched across her face.

A church member approached the pastor, tapping her on the shoulder. "Sorry to interrupt, Pastor. Could I borrow you for a moment?" the man asked.

The pastor nodded to me and walked away with the man, who brought her to a group of people on the other side of the church, leaving me to myself. I sat on a chair and stared at the window next to the altar. A ray of light shone right onto my face. I closed my eyes and felt the warmth of it as I listened to Jay playing on the keyboard over the church speakers.

I was happy. I knew, finally, what it felt like.

Enter the Labyrinth

Rain came down hard, and thunder exploded across the sky as I sat in front of the pastor again. Jay stood to my right. Everything inside me, however, seemed brighter. I felt warm inside.

I looked at the pastor at her desk, as she was going over some papers. Jay distracted her, talking to her about some mail that came in. I glanced out the window at the darkness of the morning sky. I liked it though. It was like I was looking at the world through a new set of eyes.

The pastor finally looked up, gaining my attention. "What do you want to talk about?"

I looked back at her and didn't need to hesitate to find a topic. I knew the one. "The labyrinth."

"The labyrinth?" she asked.

"The labyrinth, yes," I repeated.

"What is that?"

"It's one of the most dreaded places in the underworld," I replied. "It's where people were tested, and where the weak were discarded."

I went on to explain how there were many types of labyrinths, and they came in many sizes. The labyrinths I talked about were like nothing everyday people made here on Earth. They were alive, and filled with evil creatures, death and darkness.

I had a very personal experience in one of them when I was young. I must have been around twelve years old. I had come home with my family from a cult meeting, and I was exhausted. Images and sounds from the night's activities still raced through my mind. As my mom prepared me for bed that was all I could think about. In my mind, I kept seeing the blood of people gushing from their bodies as cult members plunged all sorts of instruments of death into them.

Their screams haunted me, and I could not get them out of my head. I kept looking down at myself thinking that I had blood on me, but I had already washed. I stood still in the middle of my bedroom as my mom helped me put my pajamas on. Frozen as the images of people dying played in my mind, I relived the harrowing moments. I could still feel the blood splattering on my face, could hear their voices crying out for help… Their faces kept coming to me, over and over. I was tormented by the fact that I was guilty of these horrible acts.

I knew that the people did not deserve to die that way, and remorse filled my heart for them, but I was afraid to show it. I looked, and saw my mom's mouth moving, then I realized she had been talking to me, and I had not been listening. I shook my head a little bit and realized she had been telling me that I had put the pajama top on inside out. When she asked me what I had been thinking about, I said nothing. I still could not shake myself from what had happened, and had taken part in.

After I climbed into bed to sleep, I was afraid to close my eyes. I saw the victims' hands reaching out to me and heard them begging me for help. There were so many people, both young and old, and I knew I had no power to help them. I knew that if I ever tried to help any of those people, I would be putting myself in danger. Not even my parents could protect me.

A little time went by, and I wandered off to sleep somehow. Before I knew it, I was pulled out of my body by a force I had not experienced before. I looked around and saw nothing, but I knew what I had felt. Something or someone had pulled me out of my body. In the spiritual world, I felt I could do anything I wanted, and that I could not be held accountable for it. I felt like a god. I was not easily intimidated—the powers I had been given made me bold. I looked around my dark room and I could feel a presence.

"I know you're here. What are you looking for?" I asked.

"You," a faint, eerie voice replied.

"I want to see you," I said. "Who are you?"

The shadows in my room merged, coalescing into a larger form, until they presented in the shape of a boy enveloped in darkness. I took a closer look, and realized it looked like a demonic version of me. It had red eyes and loomed larger, but I could tell it was supposed to be me. The shadow and I looked at each other face to face, hovering in the middle of the room.

"I am sent to bring you to tonight's trial. You must follow me. If you heed my instructions, you will live," the shadow said.

I had no idea what the demonic presence was talking about.

"We already did our rituals. What trial is this?" I asked.

In the devil's kingdom, only after being tried repeatedly, were you ever entrusted with certain powers and stature. But they tested you again and again to see if you'd stay faithful.

"What is this about, I don't understand?" I pressed further.

"Your time has come. You must walk through the riddle," he rasped, his voice sounding like a death rattle.

"The what?" I asked.

"It's a test. You will soon see." The shadow reached out and touched my shoulder, easing my apprehension. "Arrangements have been made on your behalf, that you may have a chance to pass this night… That is why I am here".

I immediately understood what he was talking about. Without words, he gave me understanding in my spirit. I knew intrinsically that my mother and grandmother sent him to help me get through whatever trial the specter spoke of.

"I will hide in the shadows and guide you. Tell no one of my presence…" He then looked around the room as if he could feel something happening. "Remember what I said." He flowed into the shadows of the room and disappeared.

As soon as was gone from my sight, a red light began to glow on my left. I turned to see what appeared there, and the red light intensified. It had moving, bright purple lights around it, illuminating the room. It suddenly expanded and looked like a rectangular doorway in the middle of the room.

I had never seen anything like that before. I could see into it and realized that it was a portal. The other side looked like Hell. I could see scorched earth, cave walls, and rock formations. I felt the mystical powers of darkness coming through the gate in great force, together with smoke and embers. Everything glowed by the light of innumerable burning fires.

"Come through," commanded a deep voice from the other side of the portal.

Then I saw a tall, dark demon with massive bull-like horns come toward the gate from the other side. The demon's skin was pitch black. He had a bull's legs as well, and several long, silver-looking tails. With his muscular and hairy upper body, he reminded me of a minotaur. The hair was long on his back and legs, but his private parts showed through his hair. He was an image of obscenity, as though he was meant to offend just to look at him. He had very big hands, each finger extending into sharpened claws.

Strangely, his head was small compared to the rest of his body. He had a human face, with bright glowing red eyes, which matched the dark red horns sticking out of his head. The only thing he was wearing was a torn, worn-out vest with small, embedded squares in it that looked to be ancient.

He reached out his hand to me, and red lights with purple smoke flew out of his hand and struck my chest. I felt his magic run throughout my being. Something happened to me, leaving me feeling different.

I looked at myself and noticed that my hands seemed altered. A closer inspection showed me that I was transforming into many different people, one after the other. I put my hands up to my face, and it no longer felt like my own. It kept changing shape, leaving me feeling utterly confused.

The demon held out his hand through the gate and beckoned me toward him. We had not even touched, and I already felt as though I had done something perversely wicked. I flew over to him, and he grabbed me by my hand and helped me through the gate.

"I am lust incarnate," he said as I crossed the gate. "I will give you the power to seduce women…and men."

He looked into my eyes, and I felt as though I was melting before him—I was completely mesmerized by him. He began to meld with me in midair, all the while changing my shape from that of a boy, to a girl, to an old woman, to a man, one appearance after another. It seemed innumerable how many shapes I was changing into.

I was completely out of my mind.

As he fostered these changes in me, we flew toward something, I was not even paying attention to where he was taking me, but we were traveling at blinding speeds, flying through underground caves, hills, and valleys.

"Your lustful desires will never be quenched—you will never have enough," he said.

Then he transformed himself into many different variations of men and women—cycling through different ages, skin colors, and ethnicities, until he finally changed back into his black demon form.

I grabbed him by the horns as we traveled through the air. It felt like I was no longer in control of myself. He looked down and I followed his gaze to see what he was doing to me.

Our bodies had melded together into a blob of body parts and flesh. I did not know where he began, and I ended.

He suddenly pulled away from me, breaking off a part of himself and leaving it inside of me. I could see the hand through my body—moving around with me. Then it traveled to my belly where it turned into a snake, and it coiled itself inside me before disappearing.

It was at that moment that I caught a new light, an unexpected glow about me. My whole body was in flames as I was burning with the fires of hellish lust. The fire was not burning me though. It emanated from me—from my heart to my spiritual shell, and outward from there.

The demon grabbed me and embraced me. We were both engulfed in what looked like green flames then. I felt like I was having sex with millions of people at one time. My morphing transformations became violent and fast, until he finally pulled away from me.

The flames went out, and we landed in front of a towering wall. He landed on his hooves; I landed on my hands and knees. I did not look around right away, still trying to collect myself after such an explosive ordeal. I was back to my own form, and all I could think about was sex. I wanted more of what I felt, and with as many people as possible. Every shape he changed me into felt different, and I knew then that I had become a slave to those cravings. I had just been taken to a higher level.

I was still on my hands and knees, trying to gather the energy to stand. As the demon looked straight ahead, I climbed to my feet and stood beside him. From there, I was able to finally see where I was.

The place was surprisingly cool, but moisture hung thick in the air. The ground was grayish, and rocky. It felt as though blackness surrounded me, and I couldn't see very far. The towering wall in front of me looked like one large piece of stone, lit with torches to the right and to the left. As far as I could see, it seemed to stretch on endlessly.

The demon raised his hand and suddenly huge black metal double doors—like the ones on medieval castles—appeared. He whispered something I could not understand toward the doors, and they opened outward.

After they spread ajar, I could see another, smaller black wall. That wall was alive though, moving as if it was breathing, and it was covered in what seemed to be feces, moss, and other disgusting substances.

The demon stepped aside, gesturing toward the opening in the foul partition. "You must travel alone and use what skills you've learned to survive. Get to the other side and you will be rewarded. This is your time. Prove yourself worthy."

"What is this about?" I asked.

"Everyone must prove themselves worthy of the power they seek, and sometimes worthy of the power they've obtained. And you must prove yourself trustworthy. Your actions through this labyrinth will reveal your true heart," he replied. He hesitated for a moment before he swept his hand against my back, ushering me forward. "Begin!"

I slowly walked past the doors, noticing how ancient they looked. A variety of demonic engravings were etched into the dark iron or steel—it felt as though it was comprised of metal I had never seen before.

The doors and walls towered above me, leaving me in awe. But I could only pay attention to them for so long. As I drew closer to the smaller doorway, I noticed little crawling insectoid creatures moving all over the black wall. Snakes and centipedes wove their path through the wall as well.

I knew that there was no way to get out of my task. I had heard of people in the cults trying to get away with not going through a test, or a task they were given. Those people were usually killed…

The only option was to forge ahead.

The black wall rose high into the air, disappearing into the darkness of the cave, beyond where I could see. Then, as close to it as I was, I was affronted by a rotten smell that was so noxious, I was immediately overcome with nausea.

I leaned up against the black wall and a small army of little creatures crawled onto my arm, catching me off guard. I screamed and shook them off as fast as I could. Though I considered just turning to run, I knew better under the watchful gaze of the demon.

So, I collected myself and willed the smell away from me. I focused on the task at hand and walked through the main doorway.

There were three paths leading to corridors in front of me: straight, left, and right. I could hardly see anything in the dim light, and in many places, it was pitch black. The floor was mushy and wet, and I flinched at the initial feeling of it beneath my feet.

I did not know which way to take. I was going to go right, but then something caught my attention. The shadows by my feet were moving, and a voice spoke out to me from there.

"Choose the left corridor. I will lead you there."

I recognized the voice, knowing that it was the shadow demon hiding in my room, who said they would help me.

"Okay," I replied.

The shadows at my feet flowed toward the floor of the left corridor, up the wall and close to one of the torches on the wall, then it combined with the darkness beyond the light.

I walked toward the left then. As I passed the middle doorway, I heard a growl, so I hurried my pace. I took a few steps in and looked back. In the darkness of the other two entranceways, I saw a horde of yellow and red demonic eyes piercing the blackness. I caught a glimpse of muscular, hairy arms, and hands with long razor-sharp fingernails. I heard growls and unholy noises. I began to see mouths opening in midair in those other two entranceways, with long sharp teeth catching the light of the nearby torches. They began to call my name.

"Nick, come here," one said.

"We love you, Nick," said another.

"This way, Nick," said a creepy voice.

I was already frightened when I heard a deep, guttural growl, and it spurred me on quicker down my selected path. I did not know what the creatures would have

done to me if they had caught me. I knew I had to

concentrate and not panic. Another surprise could catch me

off guard at any moment.

I looked around for my shadow friend and saw him

moving by a wall at the end of the corridor. I could only see

him when he moved, but his presence seemed to emanate

like a beacon for me. I finally reached the end of the

corridor, where a door was fixed in the wall. I stood at the

threshold and hesitated to move any farther forward.

"Go on, enter," said the shadow.

Reassured, I went through the door and saw a small

square room that stretched on for about ten feet. It was

pitch black, with the only source of light coming from a pit

in the center of the room. There was one doorway in the

middle of every wall in the room, but there was no way to

get to them because of the pit. It looked like molten lava

was at the bottom of the pit. The walls in the room were completely black, but a reddish hue filled the room, revealing the rough details of the walls and the ceiling. I could tell that there was movement on the sides of the pit below, something living in the walls. There were small ledges that led to the doorways to my right and left. I tried to levitate, but could not fly across, leaving me confused about my options.

"What do I do now? Where do I go?" I asked the shadow.

He manifested from the wall as a mass of black smoke. The shadow pointed to the aperture right in front of me. "Through the fire," he said.

"No, I don't think so," I replied.

"Sacrificing yourself to achieve a goal is sometimes necessary. That is the meaning of this room," he said. "Do not care for your safety, or yourself. Care only for the mission. It is the only way."

I looked down into the pit. I hoped the shadow was right—he had been to that point—but I still knew jumping into the hole would be dangerous, and that something needed to catch me in order for me to survive. I looked at the shadow, and it nodded in approval.

Blowing out an anxious sigh, I jumped in. As I fell feet first, I wondered for a second if I had made the right decision. As I descended, dead people with decomposing hands and arms reached out to try and grab me from the sides of the pit. I tried to ignore them, but as I looked down, I saw the drop was much farther than I had thought. Even then though, I fell faster and faster until I reached terminal velocity. I saw the fire getting closer and closer, and I started to feel the heat, when suddenly the lava came up to meet my feet, and it pushed me upward without burning me.

The lava became a pathway and then a stairway toward a doorway across the room. I walked up toward that egress and walked through it. I turned around to look at the pit and watched the lava return toward the bottom, moving like a tongue, touching the sides of the pit.

I found myself in front of a long, dusty black corridor that had many old wooden doorways along its sides. It was stifling, as the air sat heavy, no doubt fighting against the atmosphere in the room behind me. The far end of the corridor was lit only by a single torch, right beside one of the doors.

I began to walk down through the corridor, opening one door after another. Each one that I opened led to other corridors—some long, or short, or leading to stone stairways. But I opened one door, and it was pitch-black inside. I could not see a thing in that place that was completely void of any light. I reached out, and my hand disappeared in the darkness of the room, as though I had immersed it in dark waters. I closed the door and continued to search for the way out.

Each path I chose seemed to offer no clue as to how I should progress. After checking all the doors out, I realized that only one was significantly different than the rest. I went back to check out the one with the darkness behind it. I opened the door and looked carefully through it. When I leaned into the room, amid the void, I saw a faint, tiny light, which seemed to be a great distance away from me. I considered that the blackness or the light was the key to this test.

"Shadow? Are you there? Is this the way?" I asked.

"Yes," said the shadow. "Embrace the darkness."

"What's in there?" I asked.

From the darkness of the corridor, the shadow demon materialized in front of me. He gestured for me to walk through the doorway into the void. With his mischievous eyes and his crooked smile, it wasn't easy for me to trust him, but I knew that I had no choice.

I slowly walked into the darkness, and it swallowed me up. I looked back to see the hallway I had come from, and it was gone, the doorway disappearing beyond the endless void around me. I turned around and could still see the faint, little light in the distance though, way up high.

I stepped forward, but a powerful force lifted me up. I looked down, and could see nothing, but I felt myself rising closer to the light I had seen previously seen in the distance. As I flew upward, I felt like I was passing through black clouds of tangible darkness. I saw the billowing blackness pass through my body as I floated forth. I glanced at where I was going, and spotted a cliff, and a rocky wall with a single doorway a few feet back, lit by a torch affixed at its side.

The force lifted me up to the cliff, dropping me safely on the ledge. The soft, dim light of the torch revealed a black, scorched earth and stone floor. The only way for me was through the single doorway.

I knew I had not been there long, but in my mind, it felt like I had been wandering in the labyrinth for an eternity. I wondered how long I would be there. Would I be trapped for days or weeks? Would I even make it out alive?

"Shadow…where am I? How big is this place?" I asked.

"Just follow my instructions," said the shadow. I heard its voice coming from the darkness behind me.

"I'm tired," I said.

"Go through the doorway. You must keep moving," the shadow replied.

I slowly walked through the doorway and entered a purple, cavernous tunnel. Dim amber bioluminescent glows led my way. I followed the path for a little while, and it eventually opened into a large circular room.

The floor looked to be comprised of white, unpolished granite, decorated with large red emblems and writings I could not recognize in its center. There was blood all over the floor, and a silver dagger with a pearl-like handle in the middle of the room, also stained red with blood. The sides to the room looked like the rocky side of a black mountain. There were no other doors—no way out that I could see.

I was on the edge of the room looking in and did not understand what I had to do. Perhaps I had to sacrifice someone, I thought, but there was no one around.

I looked for the shadow, and he was by my navel looking up at me. Before I could say anything, he spoke to me.

"Letting go in every sense of the word is what these last few trials have been about. Thrusting yourself into the unknown helps to obtain the precious gift of accomplishment..." The shadow flew from before me and appeared once again beside the dagger on the floor, gesturing toward it. "Sacrifice yourself. It is the only forward," he said.

I could not believe it. But then I pondered, and remembered my body was still at home, I thought at first that I couldn't hurt myself if I stabbed my spiritual form. But then, the spirit world was no mere fantasy, and the actions I took there could have dire consequences.

I walked into the center of the circular room. The blood on the floor was cold as it touched my bare feet. I reached out confidently for the knife, thinking that I could easily just stab myself and that would be that. But as soon as I grabbed the knife, fear grabbed hold of me—the kind of fear you experience when the reality of death grips you and you know you don't want to die. I grew frightened that maybe my actions would really kill me. I looked down and the emblems on the floor began to move and come alive underneath me with anticipation.

I looked all around me, to see the room glow red from the spinning emblems on the floor. A large gate opened underneath me, huge, black and crimson, and twirling downward into a funneling shape. A great force from within commanded me to kill myself, and it was so strong, I found it hard to resist. I became drunk with it. The lust for blood I had felt at the cult meetings rose up from inside of me, and I grabbed the knife tighter.

Though I felt compelled to act on the dark desires within, a part of me, deep inside, remained aware. The fear of death grew in that deeper part of me, but the power that took over made me feel like I did not care.

Smoke rose up from the funnel. I held the knife above my chest, intoxicated with the allure of my coming sacrifice.

I plunged the knife into my heart, and blood gushed out like a fountain all over my face, chest and arms.

"How can there be blood? I don't understand…" I said.

I fell to my knees, feeling like I was starting to fade away. The knife protruded from my upper chest.

I tugged the bloody knife from the wound, and blood burst from the site, pouring into the funnel, which drank it with demonic glee. I fell forward to my hands and felt my mind going dark. I felt like I faded away faster then, my naked body covered in my own blood, until I finally fell on my face.

I saw figures inside the rock walls looking out at me, trying to press through. The room grew crazy with excitement, my blood spreading throughout and feeding the funnel.

"What have I done?" I whispered.

Everything went dark. The scene faded away from me and I closed my eyes, thinking it was for the last time.

Rebirth in Hell

I opened my eyes and saw myself lying on the floor of the room. I suddenly remembered what had happened, and jerked up straight, tapping my hand to my chest. There was no wound, no knife, and no blood.

I did not understand what had happened, and then I looked around, and realized I was not in the same room as before. Everything in the room looked the same—the floor with the emblems, the rocky walls, the way it was lit— except for the entranceway, it was in a different place.

I stood up and looked around. Though the room was identical to where I just came from, I felt a little bit different here. I turned to the wall behind me and could see through the amber wall to where I had just been. I saw the knife on the floor, the blood splattered in different places, and the portal that looked like a funnel, pulling closed. I had somehow come through to another side, though I was unsure how. The only certainty was that black magic had made it possible.

I felt different, like whatever it was that made me human had been taken away from me and been replaced with something vile. I felt…evil inside. It bothered me and excited me at the same time. I couldn't explain the feeling, only that I knew that my powers had increased, because I had, in a way, killed my humanity.

As I thought about that, a familiar voice spoke out of the darkness of the wall. "Another step toward immortality," the shadow said.

"What happened? I thought I died," I said.

"He had to see that you were willing to sacrifice yourself," the shadow said. "He had to know that you do not value your life over the success of the mission. You have been reborn."

I really did not know who the shadow was talking about at the time. I found out later that he was talking about the devil. At that time though, I was just glad I had passed the test.

I looked for the shadow and saw him moving in the darkness by a wall leading to an exit. He was submerged within the wall, his eyes looking straight at me. I took one step toward him, and he moved his head out of the wall and looked at me, as if he was reading me, then disappeared. I began to walk toward the exit in front of me again, and as I walked, I searched my heart. I felt weird inside and I knew that I needed to learn who I was once more. The evil that I felt inside gripped me deep, and I knew that I had no control over it. It was unlike anything I had felt before, evil in its purest form.

I walked to the exit and looked out, spotting the opening of a large cave. I stepped through the doorway and felt an immediate rise in temperature. There was not much room for me to walk. I stood near a cliff, and the whole cave was lit from below.

I walked up to the edge of the cliff and looked down to see the horrible sight spread out before me. The bottom of the cave looked like a sizable valley lit ablaze with brimstone and lava. There were people screaming and crying out in frenzied agony as they burned alive. Some demons were in the flames with the people, torturing them, biting them, whipping them, and eating them. But they themselves were not harmed by the fire.

People were torn asunder and fed to demon monsters. Their blood sprayed all over the place as they were dismembered, and the fire leaped up to consume the blood. I saw demons spewing great, consuming fires on people already ablaze. The flames ripped any flesh from their bodies, charring their bones black. There were other demons that committed lewd acts on the agonized victims, even as they ripped them apart with crude implements of steel and iron.

There were yet other demons with wings that flew low to the action, biting, clawing and stabbing people while in flight. Smoke ascended from many places, and the fires moved as if they were alive. The flames grabbed hold of the people, pulling them into the lava, and into holes in the ground.

I knew I was in Hell. Part of me was afraid and dreaded the place, but another part of me—the evil inside of me—rejoiced at the pain of those people. I turned my head and began to look for a way out. The heat was unbearable, even though I was so high up. To the left of the cliff I stood upon, I saw an exit.

Before I could make my way there, however, I looked down, and realized that one of the winged demons had spotted me. I was horrified that he had noticed me, but

I could not look away. It flew toward me, its wings bellowing the fires below. Within a few seconds, the monster was above my head. I felt the heat from the flapping of its bat-like wings. It was a hairy beast, covered all over in matted hair. It had talons on its feet, and long, skinny arms, extending to hands with long black fingernails that looked like swords. The demon gazed at me as bits of fire emerged from its mouth.

I began to run toward the door, and I felt and heard the fire strike the ground behind me. As close as it landed, some of it burned me, leaving my spiritual being singed. I ran into the corridor and went in quite a way before looking back. I heard heavy footsteps coming to the doorway as I rubbed where the fire burned me. I turned around then and saw a demon step into the doorway. He looked straight at me for a few seconds, then, to my surprise, he walked back out.

I was so relieved when I saw him stepping back out
of the hallway… I looked around and saw that I was
standing in a black corridor that was so long I could not see
the end of it.

I began to walk down the corridor, but the sights I
saw in the cave behind me still lingered in my mind. They
were people—real people—being ripped apart, tortured for
the sadism of the denizens of Hell. I collapsed onto the
ground, feeling like I could not go on. I could hear the
screams echoing in my head, as though they were
embedded in my skull, never to leave.

I don't remember how long I stayed on the ground,
trying to push the images and the screams out of my head.
After a long while, I was able to collect myself though. I
climbed to my feet, and I began to walk down the long
corridor again. I walked for what seemed like forever,
unable to see the end of the place. I didn't know how it was
lit, but there seemed to be faint yellowish light sources

coming from underneath the stone floor. They looked like dim, yellow, tiny Christmas lights sparsely placed along the path.

"Shadow!" I called out, but there was no answer. "Shadow, is this where I'm supposed to go?"

But I received no answer. I was alone, I thought. I stopped and looked over my shoulder. "Maybe I should go back and see if there is something I missed…" I said.

"Why would you go back? You're almost there," the shadow said, looking at me from the floor.

"I've been calling you," I said, a mix of fear and frustration shaking my voice.

"I know. I was not ready to answer," said the shadow

"Well maybe you can tell me what that was back there?" I asked.

The shadow finally revealed himself, coming out of the darkness on the ground to stand right in front of me. "I think you already know…" he said.

"You could have told me I was walking into Hell!"

I walked right through the shadow, then continued down the long passageway.
The shadow dispersed as I walked through it, then merged back to a single figure. Its eyes flashed pure, luminous green, and then it dissipated completely.

I continued to walk down the long passageway, and it grew quite humid. Amid all the darkness and dim light, I saw that the walls begin to appear as though they had moss on them. It cooled as I continued down the corridor, the temperature dropping enough for me not to mind the dampness that hung heavy in the air.

I finally spotted a doorway in the distance. As I hurried my pace and drew closer, I saw that the crown and sides of the door were decorated with gold and marble. Green algae, moss, and vegetation covered the entrance, everything coated in a sheen of moisture. I investigated the room, seeing that it was large, and rectangular in shape. At the far end, there was a towering green door.

Once I entered the room, I saw that the floor was polished aqua marble. The walls were as well, but they were covered with red tapestries bearing words inscribed in gold, which looked to be from an ancient language. White pillars were all around the room, with two parallel lines of pillars leading from the doorway I came from, all the way to the green one on the other end.

I walked between the pillars toward the green door. I thought that I might be nearing the end of my journey. As I traveled forth, I saw that the pillars began moving. Shapes protruded out of them, taking the form of people. Most were women, but some were men, and they were the same color as the white of the pillars. They would peer forward, pulling their heads from the pillars, and sometimes they would venture out far enough for their torsos to emerge as well. They would whisper things to each other, but I could not understand them. The shadow followed behind me on the floor, sometimes moving to the walls or to the ceiling.

I went closer to the green door, when I realized that it was moving as well. As I neared it, I saw that there was really no door at all. It was just water—rippling, moving water.

I looked into the water and tried to see what was obscured behind it. I could see movement, but I could not make anything out because of how murky the water was.

I heard footsteps behind me and turned to look. One of the creatures had come out from his pillar and was standing right in front of me. He suddenly put one hand on my shoulder, as he reached into my chest with his other hand. I was startled, but for some reason, I could not move away or defend myself—I was frozen there. He slowly pulled his hand out and began to change shape. Color took to his skin, hair grew on his head, his eyes became green… He looked like me.

I looked at him up and down. The only difference between him and I was that he had fins where his feet should be, and scales running up his legs.

"We will help you through this part of the trial," he said, and then he walked right into my body.

I was stunned, and before I could really process what had happened, all the other creatures that looked just like he did emerged from the pillars, taking half-human, half-fish forms. They slid toward me on the wet floor, and one after the other, they jumped into my chest.

As they entered me, I began to feel cold, and clammy, and I began to change shape as well. My arms and legs grew fish-like scales. My feet transformed into fins, and my hands became bigger and webbed. I lost my hair and nose. I could not stand anymore and fell on my behind. I was lying on the floor looking at the watery doorway, and I saw my reflection continually change as more and more of the creatures possessed me.

I looked back into the room and saw one last creature on the very far end of the room, running toward me. He was changing to fish form as he ran, and just before he transformed completely, he jumped and slid toward me. With great force he collided with my spirit, merging into me and pushing me through the doorway, into the water.

I was floating. I looked down at myself and my legs were aqua green, and completely scaly. I was scared at first, but then as I looked around, I began to feel at home in the water. It was almost as if I had always belonged there. I mentally tried to kick my feet, but the fins that had replaced them moved instead, and it felt like the most control I had in the water. I swept my webbed hands forward, easily moving through the area.

I found myself in a large underwater cavern, so grand that I could not see the end of it. I moved through the cold water, looking straight ahead, and I could make out the shape of structures in the distance. Beneath me there was complete darkness, but I could see the distant cave walls and the ceiling all around me were covered with stalactites and other natural stone outgrowths.

I was able to move swiftly through the water, without any resistance. I swam forward, and a large downward-facing horn-like structure could be seen in the distance. I saw many lights coming from the object. The farther I went, the more detail I could see. The structure looked like a bent cone, narrowing downward from the ceiling of the cave. It looked lighter brown than the walls of the area, and as I swam closer, there were many creatures swimming around it.

There was also a large school of what I thought to be fish that swam quickly from one side of the cave to the other. Sometimes they formed a halo around the horn structure. They looked like writhing black clouds, viciously and violently moving about in the water.

As I swam closer to the formation, the school of fish scattered away from me. I heard a loud, deep rumbling from somewhere inside the cave, shaking me to my core. I looked around and I saw a large eel-headed creature swimming toward me. It had colossal, muscular arms, and webbed feet, and was certainly one of the strangest creatures I had ever seen.

I began to swim away, but I saw another creature swaying toward me from the other direction. It had a fish's body, but its head was merely skeletal remains, with giant sharp teeth shaped like the ones in a piranha's mouth. I darted from them both, but they followed me. I swam past the horn-like structure, and toward the other side of the cave.

As I swam, I looked back and saw that they were no longer following me. For some reason they were just watching me swim away from them. Relieved at first, I continued to swim into the darkness. Everything grew colder and darker the farther I swam.

Something inside me told me that was not the way. I felt danger all around me, but I knew the creatures were waiting for me if I went back. Unable to summon the will to head back the way I came, I continued.

As I stared into the abyss that I was swimming in, I became more fearful of the darkness that surrounded me. I tried looking at my hands and could hardly see them anymore. As I looked back to where I came from, I could barely make out the lights coming from the horn-like structure.

And then it came again—that loud and sudden rumbling, like an earthquake that shook underwater cavern. There was something in the darkness, I knew. I couldn't shake the feeling that something was in there with me.

I turned around and decided to swim back. At least I could see where I was going in that area, and hopefully the two creatures were no longer waiting for me.

I also wondered about the structure. There had to be a way inside. After all, I saw lights in there. Where were they coming from?

As I made my way back, I saw a black cloud come toward me from my right. It was the school of fish! They swam toward me at an incredible velocity, and when they arrived before me, I saw that they were not fish, but miniature human skulls with fish tails attached to them. As they passed by me, they would sting and bite me. All I could do was try to swim past them and cover my face as they swarmed me. Then as quickly as they arrived, they finally swam away.

I heard the rumbling again and when I turned back to look, a titanic mouth filled with razor-sharp, spear-sized teeth sped toward me from the darkness. The mouth was bigger than a house… It was a gigantic, monstrous leviathan. I darted away as its mouth clasped down, creating a shockwave that shook the whole cave. Its dead black eyes looked at me with resentment, and it came at me again.

I swam as fast as I could to get away from the monster. It came at me again with those piercing teeth, trying to chomp down on me. It was not until I fled from the thick darkness and swam closer to the middle of the cave that it stopped trying to kill me. I kept going until I reached the horn structure. When I looked back, the leviathan looked at me, furious, as it retreated into the darkness. Then it was gone.

I looked around, anticipating any of the other many creatures to come after me again, but none came. I searched for an entrance into the horn-like structure then, taking in the features and rock formations on it. The lights I saw from a distance were small windows, covered with a hazy film. It wasn't glass, but something else. I pushed right up against one of the windows but could not see clearly through it. I did see figures within moving around, though.

I touched the strange formation, and could tell it was a type of rock, covered in a slick, gelatinous substance. I swam around and around, until I reached the bottom. It was there I found an entrance. The very tip of the huge structure was hollowed out, and I was able to swim upward into it.

As I ascended, I could see the surface of the water. There was an open room up above. It was still far from me, but when I finally reached the surface and looked around, I realized I was in what looked like a swimming pool. The room itself looked like the inside of a residential pool house. It was dimly lit, and I could see the reflections of the water on the white ceiling above me. The pool was bordered in granite, with a series of steps leading out of it from one end.

I swam to the steps, and pulled myself out of the water, my fish legs still dangling. There was a table at the top of another set of steps a bit further into the room, and as I crawled to take a closer look, I began to revert into my human form. I looked down and saw my legs forming once more, and then my arms. The scales retreated into my body, giving way to soft flesh. I was happy to see my own body again and breathed out a sigh of contentment.

I stood up and walked over to the table. It was disgusting—dark brown dilapidated wood was covered and stained in blood that dripped onto the floor. There were all kinds of dirty operating instruments on it.

I wondered how many people suffered there and thought of all the pain that served as someone else's pleasure.

I heard a faint scream coming from behind me then. I turned and saw a doorway into another room. I hadn't seen that doorway before and found that lapse puzzling. I could see a light from a side room that was further down the hall. I was intrigued because I also saw the shadows of people moving around in the hallway. I walked closer to the doorway there and could see that the granite extended all the way around the pool, with a walkway and stone railing. As I reached the doorway, I heard moaning, whispering, and laughing.

I looked at the shadows on the wall and could not believe it. Were there really people down there? I walked down the hall, and the moaning grew louder. The talking became audible, but I could not understand what I heard, because it was in another language. But I could tell that people were engaged in violent sexual acts. I walked down the hallway, and reached the room's doorway, daring to peer in.

I saw something I would not soon forget.

It was like someone's mansion. I was standing at the entrance of what looked like a grand living room. There were fireplaces on both sides of the room, which provided most of the light, other than what looked to be dimly lit gas lamps on the walls. There were animal pelts strewn across the floor, and the walls were covered with what looked like taxidermized animal heads and bodies of all different types of wild beasts. The room looked like a lodge, like something you would find in a hotel up in the mountains. There were naked people everywhere on the floor. They were on top of each other in layers—people of all different nationalities, sizes, and shapes, writhing in a huge orgy.

The people's flesh moved in wave-like motions. Their movements looked like slow ripples in a pool.

I entered the room and knew that they were people from all over the world—all servants of Satan.

They were being rewarded for the evils they did on Earth.

I looked up and saw a deer head looking at me. The animals were alive!

I stared at the deer, and it seemed to smile at me. Then I saw it look back down at someone. All the beasts inside the room moved about—not stuffed, but very much alive. Some were able to walk around over the people on the floor. As bears, horses, lions, monkeys, and other creatures would walk around the room, they would be grabbed by someone on the floor, or they would jump on someone, and the people would pull them into the foul orgy. When the person finished, the animal climbed to its feet, only to walk to someone else.

It was a filthy house of debauchery.

I walked through the large room toward the other side, where there was another doorway that I felt drawn to. As I walked, the scene of animalistic lust and sex began to turn into something gruesome. Some of the people began to move abruptly, in an unnatural way. There seemed to be something gray and blue inside of them that reflected out through their flesh—some type of spirit that was glowing through them. Some people mutated into beast-like creatures. They would grow hair all over their bodies yet retain their human face. Others would completely transform into demon-like creatures.

They began biting and eating each other as they mated. The animals joined in and did the same. Body parts and blood flew everywhere. Horrified, I ran toward the door on the other side of the room. As I raced forth, I watched as people were devoured. Limbs and hunks of flesh flew past me—a few even hit me—but I kept running. Some people shook violently as they laughed at me running by. I saw a woman eating a man's brain from his open skull, while a creature exposed the spinal cord of a man by ripping his flesh open like a tattered cloth. Horror and fear kept hitting me in waves. I remember one woman looking straight at me and pointing. She laughed at me as a bear devoured her lower body, her own blood squirting all over her breasts and face.

I did not understand what they were laughing at. I ran faster than I could ever remember running before.

As I approached the door, I felt the atmosphere of the room change abruptly. I reached the doorway, and I looked back, and everything had somehow gone back to the way I first saw it. There was no blood, no one being eaten, people were still enthralled in intimate moments without hurting each other. I could not understand.

I stood there, still shaken from the horrific scene. I saw the woman that was being eaten by the bear, and she was not hurt. As she was being licked by a big heavy woman, she felt me looking at her, and turned to look back at me. Her eyes transfixed on me, she pulled away from the big woman, stood up, and gazed in my direction. Her curly black hair moved as if a gust of wind had struck it. She swept out her arms and smiled at me.

In that moment, the creature with the skeletal fish head and razor-sharp teeth that was chasing me in the water earlier jumped up from within the crowd and made its way toward me. I saw the sharp teeth coming toward me and I turned to run, only to realize that I could not move as fast as I once did. It was as if something was trying to keep me from getting away and had somehow magically slowed me.

I caught a glimpse of the woman that stood up and smiled at me. Her blue eyes had become black, and there was a dark, revolving cloud around her. She was doing something to me.

I turned toward the doorway, and very slowly stepped through it.

The creature was almost on top of me then.

Once I crossed the threshold, I moved normally again. I took a few steps though and stumbled forward. I did not realize that I had entered a sloped floor leading down into a pit. I fumbled and tried not to slide, but there was nothing to hold on to. I fell face first down into a circular pit. At the bottom I could see water, but as I tumbled, I saw that the creature jumped in after me.

I smacked against the water so hard that I didn't realize that the moment after, I changed back into my sea form. Instinctively, I swam forth, though I did not know where I was going. I did not recognize anything at first, as the water was darker than I expected.

As I swam, I realized I was once again inside the underwater cave, just a few feet away from the horn-like structure. I swam through the cold water, toward one of the cave walls. The creature was right behind me, opening its terrifying maw.

I swam as fast as I could toward a black cavern that I spotted in the nearest wall. I thought of hiding in the cave, hoping that the creature would not follow me into the darkness. I whirled forth until there was a sudden shift in the water.

I was being pulled into the cave.

I saw a large hand reaching out toward me. I tried to swim backward away from it, but something was sucking me in. Then, I felt the arms of the creature I was trying to get away from. They wrapped around me, and I was sure that I was going to die. I froze as the creature carried me out of the cave, and then upward.

I could not move. I was at the mercy of the fish-faced monster that grabbed hold of me. It carried me through a small cave opening in the ceiling. It swam fast, until we reached the surface of another underground cave. It carried me to the shoreline and released me from his grasp. I was surprised, but I swam to the black-sanded beach, and raced out of the water on my own two legs.

I looked back, and the creature stared at me from the water. Its large black eyes pierced right through me. A chill rattled my spine. Somehow, I knew that it wanted to reach me, but it was not allowed for some reason.

But then, I heard it telepathically communicate with me. *I was just trying to show you the way, but you kept running from me*, the creature said to me as it linked with my mind.

"How could I have known?" I replied.

It was quiet then, perhaps even regretful or dejected. "Maybe we'll see each other again," it solemnly spoke.

Slowly, its head sank into the water. A moment later, it was gone. I had processed too much over the short time that I had first emerged from the water, and my brain felt as though it was ready to shut down on me.

I looked around and saw that the small cavern I was in was completely black, even the water looked dark beyond what I had seen before. The only light in the room came from one torch by a doorway on the side of the cave wall. It looked like part of the labyrinth.

I wondered when I was going to finish stumbling through the maze. It seemed like I had been there for weeks.

Tired, I entered through the doorway. The coldness of the water quickly faded from my body, as it was warm inside that part of the maze. I walked down a hallway, and the bottom of my feet became covered in something sticky. I did not know what it was, and at that point I did not care. I ignored it as I trudged down the hallway, just wanting to go home. I did not care about anything—I just wanted the stupid test to end. Getting out of there was the only thing on my mind.

"Not many survive the water pit," a voice rang out behind me.

I spun around and saw the shadow demon standing right behind me. It had taken my form again.

"I want to go home," I pleaded.

"Soon enough," he said. He stepped through me then and continued forward, beckoning me forward as he led the way. "Why didn't you join the party?"

"The…party? I don't know, I was just surprised for the moment," I answered.

"But you did not join, even after being invited," he said.

I knew what he was talking about, reminded of the deer head on the wall that seemed to encourage me to join in the depravity that unfolded within the manor house.

"I just wanted to get out of there. My objective is to finish this thing, not to get sidetracked," I replied.

When I said that, I realized that that was exactly what the orgy was intended to do. It was meant to test me and see if such distractions would keep me from finding my way out of the labyrinth.

And I realized the shadow had pressed me on that point so that I would understand.

"Good," he replied.

A Fantastical Exit

He continued leading me forward, but he became an insubstantial black veil once more, clinging to the darkness of the walls. He meandered from shadow to shadow in the long corridor, moving us through a maze of halls and doors. I heard noises, and faraway screams sometimes, but he kept us moving. We slowed down a little bit, and I realized that the noises I had heard were footsteps. I heard whispering voices around us, but I could not understand what they were saying.

"We're getting closer," he said.

I followed slowly, and cautiously, hearing growls and noises all around me. I could make out faces piercing through the walls. Some looked human-like, while others looked as far from that as you could imagine.

I looked up and was startled to see the face of a woman looking straight at me in the distance. Her features appeared behind one of the doorways. I only saw her face at first, the woman looking like a ghostly apparition. Her skin was pale, and she had wild, long, curly white hair. Even her eyes were completely milky white. She motioned for me to come to her, but I knew the duplicitous nature of everything within the labyrinth, so I hesitated.

"You can trust her," said the shadow.

I slowly walked down the corridor. The woman's eyes were piercing, and her stare was intimidating. As I approached, her expression toward me slowly changed. She seemed to relax. She was still partially behind the doorway when I reached her, but I could see her bare shoulders. She had a concerned look in her eyes then. I realized that her features had completely changed. Her curly white hair changed to a golden blond, and her eyes had become a deep yellowish green, reminding me of a cat's eyes.

"I am one of the ancient ones," she said in a deep, lion-like voice. "It has been a long while since someone made it this far. I have been sent to help you, and I can be your ally, and fight by your side. But there is a price for my allegiance.

"I know these caverns and hallways better than many. I have lived here longer than you can comprehend. You could die and be trapped here until your body withers and rots…or you can accept my offer, allow me to protect you, and live. It only gets harder from here." She smiled and displayed rows of big, cat-like fangs.

I looked around for the shadow, but I didn't see him anywhere. When I looked at the woman in front of me, I realized that her head was bigger than anyone's I had ever seen before. She was a giant of some sort. I hesitated to answer her, unsure of what I should do.

"Well don't just look at me. Say something," she growled.

"What is your price?" I asked.

The woman was surprised by my question, but she seemed impressed by my curiosity.

"Very clever… You looked like a smart boy. You also look like someone who's been hurt, so I'll make it simple for you: Three human babies," she said.

"Three what?" I asked.

"Three human babies…if I am to help you. They cannot be more than a week old," she replied. A hungry look seemed to take over, contorting her features.

To me, human life was not that important at that point in my life. I had seen people kill and be killed in so many ways and so many times. The fact that she was asking for babies was not that out of the question for me. And my shadow friend said to trust her.

"Okay, that's fine," I said, thinking that I could just get any three babies that the cult held hostage. "I'll give you the children, but only once I'm free of this place."

She licked her upper lip. "I will keep you from being destroyed, but I cannot guide you, only defend you. Deal?"

"Deal," I replied.

She slowly stepped out from behind the doorway, and I saw something I had never seen before. She had the lower body of a lioness, but a human torso extended up from where her catlike chest ended. Her majestic presence reminded me of a centaur, but her golden fur left her seeming even more unique.

She gracefully moved out from the door, revealing her body in full. She walked on four legs, ambling forward like a lion, her footpads tapping against the floor. She raked her human hands through her hair then. She was not wearing anything, but her long curly hair covered her breasts.

I noticed something else though. She bled perpetually from her hindquarters, blood trickling down her legs onto the ground.

She saw me looking, searching for wounds that were hidden beneath her fur. "The keeper of the labyrinth did this to me. It is how he keeps me bound to this place. But not to worry, I can protect you from the dangers you will face."

I wanted to walk away—desperately wanted the nightmare to end. Anxiety gripped me, and she saw it. She pierced my gaze with an uncanny intensity, her cat-like eyes seeming like they would bore a hole right through me.

"What is your name?" I asked, trying to press past raw nerves.

She walked up to me, patting my head as she circled around me. Her tail touched me and grazed my face, and I realized that she towered above me, standing eight feet tall or higher.

"I am Ada-Sha," she said.

She walked toward a doorway I had not seen at first. Her stride was graceful, and she did not make a sound. She still dripped blood from her hindquarters, but it seemed to evaporate as it hit the ground, as if the ground lapped it up—just more of the dark magic that could be found in that place.

She reached the doorway and stepped aside, sending another toothy grin my way. "You lead," she said as she gestured toward the next corridor.

I walked past her. She had to crouch a bit to get through the doorway but remained close behind me. We walked down a narrow corridor, where we heard thumping, almost like the sound of distant horses running. I looked up at Ada-Sha and even though she did not return my glance, I could see that she knew what that was.

"Stay close," she said.

The sound grew louder and louder, faster and faster, and we just continued to walk like there was nothing wrong. I was already worried and thought of running. I couldn't help but wonder if she would betray me. What if she was just slowing me down, so that something else could get me?

"Climb on my back," Asa-Sha said then.

"What?" I asked.

"Get on. Quick!"

As she crouched down, I hopped atop her. She wrapped my arms around her waist and as I held fast to her furry body, she charged forth. I could not believe how fast she was. We made it down the hall in no time, but then she skidded to a halt.

"Why are you stopping?" I asked.

"Which way?" she asked.

I did not know. The corridor split into two paths: toward the right there was another long hallway and then darkness; toward the left there was a blue light shining in the distance. I looked back and could feel a terror racing toward us as the thumping grew louder and louder.

"Quickly now," Ada-Sha bade.

I looked and was frozen by fear. I felt dread hit my chest like a hammer, and I could not shake it. The thumping was so loud that it rang in my ears, and as we looked toward the end of the corridor we just came from, it grew worse.

"Make a decision!" she yelled.

Billows of fire licked the walls at the doorway at the other end of the corridor we just came from. It was intense enough that it lit up the whole area. The fire dissipated, and a terrible heat wave hit us.

Something sinister was coming.

I saw what looked like the head of a giant, serpentine dragon approaching us, and I finally realized what caused the great thumping noise. Every time the creature hit the floor or a wall, its great weight produced a tremendous noise. The creature looked like a gigantic, snake-like dragon. It had huge teeth and wings, and I could not see all of its body, hidden by the narrow corridor that stretched beyond its head.

Ada-Sha turned as much as she could to face me as I sat on her back. She caressed with her hand, wrenching my attention away from the huge beast that barreled our way. "Left, or right?"

"Left," came my panicked reply.

She immediately jumped into the left corridor and sprinted forth. It felt like it would be miles to the other end, and I could see nothing but the faint bluish light at the far end. As she ran, I looked back, fearfully anticipating the dragon's pursuit. I finally saw its head reach the doorway. Its features were brightened by flames that it spat past fangs that made Ada-Sha's look like toothpicks. It entered the corridor we were in, but quickly disappeared in the darkness as my companion raced on. I looked forward, catching a glance at where we were going, and I realized the blue light grew stronger and stronger.

We approached what looked to be an ancient stairwell. The steps looked like they had been hewn from stone, and there were many different types of demonic emblems and figures cut into the designs on the walls leading up to it. At the top of the stairs, a large blue gem at upon a pillar. The gem emanated the blue light that filled the area. Behind the glowing stone was an immense door that appeared to be fashioned out of solid rock. We looked at it, almost mesmerized by it, until I remembered that a dragon was fast behind us.

I looked at my companion and she looked back at me, but before she could say anything, I heard the shadow speak.

"The dragon is the keeper of the door, and only with a sacrifice will you be allowed through." The shadow emerged from the ground and stood in front of us pointing at the corridor we had just come from.

I hated the fact that I would forget about the shadow demon. I could have used his knowledge more. But he so easily seemed to withdraw and be forgotten, and I wondered if that was a part of his power.

"What do I do?" I asked.

"Your blood is the key, and the stone is the lock…" came his cryptic remarks.

Again, I saw the fire of the dragon billowing toward us, drawing closer and closer. The thumping sound echoed down the hall.

"Fine," I said. "Whatever I have to do, let's do it quickly! It's coming! And…"

Before I could say anything else, Ada-Sha took me off her back, and set me down in front of her. She took her front paw and cut a gash on my left hand. I fell to my knee and screamed when she did that, the pain taking me completely by surprise. I looked up at her, and her eyes darted toward the gem.

I knew what I had to do.

I looked back toward the long corridor we had just come from and could see movement. Every few seconds, the dragon's face became illuminated by the fire that escaped from its scaly lips.

"Put your hand on the stone, and new life will be brought forth," said the shadow.

"Yeah, I figured it was something like that," I replied as I hurried to the blue gem.

"Put your hand on the stone now, or we all die!" Ada-Sha shouted.

I held my bloody hand and raced up the steps toward the shining blue stone. As I neared it, the light permeated the air, like a cold, damp, electric current. The light pulsed brighter and brighter with each step I took. It surrounded me, engulfing the chamber. I looked down at Ada-Sha and saw the urgency in her eyes. It was almost as if she truly cared for me.

I reached the final step and placed my bloody hand against the stone. I looked over at the door, expecting it to open right before me.

But it did not.

My hand was still on the stone when I turned around to Ada-Sha, and a devious smile swept over her face. Pain wracked my body at once. I tried to pull my hand away, but realized it was stuck to the stone. The agony surged through me, concentrating on my abdomen. It was so powerful that it brought me to my knees.

The stone emanated an array of different colors, and the light became energy that coursed through my being. I looked down the steps and saw the lioness walking up toward me. When she was at my side, she crouched down beside me, and began to pet my head.

"This was not only a test of your dedication, but it was a lesson, and an elevation. Part of you will remain with us…forever," she revealed.

I did not understand what she meant. All I knew was that the pain grew stronger and stronger. It felt like something was crawling inside my stomach, chewing through my organs.

I finally tugged my hand from the stone, and I fell to my back. I cried in pain and saw Ada-Sha leap to her feet in anticipation and excitement.

I went to touch my face, and I realized blood dripped my mouth. It poured from my lips, and then a great pain hit my stomach again. I felt like something was trying to come up my throat from my stomach. I grabbed my neck, and turned to my side, vomiting more blood. All at once, something seemed to explode from my mouth.

I looked to see what had come out of me and was in shock to see that it was a tiny, unborn baby. I was shocked and confused. Through waves of confusion, I reached to pick it up, but Ada-Sha stopped me.

"Don't touch him," she snapped.

As I looked at the fetus, the large dragon finally reached us. But when it did, it did not attack us, and it seemed to control its fire. It climbed up the stairs, setting its eyes upon the unborn child. Frightened, I crawled over to Ada-Sha.

She reached down, grabbed me, and picked me up. "It's okay," she said. "Just watch."

The dragon glared at the fetus for a moment before it looked up at me with a smile. The dragon opened its mouth and approached the tiny baby. I thought he was going to eat it, but instead he exhaled, and a strange cloud of mystical black and silver gas enveloped the baby. As the dragon continued, the fetus began to grow.

Ada-Sha walked toward it and breathed the strange fumes toward it as well. The fetus aged incredibly quickly, becoming a baby, and then a toddler, only stopping when it reached my age.

I watched in amazement at the sight of another person growing in front of me. It was a boy that looked just like me—an almost exact replica of me. As I looked at my clone, I climbed to my feet. The pain that had wracked my body was gone, almost feeling as though it had never existed. I walked toward my replica, and after taking a few steps, I watched as he opened his eyes.

I gasped.

Its eyes were not human. They looked just like the dragon's did, and its features contorted until it looked like a horrific force of evil. Even though it resembled me, I knew it was not human.

The dragon spewed out fire that engulfed the boy, but he was not consumed by it. The dragon stepped forward, and said something over the boy in a low, rumbling voice that I could not understand. The dragon stepped backwards, then lowered its head. My wicked clone, still engulfed in fire, climbed atop the dragon's head, and the creature turned around and walked away. I stood there speechless, watching the other me disappear in the distance.

"What just happened?" I asked.

"You are now spiritually bound to this place—to us—forever," said the shadow.

"You just gave spiritual birth to a boy," Ada-Sha revealed.

"Will I ever see him again?" I asked as I stared into the darkness that my child and the dragon had disappeared into.

"I hope you never have to," Ada-sha said.

The shadow didn't let me dwell on the thought for long. "Let's go," it said.

I turned toward the sound of his voice, and I saw him standing on the other side of the doorway. The stone door had opened, and we could see the other side.

We walked through a narrow, black hallway that went up and then down, twisted to the left, then to the right. It seemed to go on forever. After a while, I started to hear a buzzing sound above me. It would start to get loud, and then subside. I looked up, but the ceiling was so far from the ground that I could not see it in the darkness high above.

I looked at Ada-Sha, curiosity etched on my face. She returned an intense gaze, as if she knew what the buzzing was, but she said nothing. I hurried along faster, and as I did the buzzing grew louder above us. I looked up and spotted something flying out of the blackness before it quickly darted back into it.

"What was that?" I asked.

"They're coming. Get ready!" Ada-Sha cried.

"Who?" I asked.

Before I could say another word, a creature came down from the darkness and dove right toward me. It looked like a large, monstrous fly, and was nearly as long as I was tall. The black creature was covered in disgusting slime.

At first, when there was just that one, I was able to duck away from it. But as more descended from the darkness and began to swarm us, I knew there were too many of them.

A few of them latched onto me and tried to take me away, but Ada-Sha jumped up and fought them off. She swept me underneath her body, shielding me from the strange insectoid beasts. She looked up and breathed fire, lighting up the chamber.

There seemed to be thousands of those things up there.

As she blew her fire, the giant flies fled to safety, but more returned to attack us as soon as she stopped.

She looked at me, a somber look on her face.

"Run!"

I raced away on her command. She followed behind me, keeping the creatures away from me with her fire. We hurried up a steep, narrow staircase with black walls at its sides. Its dark, dusty steps were slippery, but I kept to my pace, desperately trying to escape. As I ran, I noticed my shadow friend underneath me, matching my speed, gliding underneath my feet.

"Go to the doorway, but do not venture into the arena," he said as if he had been waiting for me to look at him just so that he could tell me that.

I did not know what he meant. I just continued to run upward.

I soon saw a dim, amber light at the top of the staircase. I knew I would reach the top before long. I climbed the last few steps and found myself in front of a tiny doorway, and inside I could see a vast open area. I glanced back and saw Ada-Sha running up the staircase. It seemed as though she had gotten rid of the flies. But as she drew close, I could see the crazed look on her face.

"Go!" she cried. "Go!"

As she neared me, I saw thousands of flies swarming behind her. I panicked, and ran through the doorway, Ada-Sha right at my heels. As we entered, she jumped on top of me to protect me, and the flies swarmed all around us in a large circle. Ada-Sha could not keep them away from me though, their numbers far too great. All she could do was keep them from taking me.

Then I heard a large *thump* that made the earth underneath us shake.

The flies were startled as the chamber shook. They flew back to the staircase we had ascended, and all at once, the buzzing withdrew.

Another *thump* echoed out, sounding like the footstep of a mighty giant. Ada-Sha climbed to her feet and helped me stand as well.

I looked around and saw that we were in some type of circular structure. A grayish, powdery dust covered the flat ground. As I looked around and saw the way the walls were constructed, I realized this was a fighting arena, just like the shadow warned.

There were rows and rows of seats going upward, which seemed endless. All the seats appeared to be made of dark gray stone. There was one seat that grabbed my attention though, set apart from all the others, on one of the sides of the arena. This one was large, almost like a throne, and was completely black. It had some type of red designs on it, but I could not distinguish them from where I stood.

As I looked at the black seat, I received a vision of the place. I saw the seats filled with demons, and on the arena floor, human souls tore each other to pieces. Monsters would appear out of nowhere and they would grab pieces of the souls to carry them away. At the center of it all, sitting on the black throne was what looked like an old, pale, bald man, dressed in a black cloak. His attire was so dark that it made his throne look lighter. He looked on with jet black eyes as the demons screamed all around him.

Thump.

The noise pulled my focus back to the present.

I looked around and the shadow was beside me, mirroring my shape again. Ada-Sha stood just a few feet away. I looked at her, and her eyes appeared to glow orange. The only one who didn't seem to know what was happening was me. I wanted to inquire further, but I was frozen with an eerie expectation.

"Should we be running now?" I asked.

"It won't make any difference with this one," Ada-Sha replied.

Black smoke appeared from the opposite side of the arena, and it began to fill that portion of the stadium. The smoke climbed higher, and it was thick, almost like a liquid, swirling violently as it grew. Then, purple and green lights began to emerge from the middle of it.

And then an immense hoof stepped through. *Thump.*

Then another. *Thump.*

The towering creature that made those haunting sounds finally stood before us.

The colossal monster was at least four stories high. It had broad steer-like horns, and hideous red eyes. The head was that of a monstrous bull, with additional small eyes drawing back along the side of its face. As it parted its lips to shed a disturbing growl, I saw rows of jagged, sharp teeth, each of them bigger than one of my arms.

The rest of its appearance was even more uncanny: it had two mouths, one to the left, and the other to the right; it had small horns where the nostrils would be; running from the top of its head toward the middle of the two mouths were strange rows of what looked like sharp teeth. It had the shoulders and arms of a man, and the torso of a woman, with many breasts. The waist and hips were like a woman's too, but the thighs turned into hairy goat legs. It had jet black skin, and long black hairs on its legs. A horde of phalluses moved like snakes atop the creature's groin, as if they had a mind of their own. Occasionally, if they lifted high enough, I could see just as many female reproductive organs beneath, and scrotal sacks to the right and left of them.

Ada-Sha stepped backwards.

But it was too late.

The monster lunged forward, grabbing hold of her and squeezing her between its mighty claws. It brought her close to its face.

"I have been faithful, Master!" she screamed, fighting to get the words out as it squeezed the life out of her.

The monster opened its claws and Ada-Sha fell, tumbling to the ground. The monster slashed one of its long nails against a scrotal sack, and a green, oozing fell to the ground. Ada-Sha quickly leaned down and began to greedily consume it.

The monster spoke. Its voice rumbled deep, and though I could not understand the language I had never heard, I somehow knew it was casting spells with dark magic. It pointed at me with a clawed finger, and slime erupted from its mouths. Then black liquid secreted from its myriad breasts. The black milk crashed to the arena floor, splashing everywhere. Some of it covered Ada-Sha as she covered herself in the green slime that was coming out of the monster's testicle sack. It was all over her hair, face, chest and body. She must have sensed me, because she sent back a watchful gaze, and a smile stretched her lips.

Suddenly, a bright yellow glow came out of her eyes, and wings began to sprout from her back. The wings grew to a twenty-foot span, looking like those that belonged to great eagles. The monster grabbed her, picked her up, and slammed her against one of the walls of the inner circle. In fear, I turned to look back at the creature, and I saw its penises shaking like they were ready to burst. A moment later, they also cast out bursts of black liquid. The monster took a single giant step toward me, and one of the phalluses was within reach. It spewed an enormous amount of black liquid on me, and in an instant, I was covered in it. It felt like thick black mucus.

I was then picked up by the penis, constricted as if by a mighty boa. It lifted me up and brought me right to the face of the gruesome monster. It smelled more disgusting than anything I could imagine. Its glowing eyes burned with heat. It licked me with a nasty black tongue, before it waved me in the air, and then it brought me down between its legs. I thought the smell was bad before, but by its groin, a putrid stench threatened to make me vomit.

The hairs there were sticky and caked together with feces. Its vaginas were gray with black spots, and they quivered constantly. Upon being brought so close to them, I saw that they seemed to have tongues that came in and out of them. One of the pink tongues grabbed me by my head, wrapped itself around me and inserted me, feet first, into itself. There was slime all over me, and it dripped down toward my head, and onto the floor.

I felt the tongue begin to wrap itself tighter around my body, moving slowly as it secured me inside the vagina. Only my head was sticking out. I looked down, and I could see my shadow companion moving about below. He tried to communicate something to me, but I could not understand.

I thought I was going to die in that surreal, horrifying situation. As I looked down, I began to give up hope of ever returning home. I would just go from one situation to the next, and I would never make it back.

Thump.

The creature began to move.

Thump, thump, thump.

As it turned, I caught a glimpse of Ada-Sha, she had gotten up, and was looking up at me, saying something, but just as with the shadow, I could not understand.

Then billows of the black smoke began to appear, and the creature walked into it, with me inside of it. The thumps seemed far away then. I was in a daze as the creature moved through the smoke. I completely lost track of time and did not recognize anything that I saw. I spotted fires on the ground, and then rocks. Sometimes I looked at the testicles hanging from its thighs—nasty and completely inhuman, I thought—but I was so dizzy that I wasn't sure of anything. I would look down and see nothing but black, dusty dirt. As the monster continued to walk, I felt so lost.

After a long while, the monster stopped, and the smoke began to dissipate. The creature spewed me out, and I fell on the ground, covered in a mixture of secretions that I thought I would never be able to forget. I looked up, and the monster backed away, looking down at me. It then changed its appearance, shrinking down into human form.

It looked like my mother, standing naked in front of me.

I could not believe it. I was going to say something, but with a flash of its red eyes, it imparted to me that it was not really my mother.

The creature looked straight into my eyes, and then pointed behind me. I turned, and I could see many people I knew standing behind me. There were students and teachers from the school. Two of the teachers rushed to my side and helped me to my feet, but I was too weak to move. I slowly gathered strength to stand, and as they picked me up, black smoke engulfed the creature, still in human form. And then, it quickly disappeared.

My peers carried me up a hill and into the city. I was covered in horrible black and green slime, and gray smoke wafted off my body.

"I can't believe he made it out!" said a young boy.

"He's not the first, and won't be the last," said an old lady.

"It's impressive though," a young man said. "No one has made it through that one in a long time!"

"This one's different," and older man remarked. "He's special. Let's clean him up!"

They carried me into what looked like somebody's medieval shop. They put me down on the floor and started to clean me up with magic spells. As they did, dark faceless spirits came into the room to observe what was happening. One of the younger women went up to them and spoke to them.

"He made it out successfully. He was helped by a familiar shadow spirit, a lion goddess he forged a contract with, and was delivered to us by the portal master himself."

The spirits vanished as quickly as they had entered the room. They knew exactly who helped me. It was not hidden from them. I had thought it was a secret

At that point, I could not keep my eyes open. My eyelids felt so heavy, and I began to close them. All I wanted to do was to go back home, but they all seemed very happy, congratulating me, and chanting victory songs. I could hardly hear them, their voices sounded distant. Everything seemed far away in my mind.

Then, everything went black.

I remember regaining consciousness for a few seconds here and there and I heard things but could not open my eyes. I heard people's voices, and demons speaking, and I would drift out again. I somehow knew I was being carried around, taken from one place to another, but I did not know exactly where I would be.

One of those times, when I regained consciousness, I heard my mom's voice. I tried opening my eyes, but I could not, no matter how hard I tried. That time, when I went back to sleep, I was happy, because I felt I had returned home.

When I finally did fully wake, it was a slow process. First, I felt her hand on my forehead, checking for a fever. I opened my eyes and I saw her looking at me as if she was searching for something in my eyes. I looked out the window, and it was dark.

"You made it back," she said.

"How long was I gone?" I asked.

She took the towel off my forehead and put it in a bowl of ice water before returning it to my brow.

"Eight days," she revealed.

I sat up in bed and looked at her.

"Where were you?" I asked.

"You know I could not be there. That's why I sent you the shadow," she said. She lightly pushed me back down onto the bed. As I relaxed once more, I did not remember getting sick. I realized then that all the time I spent in the labyrinth, I was unconscious on the surface. I made it out though. That was the prevailing thought I had as I sank into slumber once more.

I made it out…

The Real Trials Begin

It was late. I had been talking to the pastor for hours, and we were all feeling tired. Talking about the labyrinth had completely zapped my energy, and I needed to go to sleep.

"So, how many of these labyrinths are out there?" Jay asked.

"I really don't know," I said. "I mean, I've seen several, and they are all different, but I really don't know exactly how many of them are out there."

"Well, you go home and get some sleep," the pastor said. "I pray the Lord gets you home safely."

"Thank you, Pastor," I replied.

The pastor, Jay and I gathered our things, and exited the church. It was a clear, starry night, and a cool breeze hit the trees, making the leaves sway side to side. I heard an owl in the trees, and looked to see if I could spot it, but there was no such luck.

I got into my car and waved to Jay and the pastor as they drove away. I slowly pulled out of the parking lot and drove in the opposite direction, toward my apartment. The street was narrow, but beams of moonlight shined through the leaves and hit the road below. I drove past a lonely streetlamp, and when I looked back at it in my rearview mirror, I spotted a large black shadow cross from one side of the street to the other.

I didn't really pay it any mind and continued driving. I loved the way the moonlight was so bright that night. I caught a glimpse of the full moon, admiring the celestial beauty. As I slowed down to gaze upon it, I glanced in the rearview mirror once more, and saw many dark shadows behind me. They were all up in the trees, jumping from branch to branch as they followed me.

I continued to drive, and turned onto a larger street to see if they would still follow. They did indeed, and it seemed like there were more creatures that had joined them. I saw them coming out of buildings, cars, and even tree trunks in order to give chase as I drove down the street.

I sped up, and as I looked behind me, I realized that a few cars I had just passed had turned and began to follow me as well. It was almost certainly an attack—a joint spiritual and natural attack in tandem. I had seen something like that before, only not from the receiving end.

I sped up even more, but not fast enough. A truck that was following me smashed into my car, shaking me from my route, though I kept my vehicle steady. Demons jumped out of the truck like locusts descending on a cornfield, and they latched onto my car. They gnashed at me and tried to scratch me through the side and roof of the car. My driving grew erratic, leading me to swerve a few times.

I looked to the sides of the streets, and saw demons to my right and left, following my car. I didn't know what to do, but as I began to panic, I thought of what the pastor told me: they would try to kill me if they could not turn me back to them. This was indeed what she predicted.

One of the demons caught my arm with its claws and slashed me across my left arm. I screamed, and my pain just seemed to fuel their resolve to kill me.

But I resolved not to let them win. I was not going to fail after all that I had gone through. I had been to hell and back, and I was not going to let the darkness keep me from the light. I had to believe that God would protect me.

"Jesus, help me!" I cried out.

At once, a tremendous boom rang out above my car, and I could feel the shocks of the vehicle bounce from an added weight on the chassis. The demons that had gathered on my car were thrown off with great force onto the street.

There was something on top of my car, but I could not think about it for too long. I spotted a huge, flying demon in the sky ahead of me. It tucked its wings, diving down to strike me, and as its outstretched hand was about to pierce through the windshield, I saw fire strike him from above my car. The flames were so intense that the whole street was illuminated by the light. The demon, in flames, fell to the ground immobile, smoldering where it landed.

"Oh Lord…please get me out of this. Please help me!" I prayed aloud.

My prayer wasn't answered in time for the truck to slam against my car once again. I glanced at my rearview mirror again and saw a bit clearer in the lingering light of the flames. The people in the truck were agents, and they must have belonged to the secret society. They drove closer again to my car, but instead of hitting me, they brandished guns and aimed them at me.

Before they fired a single round, I saw an immense flame come down and strike their truck. The attack was so powerful that I thought the truck had exploded. It was still in one piece, but it had been engulfed in flames. Damaged as it was, the driver could no longer control it. It swerved, and then rammed into a nearby telephone pole, bursting into a ball of fire.

I slammed on the brakes, squealing to a halt. I thought at first to look at the accident, but I was more interested in the divine protection I received. I stretched my neck out of the window and looked up to see a gigantic angel standing on the roof of my car. The angel must have been at least three times my height. He was dressed in white garments atop golden armor, and he held a massive, fiery sword. He looked down at me, and his countenance was so fierce I shivered at the sight of him. His eyes were engulfed in white light, his hair was comprised of living fire, and it seemed as though divine flames moved underneath his skin. He was so bright that all the buildings in the area were illuminated by him. The angel turned his head up to look at something and I followed his gaze. I could see that I had come to a dead end. When I looked back at the top of my car, the angel had disappeared.

I looked around and didn't really know where I was. It seemed like an industrial area. There were buildings that resembled old factories, and my car idled in front of an old gate leading to one of the parking lots.

Another booming sound echoed through the area. I could see huge bursts of fire down the street where I came from, each brighter than the last. Towering flames illuminated the darkness in the trees, and I could see hordes of demons scattering from there. The angel came into view once more, and I knew that he was fighting for me, keeping the demons back.

I knew I had to run. I hurried from my car and rushed to turn and push the large metal gate open. I raced up the gravel road to a truck loading dock and climbed an old stairwell to reach its top. I could clearly see the angel fighting the demons then, the swarm never seeming to end. Still, he held them all back—not one of them pierced his defenses.

I ran around the side of the building and found a window that was low enough for me to jump through. I picked up a few bricks, and I threw them, shattering the glass. I grabbed a broken broom handle on the ground and cleared out the rest of the glass so that I could enter safely.

Once inside, I stumbled into a large open room filled with dated machinery. Everything was decades old, covered in dust, and cobwebs. I looked around, but it was dark. The only light entering the building came from the streetlamps outside. As it shone through the old windows, I caught glimpses of disturbed dust particles traveling through the stale air inside.

As I walked through the sea of machinery, a scripture came to mind. Then, out of nowhere I heard it from a disembodied voice.

"Whatsoever you bind on Earth shall be bound in Heaven and whatsoever you loose on Earth, shall be loosed in Heaven".

I stopped for a second and wondered…was that me thinking that? Before I could consider it further, I saw, out of the darkness, a tremendous axe coming out of the shadows, heading right for my face. I ducked and rolled away, springing to my feet to look back and see a giant demon come out of the shadows. He looked like a gargoyle—muscular, gray, and dressed in ancient-looking garments. As he stood there, I could see that there was gray smoke emanating from him. He looked at me with pitch black eyes, saying nothing, but I could feel immense hatred exuding from him. He looked to his left and right, and then four more demons that looked just like him emerged from the shadows and stepped forward, flanking him on both sides.

I ran as fast as I could toward the other end of the factory. The gargoyles followed me, jumping from one machine to another, gaining on me with every step. I ran underneath a large metal brace that held one of the machines, and I hid beneath it. I heard them slow and stop their pursuit, prompting me to sneak from the shadows of one machine to another, slowly moving from my original hiding place.

I heard them walking, their steps rattling the metal floor beneath them. Each stomping pace forward made me ache inside. It seemed they could not find me though, and they spread out throughout the factory to search. As I waited there, listening to one of them draw closer, I looked around and realized that I was nearly out of room, almost up against a wall.

I prayed and prayed, but nothing happened. No angels appeared; no lightning; no thunder.

Nothing.

I heard the heavy steps drawing closer, and wondered what I could do. Then I remembered the scripture I heard just a few minutes ago, resonating in my mind. I realized that they were instructions. I believed that God wanted me to fight back.

I crouched there, asking God for courage, finding it difficult to work past my fears. I slowly rose and saw one of the gargoyles just a few steps away from me. He sensed me and turned around to face me. His liquid black eyes glared at me, and another plume of smoke seemed to pour out of him. The demon bared his large sharp teeth and jumped toward me, bringing his axe back to strike.

"In the name and authority of Jesus, I bind you, devil, and cast you to hell!" I screamed.

As the demon was in mid-leap, a large, black, smoky funnel appeared on the floor. Chains lashed out of the funnel toward the demon like whips and bound him tightly. An invisible force dragged the demon into the funnel, and it suddenly disappeared just as fast as it emerged.

I looked around and saw the other gargoyles in different parts of the factory floor, looking straight at me. They were completely enraged then, and violently rushed after me.

But they were no longer alone.

Jumping from one machine to another, they were followed by a trail of poltergeists that hurled everything behind them all over the room, creating a vast cloud of dust and metal.

I lifted my hand up and pointed my index finger toward them, shouting with all my might. "I bind all of you in everlasting chains and fetters, and I cast you down to hell where you belong. In the name and authority of Jesus!"

Before I finished, smoke funnels opened, and I could see through to the other side of the closest one, and all I saw was fire on the other side. The demons—gargoyles and poltergeists alike—were bound in gigantic chains that emerged from the funnels in a split second, and then they were dragged down into the hellfire that awaited them.

I stood there for a moment as everything grew still. I stared at the cloud of dust settling before me.

I knew I had to leave.

All the doors were blocked by heavy machines then. The demons moved everything around in the chaos, and I no longer had a clear exit.

I looked around and saw a staircase leading to an upper floor on the other side of the room. Everything between me and my way out was a mess. It seemed like every piece of machinery was flipped upside down, turned around, or broken into scattered pieces.

I walked through the wreckage left behind by the gargoyles. The light of the streetlamps barely entered that part of the building, and as I approached the staircase, shadow spirits emerged from the dark corners of the room, out from behind the blackened ceiling, and from behind machine parts scattered on the floor. They revealed themselves to me, and I realized I was surrounded. The shadow forms were tall, peering at me with red eyes. They were like black smoke, some beginning to resemble humans, but they quickly changed to more ghastly, monstrous, unrecognizable forms.

Before I could say anything, they all attacked at once. I felt pain all over my body. As the shadows surrounded me, they bit, scratched, and clawed at me. I fell to the floor in agony. My backbone felt like it was breaking, my chest felt like it would be crushed at any moment, and I could hardly breathe.

In a moment of panic, in the briefest of times between blows from the shadow monsters, I found a chance to cry for help.

"Jesus!" I yelled. "Jesus!"

The shadows backed away but continued to circle around me. The pain I felt subsided. I don't know why, but I remembered a sermon the pastor preached about the blood of Jesus. I saw the pastor in my mind preaching it.

It's in His blood! There is power in the blood of Jesus! Plead the blood of Jesus on your situation, plead the blood of Jesus on yourself, and plead the blood of Jesus against your enemies. His Blood will cleanse your sins, it will sanctify you, it's a protection for you, and fire against the enemy of God! Praise God Almighty!

There is power in His blood that He shed for us. An understanding came to me...

I slowly rose to my feet and began to plead the blood of Jesus against the shadows. Out loud, over and over, I called upon the Lord.

"I plead the blood of Jesus against you!"

As I yelled, the shadows backed away farther and farther, screaming in pain. I realized then that they were being burnt.

It was working.

"The Blood of Jesus prevails against you! I plead the Blood of Jesus against you!" I screamed.

The shadows fled from me, writhing in pain as they burned. Before long, they had faded back to their infernal realm, leaving me in peace once more.

I looked around, noting that everything was still again. I took a few steps toward the staircase, and waited, looking around to see if another ambush was ready to spring. But after some time of seeing none of Satan's minions, I dared to hope.

I finally reached the stairs. I hoped that maybe I would find a way out. Maybe there was a fire escape, or an egress to another room that would lead back to an exit door. I had to find a way to leave the terrible place.

I walked up the steps, one after the other, glancing about, but also looking up toward the second floor. Dust was everywhere. I finally reached the top and I saw desks and chairs everywhere, neatly arranged in rows. File cabinets were lined on one side of the large room, and there was what looked like a waiting area on the other side. I knew it used to be an office space.

I walked a bit farther, leaving a trail of neatly placed steps behind me on the film of dust on the floor. The air was stale, and I began to feel a heaviness in my chest. I stopped in the middle of the room to catch my breath.

Without warning, all the desks and chairs were pushed away from me by an unseen force, and I was left in what looked like a circle of office furniture. The room darkened, and I began to see stars. The whole room was transformed into what looks like outer space. I saw planets and galaxies far away. There were stars of varying sizes all around me. I didn't understand what was happening, but as I turned around, I saw even more stars and realized I was surrounded. Then, out of the midst of the stars, I saw a figure approaching me. It, too, was comprised of starlight and stardust, but it also seemed covered in a shroud of the blackness of space.

The figure drew closer to me, and then the stars within it began shining brightly, until the whole figure seemed like one unyielding supernova. As it approached me, closer and closer, I could no longer behold its mighty splendor.

I stepped back as the figure of light transformed into what looked like a tall, beautiful man, dressed in a long white robe, decorated with gold.

It was at that point that I recognized him.

How could I not?

"Why did you leave me?" the devil asked. "Did I not give you all of what I promised?"

I just stared at him. His lavender eyes seemed filled with innocence. His long blond hair and clear white skin glistened before the stars and space.

"You tried to kill me," I finally replied.

"Oh that! Well…how else could I get your attention?" he mused. "You are more special than I thought, I admit it. Come back to me. Come back, and I'll give you more than you ever dreamed of. I'll make you more famous than you could ever dare to imagine…"

Then, as he waved his hand, I saw a vision of myself standing in front of massive crowds, singing, and they were all jumping up and down as I entertained them. Crowd after crowd, city after city. I watched myself travel the world. I was a major pop star.

"I will make you rich beyond your wildest dreams," he said.

And as he waved his hand again, he showed me houses, buildings, lands and ships that I would own in different parts of the world. I had my own fleet of airplanes.

Then, slowly, the vision faded.

"All you have to do is proclaim your fealty, and kneel at my feet," he insisted.

He pointed to the floor in front of him. As he pointed, all the visions disappeared, and we were back in what looked like outer space. It seemed as if a spotlight shone on the floor before him. He was dressed in pure gold then, wearing a golden crown. Even his hands were covered in gold and precious stones. I looked at him, and I looked at where he pointed—where he wanted me to kneel.

"Yes, my son," he softly said. "I will welcome you back. Bow before me and become my servant once more."

I looked into the devil's eyes. They twinkled with excitement as he sized me up.

"No," I said.

He looked at me and smiled. He transformed himself into a gorgeous woman wearing only a see-through gown. I looked around and noticed that I was surrounded by naked women and men, moving sensually toward me. I could not run away even if I wanted to—I was surrounded. The carnal desires of the people engulfed me. I became dizzy for a moment, and I knew they were trying to appeal to my past, and the very thing that I had grown to love the most: sex. I stood there not knowing how to cope. I felt wave after wave of lust hitting me. The devil then transformed into a handsome man, then back to a woman, and then to an androgynous mixture of both sexes, before he slowly approached me.

Then, in that moment, I remembered all the pain I endured when I served him—all the continual lies that I had been told down through the years. I had been abused, used, and discarded more times than I could count. I knew that his offer was a trap. It wasn't real. He did not have any good intentions for me, and death was on the other side of those naked bodies coming toward me…

"No," I said sternly as I held out my hand, gesturing for them to stop.

"But don't you miss me?" he whispered.

"You cannot offer me eternal life," I screamed.

"What?" he said as he stopped walking.

"The only one that can truly give me life, is Jesus," I said.

"Don't you bring Him into this," the devil said. "This is between you and I."

"You are not God," I said

He growled at my continued defiance. He turned back into a lavender-eyed man, dressed in white.

"I was so messed up," I said. "I lived and felt the darkness inside me. I was drowning in pain and sorrow when I served you. Jesus saved me form all of that!"

"Stop it!" he yelled at me.

"Jesus saved me…from you!" I shouted.

"No!" he screamed as he fell to the ground.

The light he was emanating was gone, and he began to change to what looked like an old, frail man. At that point all the naked people transformed into their true demonic, monstrous forms, and fled the room through air vents, and cracks in the floor and walls. They vanished, leaving the devil by himself.

"Jesus loved me when I was nothing," I said. "He gave me meaning and purpose. He gave me a new outlook on life. He transformed me. I can think and reason on my own now," I said.

"Shut up!" he cried as he fell on his face.

The devil continued to grow frailer with every rebuke I sent his way. He looked tiny within his dirty black cloak, and he brought his hands to his ears as if to protect himself from my words.

"I will never serve you," I said.

He looked up at me, the old frail man with translucent hanging skin, and sunken, jet-black eyes, and I saw that his rage and disappointment were limitless.

"You will never be anything—you will have nothing!" he screamed.

"I have Jesus!" I screamed back.

He screeched in pain as he crumpled to the floor. Though he seemed weak, and weary, his scream was so loud that the furniture and the windows rattled. The glass broke, and I reflexively brought my hands to my face to protect me from any shards flying into the building.

"Jesus has me," I shouted, somehow finding the strength to be louder than the devil. "When it is my time, I will go to Heaven—the same place you were cast out from!"

His despondent screams were uncanny, then. An unexpected, unseen force pushed him backward into a corner of the room. He convulsed uncontrollably, as if something invisible struck him repeatedly. He tried to get away, but the blows hit him so hard across his body that he couldn't even crawl away. The unseen force beat him to pulp, and I knew that it was the power of God. Finally, he was hit so hard, that he went flying out a window into the night sky, disappearing from my sight.

I looked around the room, and everything had grown still. The chairs and desks were piled up around the room, but the dust in the room had settled. I stood there alone in the dark, and the moonlight coming in was the only thing that lit the room.

"You're not alone," I heard a voice say.

"What?" I asked.

"I have always been with you, and will forever be with you," the voice said again.

I knew, then, that it was the voice of God.

I looked around but I didn't see anyone.

I stepped forward, looking down at my feet so that I didn't hurt myself on the piles of furniture or the shattered glass. It was then that I saw a glimpse of a man dressed in white walking beside me. But in an instant, he disappeared.

When I looked up, I was surrounded by angels dressed in beautiful white robes that emitted glorious, almost blinding, light. A heavenly luminescence was everywhere. There were so many of them that I could not begin to count them. They were all around me, even outside the windows. I saw them floating in midair, looking at me. I felt love—an intoxicating feeling of love—and happiness swept over me, like I had never felt before.

I was lifted up and out of that room. Level after level, I ascended upward. The angels summoned a vertical tunnel as they surrounded me. Suddenly I passed through the roof of the building and into the night sky. The company of angels was still around me as I ascended into an even brighter shining light. And then, all at once, all the angels around me begin to sing a beautiful melody of praise, and it permeated my being as I ascended.

I closed my eyes.

Maybe I was dead and going up to Heaven.

For some reason, I felt it didn't matter. Their voices were amazing, and mesmerizing. They sounded like water, and air, and beautiful instruments playing at the same time. The melody continued to move through me as I surrendered to the wonderful feeling of peace and wellbeing. I lost myself within it.

I opened my eyes and saw beautiful hills of grass, and towers of pure gold and light in the distance. There were flowers everywhere.

I turned around and spotted a group of people wearing gleaming white robes. They grinned at me and even their smiles seemed to shine.

Then as if it had been a dream, I opened my eyes, and I found myself sitting on the grass right next to a sleeping, homeless man. I realized I was outside the factory building, just across the street, in what looked like an empty field. The sun rose with the morning. I slowly stood up, and heard the birds chirping, and a cool breeze passed by my face.

Everything seemed different for some reason. I looked at the sleeping man and cleared my throat.

"Excuse me. Hello?"

The man slowly rolled toward me, blinking away the fatigue that still gripped him. "Who are you?" he asked.

"I'm Nick," I said. "Do you know how I got here?"

The man gestured for me to give him a hand getting up, and I extended my hand to help him. But when he took my hand, I felt God's love pass from me to him.

The homeless man gasped, and his eyes grew wide, and he looked around. "Who are all these people here?"

"What people?" I asked.

The man climbed to his feet and skittered away from me while looking back.

"Where did they all come from? Who are these people?" he screamed as he ran.

"What are you talking about?" I asked, but he withdrew further and further away.

I didn't know what that man saw, but I knew one thing: I would never be the same. I saw everything through a new lens. Everything seemed brighter, crisper, and I felt clarity that I had not felt before in my mind. I saw the factory in front of me and wondered about all the things that had happened. I walked a little toward the sidewalk, and looked down the street, and saw the charred vehicles, and burnt markings all over the place from the night before.

I paused, and realized I still felt that feeling of love. I felt good. I felt…whole. I knew where I had been. But most importantly, I knew where I was going to go.

It was only the beginning.

The End